Goodbye, Perfect

Sara Barnard

MACMILLAN

First published 2018 by Macmillan Children's Books
an imprint of Pan Macmillan
20 New Wharf Road, London N1 9RR
Associated companies throughout the world
www.panmacmillan.com

ISBN 978-1-5098-5286-4

1 3 5 7 9 8 6 4 2

A CIP catalogue record for this book is available from the British Library.

Typeset by Ellipsis
Printed and bound by CPI Group (UK) Ltd, Croydon CR0 4YY

'*Beautiful Broken Things* is a book that the YA [illegible] desperately needs – a book about the beauty, passion and extremities of female friendship' Alice Oseman, author of *Solitaire*

'Starkly realistic and ultimately uplifting, *Beautiful Broken Things* is a compelling tale of pain and redemption, growing up and growing together, and finding empowerment and strength in friendship' Catherine Doyle, author of *Vendetta*

'Stories about female friendships are hard to come by, especially ones with no romance, but *Beautiful Broken Things* fills that gap in an intensely compelling and passionate way' Lauren James, a[illegible]

'A go
rebuildi
best-friends

'Armed with a pe
and fabulously down
clear that contemporary
sweet; that books with serio
by what we think we know ab
some stories don't have to involve
Arianne, Daisy Chain Book Reviews

'*Beautiful Broken Things* is a stunning look
between three girls. It feels so, so realistic' Jim
Moon Lane

'Barnard has a real talent for honest, flawed characters who
cannot help but fall in love with' *Bookseller*

'Stunning' *Guardian*

Books by Sara Barnard

Beautiful Broken Things
A Quiet Kind of Thunder
Goodbye, Perfect

For all the BHGS girls in form G, '99–04,
in memory of when we all believed our labels.
And to all the girls right now who still do:
you're so much more than what they tell you.

ONE WEEK BEFORE

'Do you ever think about just . . . running away?' Bonnie asked.

'Running away from what?'

'You know. Life.'

'You can't run away from your life,' I said, settling back against the cushions. We were in her bedroom trying to revise, me on the futon, her on the bed. 'It'll always be there when you get back.'

'Not if you don't go back,' Bonnie said. 'If you start a new life.'

I shook my head. 'I don't think you can ever really start over. Because if you're trying to do that, you're basically trying to run away from yourself. And you can't. You're stuck with you, forever. Wherever you go.'

Silence.

'Why're you asking, anyway?' I asked, craning my neck so I could see her, sitting across the room from me.

She shrugged. 'Just . . . argh, exams, you know?'

I smiled. I knew. 'Oh yeah, I'd run away from exams, definitely. But only if you came with me. And Connor.' My boyfriend. I considered, then added, 'And Daisy.' My little sister. 'And we'd need to be back in time for LeeFest.'

'That's a holiday you're describing,' Bonnie said.

'Even better,' I said. I turned a page of my Biology textbook and sighed, feeling the familiar sink in my chest at the sight of all the stuff I would never learn nor understand. 'Maybe it should just be you who runs away, then.'

'Maybe,' she said. I could hear the smile in her voice.

'Give me a heads-up when you go,' I said. I was trying to read about genes, but I was thinking *jeans* and how I needed new ones, and whether I should go for the embroidered ones I saw down the market. 'Send me a text. Or a postcard.'

'OK,' she said.

'Promise?' I prompted.

'Promise,' she said.

Saturday

1

The police arrive when I'm in the shower.

I don't realize straight away, of course, because when I shower on a Saturday afternoon I make the most of it. So around the time they're walking over our threshold, I'm covered in a tea-tree-and-minty lather, eyes closed against the bubbles, singing a medley from *The Lion King* at the top of my voice.

The singing might be why I don't hear my adoptive mother, Carolyn, knocking on the bathroom door. And *that* might be why she chooses to break the most sacred of McKinley household rules: she walks right in and bangs her fist on the glass of the shower door.

I scream, obviously.

'Eden!' she yells, which is pretty unnecessary considering (a) she's already got my attention, and (b) it's not like there's anyone else in the shower she could be talking to but me.

I should say here that this is very unCarolynlike behavior, and it's that weirdness, more than the actual request, that makes me turn off the shower, open the door just enough to poke my dripping head out and demand, '*What?!*'

'Can you finish up and come downstairs, please?' she asks, back to her usual calm self, like this is just a normal, reasonable request.

'Why?'

'The police are here,' she says. 'They want to talk to you.'

I feel my entire face drop, my eyes go wide. '*Why?*' I say again, more panicked this time.

'I think you know why,' she says, which is terrifying. 'I need you downstairs in five minutes, OK?'

I go to close the shower door again – partly out of obedience, but mostly so she can't see my face and whatever might be written across it – but Carolyn puts out a hand to stop me.

'Bonnie's mother is here, too,' she says, then lets the door slide closed, right in my stunned, guilty face.

I do know why. That's true.

Not because I was expecting them, or because I've done anything wrong, but because this morning I got this message from my best friend, Bonnie: **I'm doing it. I'm running away with Jack. EEEEEEKKK!!!!! Don't tell anyone! Talk later! Xxx** And by 'this morning', I mean at 4.17 a.m.

OK, I realize this might sound a bit alarming out of context. Especially with the whole police-at-the-door thing. But when I read it a few hours after it was sent – bleary-eyed, still half asleep – I was just a bit confused, maybe a little annoyed, mostly because Bonnie and I had made plans to go to Canterbury today, and her unexpected bailing meant I was suddenly planless on a Saturday. She'd agreed that this would be our free day from revision, our chill-out day, practically the only time she's allowed in the ridiculously strict revision schedule she's been sticking to since April. Our first exam – Biology – is on Wednesday. Five days away.

I replied just the way you might expect me to. **Huh?**

Can't talk right now, but I'll call later! Just say you haven't heard from me if anyone asks! I'm on an ADVENTURE! <3 xx

I didn't think for a minute that she really was running away, because that's just not something Bonnie would do, and even if it was, she's got no reason to leave. So I chalked her messages up to exaggeration – *maybe* she's staying out for the night with her secret boyfriend (more on him later) without telling her mother, at most – and put my energy into salvaging my Saturday.

I carried right on thinking that all morning, which is why, when her mother called Carolyn to ask if I'd heard from Bonnie, I said no, as promised.

'I thought the two of you had plans?' Carolyn asked, her hand cupping the phone to her chest.

'We did,' I said. 'But she changed them last night. Didn't say why.'

'Last night?' Carolyn repeated.

'Yeah,' I said.

'And you haven't heard from her since?'

'Nope,' I said. I didn't think twice about lying for Bonnie. As far as I was concerned, she'd asked, and I'd agreed, and that was that. I didn't need any more details or context. A promise is a promise, and a best friend is a best friend. But I had to try and make it believable, and also get the attention away from me, so I added, 'I wouldn't worry about it, though. She's probably with Jack.'

Carolyn's eyebrows went up. 'Who's Jack?'

'Her boyfriend,' I said, telling myself that Bonnie could hardly expect Jack to stay a secret if she'd 'run away' with him. 'That's probably where she is,' I added. 'I'm sure she'll be back soon.'

That's literally all I know about her secret boyfriend, by the way: his name, and the fact that he's a secret. I'd actually been sure 'secret' was just Bonnie-speak for 'imaginary', especially as I was never allowed to meet him, or even see a picture. But apparently not.

Thinking that made me a little uneasy, so I tried to call Bonnie to ask for more details on the whole running-away thing, but she didn't answer. I sent her a message – **You're OK, right?** – and it took her a few minutes but she finally replied: **More than OK. Don't worry! xx**

I relaxed, because there's no one I trust more than Bonnie, and if she says she's OK, then I know it's true.

So, I knew from this that Bonnie's absence had been noticed by her parents, which I thought was a bit weird, even then, because how could they know so quickly – and know enough to be so worried that they'd call Carolyn – that she'd even gone anywhere? But I didn't think about it for very long because, like I said, it's Bonnie, and Bonnie doesn't get into trouble. Not real trouble. And that's not an opinion – it's a fact.

Here are a few things about Bonnie Wiston-Stanley, aged fifteen and three-quarters:

- She likes Caramac bars broken into little pieces and stirred through vanilla ice cream.
- She's in all the top sets at school, and pretty much top of those, too.
- She's Head Prefect and everyone expects her to be Head Girl when she goes to sixth form next year.
- She plays the flute, and not just in a has-to-because-her-parents-make-her way, but actually properly plays it, like with grades and everything.
- She wears glasses with thin brown frames.
- She has freckles, which she hates even though I think they suit her.
- She never used to wear make-up, not until a couple of months ago.
- She's the best, most steady, most reliable friend in the world.

I guess you'll want to know about me, too. What are a few things about me? Well, my name is Eden. Eden Rose McKinley, in full. I like plants and flowers and things I can grow with my hands. I was adopted when I was nine years old. I live in Kent. I have a boyfriend called Connor. I once got suspended for drawing moustaches on the portraits of the senior staff in the main entrance hall during a fire drill. My teachers call me 'spirited' when they're trying to be nice, and 'disruptive' when they're not. One day I'm going to get a tattoo of a dandelion on my shoulder. I used to have a recurring dream that I was being flown around in the beak of a pelican. I like cannoli better than anything else in the world. I'm not always as nice as I'd like to be.

There. Now you know about us both.

Anyway, so yes, I do know why the police have turned up at my doorstep, but I know it in a very basic, process-of-elimination way, not in a proper knowing way. For one thing, I've got no idea why the police are involved at all, and even less why they'd want to speak to me. Why would the police be involved in a teenage girl going off with her boyfriend for a bit without telling her mother? Since when is that a crime?

Shit, maybe I shouldn't have mentioned Jack. Maybe that's what this is all about. But I'd got so used to thinking of him as not real that even saying his name out loud hadn't quite felt real. She'd never told me anything concrete about him, never shown me a picture, even. Just given me titbits vague enough that I'd assumed they were lies; *bad* lies, at that. How old is he? *Older*. How did you meet him? *A flute thing*. I'd figured she was jealous of Connor and me and had made up her own imaginary equivalent, and who was I to spoil that for her?

I know that might sound a bit unlikely, but Bonnie has been known to have a pretty wild imagination when it comes to things like boyfriends. It's like a combination of wish-fulfilment and too much fanfiction. When we were fourteen, she returned from summer camp full of stories about her new boyfriend, Freddie. I believed her, because why wouldn't I, and it took almost six months for me to finally catch on that the whole thing was basically a fantasy. Freddie was just a boy she'd had a crush on and then kissed on the last night of camp. Not exactly a love story.

So as far as I'd been concerned, 'Jack' was either entirely imaginary or just a friend from orchestra or something that she *wanted* to be her boyfriend. Otherwise, why wouldn't I have met him?

I get out of the shower and head for my room, trying to get my head straight. It's not long after four, which means it's about twelve hours since Bonnie sent me her first message, and six since her mother started making calls. It doesn't seem like long enough to get so freaked out you'd get the police involved, but then, what do I know about parenthood?

I towel off in a kind of fast/slow hybrid, because I'm not sure whether I want to hurry up and get downstairs, as instructed, or put it off for as long as possible. I take my time towelling my hair, thinking back to everything I've done over the last twelve hours, just in case they ask.

The answer is, not much. I made French toast for my little sister, Daisy, because she's grounded at the moment for getting into trouble at school, and I felt sorry for her. It wasn't long after that when Carolyn started asking her questions about when I'd last spoken to Bonnie, and I'd figured it was a good idea to get out of the house, so I did. And by that, I mean I went to see my boyfriend. My lovely, non-secret boyfriend, Connor.

I tried to call him before I left, but he didn't answer, so I just sent him a text to let him know I was about to turn up on his doorstep. We have the kind of relationship where that kind of thing is OK, so I knew he wouldn't mind.

It took me about fifteen minutes to walk to Connor's house – we both live in Larking, which is a boring little market town in Kent – and he was already waiting in the doorway when I started walking up the drive. He was half dressed, his jeans hanging low, revealing a strip of blue boxers. He was shirtless, his hair sticking up at all angles, his eyes morning-blinky. But still he was grinning, his face lit up, like every time he sees me. When I took the step up to walk through the door, he leaned down and dropped a kiss on my lips. He tasted of peanut butter.

'Hey,' I said. 'You just got up?' This is unusual for Connor, who's usually up before 7 a.m. every day of the week.

He shrugged. 'I was up most of the night.'

'Oh, shit,' I said. 'Sorry.'

'It's OK; everything's fine now.'

'Um, what happened?' I wasn't sure how to ask this – or whether I even should – but he didn't seem annoyed.

'Mum had a fall,' he said.

'Shit,' I said again. Connor's mother has rheumatoid arthritis, and he's been her carer since he was eight. His gran lives with them and helps look after them both, even though she's in her seventies and probably needs more care than Connor does, nowadays.

'She's fine,' he added. 'I mean, not fine. But, you know, fine enough. We had to go to hospital, but it's nothing major, just a couple of fractures.'

'A couple?' I repeated, horrified. I tried to remind myself that in Connor's house this qualifies as 'nothing major'. But I couldn't help but think of how *completely major* it would be if Carolyn had to spend half the night in hospital. I wouldn't shut up about it for weeks. But this didn't even warrant a text.

Connor smiled at me. 'Just a couple,' he said. 'She's sleeping now. So's Gran.'

'You can go back to sleep, too,' I said quickly. 'I can go.'

He shook his head. 'No way. Stay, obviously.' He leaned down to kiss me again – he's just taller enough than me that he has to lean when we kiss, which I love – and we stayed like that for a while, broken bones and runaway friends skittered from my mind.

Connor and I shouldn't be a perfect match. Him, the shy ginger kid, and me, the wild(ish), difficult one. But the thing about Connor is he isn't actually that shy at all. And I'm not wild or difficult, not really. Sometimes it just takes that one person to see beyond what everyone tells them they're meant to see.

Here are a few things about Connor Elliott, aged sixteen years and six months:

- He was bullied from Year 7 to Year 9, but he doesn't ever talk about it, even now.
- He loves birds and wants to be an ornithologist, and he's proud of this, not even slightly embarrassed, even though the other kids have always tried to make him be.
- He can tell what bird it is just by the sound it makes.
- He knows how to cook.
- He's dyslexic, like me, but he tries harder and he actually likes to read.
- He has blue eyes and hair the colour of paprika.
- He broke his nose when he was nine and now it has a bump on it.
- His mum and gran say he's the best boy on the planet.
- I agree.

No one thought we would work, let alone last. But here we are, over a year on, happy. We're like veterans of a teenage love story.

I didn't stay at Connor's long, because even though he tried to hide it he was clearly knackered. We spent a lazy couple of hours in his bedroom, watching TV, kissing and playing *Portal*, which is the only video game I ever agree to play with him, even though he insists it's old now and I should give some newer games a chance. Every now and then, he left to go and check on his mother and gran – both still sleeping off the previous night's stresses – and to replenish our bowl of tortilla chips.

'I should go,' I said finally, after he'd literally fallen asleep on my shoulder twice.

'Nah, stay,' he started to say, but he broke into yet another massive yawn instead. When he was done he laughed, sheepish. 'OK, maybe I'm a bit tired. Don't go, though.'

'I'll see you tomorrow,' I suggested. 'When you're a bit more awake.'

He made a face like a little boy refusing a nap. 'But you're here,' he said. 'It's a waste of Eden-time.'

I rolled my eyes. 'Can it, you soppy div. Go to sleep.'

'Cuddle first?' he suggested, pulling back the covers and burrowing under them.

'You're so macho, Connor,' I said. 'I can't handle what a manly man you are.'

He laughed, pulling me under the covers towards him. His skinny frame was warm and cosy, impossible to resist. Connor is comfortable with himself like no other boy our age I've ever met. Not in a loves-himself way, either. More like he has his priorities, and he knows what matters, and what matters isn't wasting energy on worrying that he isn't the model of masculinity. It's basically the thing that made me fall in love with him in the first place. That and the fact that warmth comes off him like a radiator in winter.

Anyway, that was it with Connor today. I didn't even tell him about Bonnie. I must have left his house sometime after two, come home, mooched for a bit and then decided to have the proper long shower that Carolyn ended up interrupting.

And now here I am, in my room with the police downstairs waiting for me, stepping into my jeans and deciding that, yes, I'll carry on telling the small lie, as promised. I can't see what difference Bonnie's message from earlier would really make to anything, anyway, and I don't want Carolyn getting mad at me for lying to her this morning.

Carolyn's head appears around my bedroom door and I jump, almost tripping over my own feet.

'Are you nearly ready?' she asks.

'Let me just do my hair,' I say.

'Eden,' Carolyn says warningly.

The tone in her voice, together with the situation, makes me feel suddenly panicky. 'Why do the police want to talk to me?' I demand. 'I don't know where Bonnie is. I really don't!'

'They're not expecting you to know,' Carolyn replies. 'They just want to talk to you. And anyway, if you ask me, Bonnie's mother is the one you should be more concerned about. The woman's practically hysterical.'

'Why do they think I'll know *anything*, though?'

'Because you're her best friend. God knows, if you disappeared, Bonnie is the first person I'd want to speak to.'

'No, I mean, why are they freaking out like this? Why are the police even involved? She's probably just off with her boyfriend somewhere.'

Carolyn lets out a little noise I can't interpret, and I frown at her, trying to get a reading. What is going on? None of this feels right.

'I know Bonnie's usually Miss Responsible, or whatever,' I add.

'So yeah, maybe it's a bit unusual. But not police-unusual.'

Carolyn doesn't answer this, just glances behind her at the empty corridor and then back at me, raising her eyebrows in a silent 'hurry up'. 'The police are going to ask you why Bonnie has run away with Jack,' she says.

'Why would I know—'

'There's no point in wasting your breath telling me,' Carolyn breaks in. 'You're just going to have to repeat yourself. So let's go downstairs and speak to the police, OK? I'll be right there, and you don't need to be nervous.'

'I'm not nervous,' I say, surprised.

Carolyn mutters something, which I think for a second might be 'I am', but she's already turning away and heading down the hall, so I follow.

There are two police officers waiting for me when we get downstairs. One is a man, grey and gruff, who does all of the talking. The other is a woman, younger than Carolyn, who takes notes in almost total silence.

'There's no need to be nervous,' the man says, after we're done with the introductions and preamble. His name is DC Delmonte, and it's making me think of peaches. 'All we need from you is the truth.'

'I don't know anything,' I say. Actually, I've already said this four times. No one seems to be listening.

Matilda, Bonnie's mother – who's never liked me, by the way – let's out a loud 'hmm'.

'I don't!' I insist.

'Just tell us what you *do* know,' DC Delmonte says. 'Even the things that may seem . . . insignificant. When did Bonnie meet Jack?'

'I don't know,' I say.

'Well, how long have they been in a relationship?'

'I don't know,' I say.

'Did Bonnie ask for your assistance in keeping their relationship a secret?'

'What? No. Why would she?'

'Have you spoken to her today?'

'No.' WhatsApp messages don't count as speaking, do they?

'Did you speak to her yesterday?'

'Yes. But just to talk about revision.'

'Did you talk about Jack?'

'No.' Why are they so obsessed with Jack? Is this all because I mentioned his name to Carolyn this morning?

They're all looking at me like they're waiting for me to say something very specific, but I have no idea what it is. It's like having an in-joke described to me by the group of people it involves in painstaking detail, and everyone's waiting for my reaction to the punchline.

'What the hell is going on?' I ask finally.

'Eden,' Carolyn says, her voice straining with the clear effort of staying calm. 'Do you know who Jack *is*?'

There's a tense, potent silence. I can hear Bonnie's mother's laboured breathing, her eyes brimming and rage-filled. The policewoman has her head tilted slightly, concentration in the lines of her face, and I get the unnerving sense that she's profiling me, or something.

'No,' I say, and I hear how small my voice is in the room, shrunken by adult voices, strident and loud. And, suddenly, I'm scared.

'It's Jack Cohn,' Carolyn says.

'Who?' I ask. My brain is too frazzled, too anxious, to process the information. I don't know anyone called Jack Cohn.

'For God's sake!' Bonnie's mother shrieks in a sudden burst of frustration, so unexpectedly that I actually jump. She takes a step towards me and I shrink back. Why is she so angry at *me*? I'm not the one who's disappeared. 'Just tell us where they are, Eden!'

And that's the moment that Carolyn says it, and everything I thought I knew shatters. '*Mr* Cohn, Eden,' she says. 'Jack is Mr Cohn.'

An image pops into my head, then. Waiting in the music block for Bonnie to finish her flute lesson. Leaning against the whitewashed wall, my head resting underneath a nameplate. *Mr J. Cohn: Head of Music.*

Mr Cohn, Music teacher. Mr Cohn, form tutor of my little sister. Mr Cohn, full-grown adult man.

Mr Cohn, my best friend's secret boyfriend.

Holy. Shit.

2

Just under a year ago, the summer before Year 11, Bonnie told me very seriously that she wanted to learn about alcohol, but sensibly. 'In a safe environment,' she said. Which turned out to mean my bedroom. She supplied the alcohol, turning up with a bag full of bottles. She'd brought vodka, gin, white wine, red wine and, bizarrely, Frangelico.

'That'll do,' I said, laughing. And when I saw her face, so earnest and confused, trying to interpret my words, I laughed so hard there were tears in my eyes.

'I wanted a cross-section of an average off-licence,' she said. 'Is that wrong?'

'Nah,' I said. 'Not if you're a forty-year-old woman.' And then I laughed some more, and finally she stopped looking all saintly and confused and started laughing too.

When we got to my room, she sank to her knees on my carpet and started arranging the bottles in a little semi-circle, studying the labels as she went. 'Did I miss some?'

'Bon,' I said, trying not to crack up again. 'There's no beer. Or cider. Or anything anyone our age would actually drink.'

'*Oh*,' Bonnie said, realization dawning on her face. 'Oh, *beer*.' She turned to look again at her arrangement of bottles. 'Whoops.' She actually said 'whoops'.

And then we both laughed some more, and I went downstairs to ask Bob, my adoptive dad, if he had any beer we could borrow for an experiment, and it turned out he only had bottles of real ale, and we decided it would do. And my adoptive older sister, Valerie, home from uni for the holidays, overheard and supplied a bottle of amaretto to sample.

Bonnie, being Bonnie, had brought her notebook with her. It was a proper Moleskine one with a black leather cover, an annual Christmas present from her parents since she was old enough to write sentences. She showed me the system she'd prepared, so proud of herself, ready for her sampling. Honestly, anyone would have thought she was a professional alcohol tester, or something.

The thing was, Bonnie's mother had a habit of picking up Bonnie's notebook and leafing through it at will, so Bonnie was paranoid about leaving the evidence of her debauchery for her to find. Her solution, naturally, was me, which is why I still have the notes Bonnie made as the two of us made our way through the selection.

Ale
Note 1: Sampled first so it doesn't lose its fizz.
Note 2: Eden says beer/ale doesn't have 'fizz'. Will look up later what it is if it's not fizz. Bubbles? (Like Champagne?)
Volume: 4.9%
Taste: Bitter, horrible aftertaste.
Comments: Couldn't drink a glass of this, eugh.
Eden says: Get used to it.

Vodka
Volume: 37.5%
Taste: Like nail-varnish remover.
Comments: OMG! EUGH! WHY WOULD ANYONE DRINK THIS FOR FUN?
Eden says: I can put Coke in it and it won't taste so bad. Noted!

Gin

Volume:	40%
Taste:	Not as bad as the vodka.
Comments:	Kind of like sparkling water, in an alcohol-y way. Maybe this is the one for me?
Eden says:	Gin is what old women drink. ☹

White wine

Volume:	11.5%
Taste:	Kind of sour. Sour juice.
Comments:	Drinkable! (Sort of.)
Eden says:	You should have found the cheaper stuff.

Amaretto

Volume:	28%
Taste:	Strong. Almondy.
Comments:	I don't like almonds ☹
Eden says:	We don't want to drink what Valerie drinks, anyway.

Frangelico

Volume:	20%
Taste:	LIKE CAKE!!!!
Comments:	(1) The bottle is AMAZING. (2) IT TASTES LIKE CAKE. (3) Eden HADN'T EVEN HEARD OF IT! (4) This is it. Liqueur is the way to go.
Eden says:	Teenagers don't drink liqueur.
I say:	They would if they'd tried Frangelico.

'I want to be ready,' she said, when I asked her why she felt the whole thing was necessary.

'Ready for what?'

'Year Eleven. Parties and stuff. I don't want to be the girl who goes out and gets alcohol poisoning, you know?'

But I didn't know. It wasn't like *I* was planning to go and get alcohol poisoning either, but I hadn't given much thought to my solution to that problem beyond just . . . not drinking too much. Besides, I wasn't sure exactly how Bonnie thought her experiment would help later on, except for knowing that she hated vodka. And who needs a controlled experiment to learn that?

It was August, the height of summer, weeks before the start of the school year, and it all felt so distant to me. School seemed like a million miles away. But it was never distant for Bonnie. It was like she was one hundred per cent in it, all the time, while I had always just been waiting for it to be over.

This is what you have to get: *this* is Bonnie. Over-prepared to the point of ridicule, so desperate to be ready for things, to do things properly, to get it right. She's careful. She experiments. She discusses things with *me*. I'm her *best* friend, her confidante.

Which is why none of this makes the slightest bit of sense. Bonnie's secret boyfriend can't really be Mr Cohn. It just can't be. How would that even have happened? Why wouldn't she have told me? There's no way she could have kept something that big from me. Is there?

Bonnie had never had a boyfriend at all before last October, when she got together with Lewis Cooper. He was on the school football team and wasn't so much the school heart-throb as the school he'll-do. He'd had several girlfriends by the time he got to Bonnie, but she – usually so sensible – was sure this meant that he'd been 'getting ready' for her. She threw herself into their relationship in the same way she always threw herself into her homework and her flute practice – enthusiastically and almost obsessively. She arranged double dates with Connor and me (awkward), gave him a present for their one-month anniversary (far-too-expensive aftershave), took endless couply pictures for her Instagram (nauseating), and generally drove me crackers. (Connor and I had been together for about six months by this point, and our relationship was basically the total opposite. Like Connor, it was sweet, quiet and drama-free.)

It ended, of course. Lewis got bored and dumped Bonnie by text on an ordinary Tuesday afternoon. He didn't even give her a reason, just that 'he wasn't into it', and got right on to the next girl (Sasha Chymes, Year 10). It lasted six weeks in all, but by the way Bonnie reacted you would've thought they'd been engaged or something. She was *devastated.*

'I just wanted him to love me,' she said, in one of her many – *many* – sobbing sessions in my bedroom. 'Is that so much? Really?'

'You'll find someone better to love you,' I said.

'Who?'

'*Anyone*,' I said bluntly. As far as I was concerned, Lewis Cooper was a total waste of space, and I'd thought it even when she was besotted with him. The guy wore a visor to school, for God's sake.

'What if no one ever does?'

'Of course they will, Bon.'

Maybe I should have paid more attention, I don't know. Maybe I shouldn't have been so dismissive of what she was trying to say. I just thought she was overreacting, that she was just being a bit dramatic. Uncharacteristically, sure, but hardly the first girl I knew to have freaked out over a break-up.

But maybe I should have listened more. Maybe I should have asked why she was so worried about being unwanted or unloved.

But even if I had, how could I have guessed that something like this could happen? That some*one* like Mr Cohn could happen?

Bonnie first mentioned 'Jack' about two months or so ago, if I remember right. She'd drawn one of those silly hearts on her Maths book and written *Bonnie + Jack 4ever* – yes, it really was that cheesy – and I'd asked who Jack was. She'd been so annoyingly vague, I'd decided not to give her the satisfaction of carrying on asking. Needless to say, I never met him, and she'd never tell me anything concrete about where they went or what they did together.

There are some things that should have been red flags. I see that now. The fact that she didn't want to give me any actual details about Jack is the obvious one; why didn't I think it was weird that I never saw any pictures of him? Did I really believe that 'he didn't have Facebook'? (Well, no. But I thought that meant he didn't really exist, not that he was actually our teacher.) She'd been increasingly distant from me over the last few weeks leading up to our exams, but I'd put that down to stress. I'd really thought she was revising.

And as for Mr Cohn himself, well, the first thing you should know about him is that he was the cool kind of teacher. The one who called us all 'dudes' (as in, 'Can you turn the volume down a notch, dudes?') and wore hipster glasses and one of those man cardigans that you can only pull off if you're ironic and know how to wax your hair.

I knew Mr Cohn because he was my Music teacher in Year 7 and 8. I went through a phase of having a crush on him, like all the girls at school did, because he was funny and charming and good looking, not to mention younger than most of our other teachers seemed to be. He was especially fun to crush on because he liked to tease us, acting like he was one of us, a friend, an ally, rather than just another Sir.

The truth is I'd never thought he'd given off a dodgy vibe. He was just Mr Cohn. And I had absolutely no clue – not even the tiniest inkling – that he had a thing going on with Bonnie. I could lie and say I suspected something, or that it all makes sense now, but I didn't, and it doesn't.

It just doesn't make any sense at all.

3

I get a grilling from the police, Bonnie's mother and Carolyn for another twenty minutes after the Mr Cohn revelation, even though I'm too dumbstruck to make much sense.

'You must know,' Mrs Wiston-Stanley keeps saying, over and over. 'You must know where they've gone.'

Carolyn is the one who finally gets them all to leave. 'Maybe we should try this again tomorrow,' she says. 'When Eden's had some time to get over the shock.'

The policewoman, who's been saying nothing but has been taking diligent notes for the entire time we've all been speaking, looks at me and quirks her eyebrow a little before she leaves. I don't know if it's meant to reassure or unsettle me, so I'm just left confused instead. Has she seen through me? Maybe she knows. But how can she know? All they have on me is that I'm Bonnie's best friend.

And anyway, I don't know where they are, do I? One little text that told me she was leaving doesn't mean anything, does it? It wouldn't help them find her. I'm as much in the dark as they are.

'Are you OK?' Carolyn asks, putting an arm around my shoulder and pulling me in for a gentle squeeze.

Surprised. Confused. A little weirded out. 'OK' isn't the word. 'Yeah,' I say. 'Why did they come all the way here? Just for that?'

'I think they thought you'd know more,' she says after a pause. 'You were the one who mentioned a "Jack", and even if you didn't know exactly who that was, it was enough to send them down the right road.' *Ah. Whoops.* 'But they don't have much to go on in terms of timing.'

What does *that* mean? 'OK.'

'Do you want to talk about all of this?'

'No.' An image pops into my head of Mr Cohn demonstrating how to play a cowbell in Year 7. He'd been so enthusiastic about that stupid bell thing, striking it with an expression of such earnest joy, we'd all nearly wet ourselves laughing. The boys had called him 'Bell-end Cohn' for the entire year.

'Eden,' Carolyn says. I blink and look at her. 'It's OK to feel shocked about this. Talking about it might help. Shall I make us some tea?'

'No,' I say again, wriggling free of her arm. I have to call Bonnie. Right now.

Carolyn's face clouds over with frustrated disappointment, an expression I recognize. Sometimes I indulge Carolyn's desire for a close mother–daughter relationship. Sometimes I don't. And when I don't, I get that face.

'The police will be back to talk to you at some point,' she says. 'Wouldn't you feel better talking to me first?'

The only person I want to talk to is Bonnie. 'Maybe later,' I say.

'Eden—'

I take the stairs two at a time and go to my room, closing the door behind me. I grab my phone from my bag and unlock it, seeing two messages from Connor – **I'm more awake now!** and **Come over later?** – but none from Bonnie. I ignore Connor's messages and instead send Bonnie an urgent, all-caps what-the-hell text, and then try to call her, but it just goes to voicemail again.

Oh God, this is completely insane. And wrong, right? Now I'm on my own again, away from Mrs Wiston-Stanley's glare and the policeman's sharp gaze, I can let myself think again, and it is *not good*. Maybe I should have told them about Bonnie's message as soon as I found out about Mr Cohn? But I *promised*.

I sit down on my bed, staring off into space, trying to reason with myself. There's no need to get all panicky. This is Bonnie, for God's sake. The most responsible teenager in the world. *But she's gone off with Mr Cohn*, AND ANYWAY it's not like she's in any danger or anything. How much of a difference does it really make that her secret boyfriend Jack is actually Mr Cohn – *Mr freaking Cohn, Jesus* – instead of a guy our age? *It makes a big difference* – Yeah, it's a bit of a weird situation – *It's a totally weird situation* – and I guess it makes sense that she'd want to get away from the drama for a while, now it's all blowing up – *But it's blowing up because they've run off together – OH MY GOD, THEY'VE RUN OFF TOGETHER* – and she'll be back soon, obviously. There is no reason at all for me to grass her up. It's not up to me. *But everyone's really worried* – I can just wait for her to get back and then it can all get sorted out. *Maybe I'm a bit worried too*. I wonder where they've gone. *I wonder where they've gone*. I hope she's OK. *God, I hope she's OK*.

I text her again, pointlessly. I try and think about what she'd do if it was me who'd buggered off instead of her. Imagining the look on her face if I tried to pull something like this makes me smile, but then I remember that she really *is* pulling something exactly like this, and the smile drops off.

This is not how my Saturday was supposed to go. I'm just wondering whether I should ask Connor to come over so I can talk to him about all of this and/or let him distract me, when my door comes flying open, slamming against the wall, and a short, blue-eyed nightmare bounds across the floor and jumps on to my bed.

'Ohmigod!' she yells.

'Daisy!' I snap, getting up and inspecting the wall for puncture wounds. 'For God's sake.'

'I can't believe your Bonnie's done a runner!' she says, eyes wide with excitement, sitting up on her knees on my mattress.

'Go away,' I say, but I don't mean it and she knows it, because she doesn't move.

'Do you think they're shagging?' she asks.

'Daisy!'

'They must be, right? Gross!' She says this with the same level of delight as if someone had given her tickets to Disneyland.

I give her a shove as I lie down beside her on the bed, grabbing a pillow and holding it over my face.

'Tell me everything,' she commands, drumming her hands on my leg.

'I don't know anything!' I say, my voice muffled, glad she can't see my face.

She snorts. 'Yeah, right.'

I lift off the pillow and glare at her. 'Who even told you, anyway?' Is it public knowledge already? God, people don't hang around, do they?

'Carolyn, course,' she says, flopping on to her back on my bed. 'So. Where are they then?'

'I obviously don't know, Daisy.'

She raises a single eyebrow – a skill she perfected last year and has been unduly proud of ever since – and then laughs, scooting across the bed and resting her head on my stomach. Daisy can switch between bloody irritating and cute as hell in a heartbeat. It's as charming as it is annoying.

Here are a few things about Daisy, aged twelve years and three months:

- When she was seven she fell into a pond trying to catch a frog and has refused to go swimming ever since.

- She has ADHD and dyscalculia, which she says are just stupid adult labels for 'likes fun' and 'hates maths'.
- She makes me laugh like no one else in the world.
- She used to be all soft and sweet, but since she started secondary school she's been getting tougher and sharper.
- She's turning out to be one of the trouble kids in her year. Carolyn and Bob have been called into the school three times already.
- She has dark blonde hair and blue eyes, and no one ever believes we're sisters because we look nothing alike.
- She doesn't remember what it was like living with our real mum. She says her memories are all me, and then the McKinleys.
- I would walk over burning coals and broken glass if she needed me.
- She's the world's biggest pest.
- I adore her.

The thing with Daisy is that, as annoying as she can be, she's the truest family I have, whatever definition of 'family' you use. The way I think of it is, I have three families, some overlapping, some cancelled out by the other, but all there. The most obvious one – as in, the answer I'll give during my French GCSE oral exam to the standard 'Describe your family' question – is the McKinley family. I'm the middle child of two parents, Carolyn and Bob. They adopted me and my little sister Daisy seven years ago, and now we're part of their family along with their biological daughter, Valerie.

But being adopted means you had some kind of a family to start with, a different one, maybe even a 'bad' one. And me, I came from the Kostenko family, and that was my mother – my 'real' mother – my little sister and me. The three of us in a messy, broken little unit. In my head, where I keep my secrets, that unit still exists. Even if it's just in the past – even if I can never enter it again – it's still there. Time and adoption can't really take it away.

My third family, the tiniest one, is what exists in the centre of the Venn diagram. Squished together in the oval is Daisy and me, bound by blood, kept together through adoption. My link to my past, and my companion through to the future. Daisy can be a pain in the neck, a constant worry in the back of my mind, but she's mine, and I'm hers.

Sometimes I feel like I wandered into someone else's life, and I'm not actually meant to be here. But then I look at Daisy, and it's like . . . *Oh yeah. Here I am.*

She hangs around to annoy me for a while longer, demanding that I braid her hair, and then complaining that I've made her look terrible. She finally leaves me alone as it starts to get dark, which is excellent timing because not five minutes after she's gone my phone buzzes and I glance at the screen.

It's a new message on WhatsApp from an unknown number. Shit. What if it's . . .

Unknown

Hi! It's me! New phone! (Well, new OLD phone)
And a new old car! They'll never find us ☺☺☺☺

Oops, me = Bonnie ☺

Me

HOLY FUCKING SHIT BONNIE.

Ah . . . so you know then?

Me

HOLY FUCKING SHITBALLS BONNIE.

Unknown

Does this mean everyone knows?

MR COHN?!?!?!

OK, wow. Um. Surprise! Is everyone freaking out?

YES. I AM FREAKING OUT.

Don't freak out. It's a good thing. I'm so happy.

Where are you, Bon?

Can I tell you?

What?

Seriously, can I? Will you promise not to tell?

Of course I won't tell.

Even if my mum asks you?

Bon, I won't tell. Where are you?
And when are you coming back?

Wales.

Wales?!

Wales?! I don't know what, exactly, I expected, but it wasn't Wales. What do I even say to that?!

Me

Bon, are you kidding?

Unknown

?? No! It's perfect. There's no way they'd come looking for us here. It's not forever, just for a bit.

A bit? You mean until you come back home?

No, I mean until we go somewhere else.

Somewhere else?!

What did you think I was doing? I told you I was running away.

I didn't think you meant it!
AND NOT WITH MR FREAKING COHN.

Minor detail ☺

Do you realize what's happening here?
Your mum is going MENTAL.

Don't say 'mental' like that.

BONNIE.

'Eden?' Carolyn's voice travels from down the hall, and I jump, dropping the phone.

'Yeah?' God, my voice sounds so guilty. I'm so bad at this.

'Dinner in five minutes, OK?'

'OK!'

I reach for my phone again, my heart thudding.

Unknown

Look, calm down, OK? It's fine. I know my parents are going to be freaked out, but it's really fine. I'm fine. I've never been so happy. This is the best thing that's ever happened to me.

That's a lot of 'fines'.

Me

The police came to my house.

Unknown

Oh wow. I'm sorry, Eeds :(Did you tell them anything?

No.

Thank you xxxxxx

I swallow, looking down at my phone screen, trying to figure out what to say. What *should* I say? Doesn't she realize how wrong this all is? Should I try telling her? Before I can figure out what to type, a new message appears.

Unknown

Don't worry. Really. You know I'm safe. My parents know I'm safe. Maybe they won't like that I'm with Jack, but he'd never hurt me, and one day they'll understand that I'm happy and I didn't do this to hurt them. I love him, and he loves me, and we're going to be together.

Me

But it's our exams this week.

Unknown

Love is way more important than some tiny exams, E.

When we were thirteen, Bonnie cried during a Maths test. It wasn't even an exam, just one of those little tests you get every month or so to check everyone's been paying attention. Even more meaningless than actual exams. But Bonnie worked herself into such a state that she actually cried because she couldn't answer three questions in a row.

I'd thought it was pretty funny at the time, to be honest. I thought she was being ridiculous, getting so upset about a pointless little test. But now, with our GCSEs just days away, I want that Bonnie back. I may not have understood why she cared so much about a test, but I understand even *less* how she can suddenly not care at *all* about our *GCSEs*. Her future.

Me

I don't understand what's happening :/

Unknown

You don't have to understand. Just don't worry, and don't tell anyone!! You should delete all of these messages in case someone looks at your phone. Save this number if you want, but don't save it under my name, OK? And don't tell anyone where I am. Please, please, OK?

What do you want your fake name to be?

:) You pick for me xxx

I hesitate, then save the number as a new contact: 'Ivy'. I'm big into plant symbolism, and Ivy is the perfect name for my newly renegade best friend because it symbolizes friendship. Ivy is tough, succeeding where other plants would fail, continuing to grow even when the conditions are harsh. That's how I see Bonnie. Tough, steady and determined.

I sit on my bed in the quiet, staring at the bright screen, the word 'Ivy'. All of those incriminating messages waiting patiently to be deleted.

OK. OK, Eden. Think about this.

Everyone wants to know where Bonnie is.

I know where Bonnie is.

The thought prickles in my mind. I could tell. I could call Mrs Wiston-Stanley and say, *I know where Bonnie is*. I could be the hero. I could surprise everyone.

'Eden?' Carolyn's voice carries up the stairs.

Carolyn would be so proud of me.

'Dinner's ready.'

I don't give her many opportunities to be proud of me.

But . . . Bonnie. My best friend. Bonnie, who never questioned us being friends, even though we're so different and she could have been friends with all the other clever girls in the top sets who can spell words like 'accommodate' and 'parallel' without looking them up and who never get detentions. Bonnie, who never judges me, not for anything, even when I put apple slices in my peanut butter sandwiches. Bonnie, who shares my sadnesses and worries, who holds in my secrets and doesn't make me feel bad for the emotional baggage she helps me carry.

If this was the other way round, would Bonnie tell on me? The obvious answer is yes, based on the pre-runaway version of herself. She's too responsible to keep my location from my worried parents, too rubbish under interrogation to stay quiet even if she wanted to. But then again . . . Bonnie is loyal. Incredibly loyal. It's why we stayed friends against all the odds between the ages of eight and now. If I asked her not to tell, maybe she wouldn't, and for the same reasons that *my* instinct is not to tell.

I can't tell. I have to trust her when she says that she's safe and happy, that this is what she wants. If I sold her out to my parents – or worse, *her* parents – I'd be betraying her, and I can't do that. She'd never forgive me. *I'd* never forgive me.

And so that's that. I delete our message history, lock my screen and head downstairs for dinner.

How Bonnie and I Met

It's a Wednesday in February. I'm seven years old, two days away from my eighth birthday, and it's my first day at yet another new school. (Moving schools is an oh-so-fun side effect of being in and out of foster care.) Over the weekend I moved into my new foster family's house on a long-term placement – they're called the McKinleys, which I can't spell – and this morning my new foster sister, Valerie, plaited my hair for me. I do not feel like myself. My school clothes are so clean, they feel strange against my skin.

My teacher is called Mrs Bennet, and she keeps her hand on my back, right between my shoulder blades, as she introduces me to the class. She says, 'This is Eden. She's just moved here, and I'm sure you'll all make her feel very welcome.' She guides me over to one of the tables and points to the empty chair beside a thin girl with brown hair and glasses. 'Eden,' Mrs Bennet says. 'This is Bonnie Wiston-Stanley. I've asked her to look after you while you settle in.'

'Hello!' Bonnie says, confident and warm, like she was then. The way clever kids are before they get to secondary school.

'Hi,' I mumble. I'm thinking, *Wiston-Stanley*?

'Don't worry,' Bonnie says, putting an arm around my shoulder, her eyes bright behind her glasses. 'I'll look after you. I promise.'

And she did, right from that moment on, even when it became clear that I didn't need to be looked after. She still did it, quietly and unquestioningly. When some of the other kids laughed at me for not being able to read properly, she stopped me from throwing rocks at them (all but one – Josh Williams never tried to cross me again) and told our teacher, very nicely but firmly, that the two of us were going to be reading buddies from now on. She swapped lunches with me in the weeks before Carolyn realized that I didn't like ham sandwiches. She made us friendship bracelets with an 'E' and a 'B' charm.

I'd never had a friend like her before, never really had a proper friend at all. Before Bonnie, I'd been the often scruffy, sometimes polished, always slightly bewildered kid, watching everyone else move seamlessly through a world they all seemed to know how to belong in. It was like the other kids had sensed that, because they'd never tried to be friends with me. Not until Bonnie.

Everything about being fostered and living in a new place and going to a new school was hard, except Bonnie. She made me feel safe. I felt lucky to be her friend, to be the one she shared sleepovers and secrets and giggles with.

A lot has changed since then – it's a long time since I was the odd kid no one wanted to be friends with – but I never stopped feeling lucky for Bonnie. And that friendship bracelet still hangs from the wall near my bed.

Sunday

KENT SCHOOLGIRL 'VANISHES' WITH TEACHER

A missing schoolgirl is believed to have absconded from her hometown in Kent, travelling with a teacher from her school.

15-year-old Bonnie Wiston-Stanley was reported missing by her parents on Saturday morning when she failed to return home after staying with friends.

Kent Police confirmed last night they were urgently seeking local music teacher Jack Cohn, 29, in connection with her disappearance.

Wiston-Stanley was identified via CCTV at a Tesco petrol station on the outskirts of Kent in the early hours of Saturday morning, in a car driven by Cohn. The car was later found abandoned at a car park in Portsmouth.

Cohn is currently Head of Music at Kett Academy, Larking, where Wiston-Stanley is a pupil.

An initial police search of Wiston-Stanley's home yesterday brought to light evidence that Cohn had been in close contact with the pupil.

Speaking during a police press conference last night, Matilda Wiston-Stanley pleaded for her daughter Bonnie to get in contact with her family.

'Kett Academy governors, staff and pupils are united in concern for Bonnie and simply wish her to make contact with her family, who are naturally very concerned for her welfare,' headmistress Christine Neal said in a statement.

'The school is currently cooperating with Kent Police in its investigation and therefore cannot comment further on the matter at this time.'

GCSE exams will begin this week as normal, students were told.

4

Valerie

Is that YOUR Bonnie on the news?!

I wake up at 8.48 a.m. to this text message from Valerie, but I don't bother replying. No doubt Valerie has already rung Carolyn by now and had the news confirmed for her, and the last thing I want to do right now is to talk to Perfection-Personified about everything that's happening. Maybe it's weird, but I almost feel embarrassed to be a part of this mess, even just by association, in front of Valerie. This would never happen to her, or even one of her friends. It just wouldn't.

I used to want to be like Valerie when I was younger. She's the most together person I've ever known, and I always felt like everything would be so much easier if I was just more like her. But I realized pretty quickly that I could spend my whole life trying to be like Valerie and never come close.

Here are a few things about Valerie, aged twenty-two years and seventeen days:

- She's almost finished her final year at university, where she's on track to get a First in Biochemistry.
- Everyone calls her Valerie – she is never, ever Val.
- She took a gap year before uni and went travelling around Asia with her boyfriend.
- She came back single, because she decided she was

better on her own.

- She can speak French.
- She passed her driving test first time.
- On the day her parents adopted me, she handwrote me a letter that started 'Dear Little Sister', and I still have it.
- Her middle name is Minty, because it was her gran's pet name, and she hates it.
- 'Minty McKinley!' she shouts whenever this comes up. 'Valerie *Minty* McKinley!'
- She's never failed at anything in her life.
- We have absolutely nothing in common.

It's not that I don't like Valerie, or that she's mean or annoying or anything. It's more that I don't know who I am with her, what her role is in my life. Maybe this sounds a bit weird, but I like to know this about the people in my world. It helps me feel grounded. It helps me feel safe.

Carolyn and Bob chose me. Daisy is my blood. Bonnie and I chose each other. So did Connor and me. That's what makes them my people. But Valerie . . . She just got landed with me. The sister she didn't ask for or need. Keeping a distance from her just spares us both a lot of unnecessary grief. If she knew me as well as she thinks she wants to, she wouldn't like me, because why would she, and then where would we be? So even when she tries, I resist. It's best for everyone. Besides, there's six years and a whole world between us. It's not like it's a loss.

I haven't got any new messages from Bonnie, and no one's come to wake me up, so I know she and Mr Cohn haven't been found yet. I send 'Ivy' a quick message – **Update?** – and then lie there under the covers for a while, thinking about all the possible places they could be and things they could be doing. Are they still in Wales? Or have they gone on to that vague 'somewhere else' that

Bonnie mentioned? If I'd told Carolyn last night about Bonnie's messages, would they have been caught by now?

I go downstairs for breakfast and find Carolyn and Bob, looking almost comically serious, sitting at a kitchen table covered by newspapers. It is only at this moment that the final word in Valerie's text message registers – 'news'. Bonnie was on the *news*.

And, clearly, news*papers*. I can see her face beaming out at me from at least three front pages.

'Morning, love,' Bob says, trying out a smile.

'There's some bacon left,' Carolyn says, standing, already reaching for the cooled pan on the kitchen counter. 'Shall I make you a sandwich?'

'I can do it,' I say. 'What are the papers saying?' I'm reaching for the *Observer*, which is lying open to a page with Bonnie's face on it, but Bob puts a hand across it to stop me taking it.

'Don't worry about the papers for now,' he says, his voice as gentle and calm as it always is. 'Have some breakfast.'

'Have you spoken to Valerie?' Carolyn asks.

'No,' I say, trying not to sound as frustrated as I am. 'I figured you would. Do the papers know anything we don't?'

Carolyn hands me a plate containing the bacon sandwich I'd said I'd make myself and sits back down. 'The papers are a little behind,' she says. 'We know more than they do, so you're best speaking to us rather than wasting time reading the salacious speculation in the tabloids.'

'Salacious,' I repeat, trying out the word. It's a great-sounding word. *Sall-ay-shuss*. 'What's that mean?'

'Sordid,' Bob says. 'Sensationalist. Sexed-up.'

'Anyway,' Carolyn says, 'I rang Bonnie's mother this morning for an update. The investigation was going on all of last night, but they really don't have much of an idea of where they might have gone. She's very distressed, as you can imagine. And dealing with this level of press coverage as well . . .' She gestures at the spread of newspapers. 'It's awful in its own way, but necessary. The feeling is that it's worth identifying Bonnie, even though she's a minor, because they'll be found more quickly if there are two faces for the public to look for. Does that make sense?'

I nod, even though it doesn't really. It seems so extreme, so *real*, to see it in the papers. 'What happens once they find them?' I ask. 'Will they be, like . . . in trouble?'

Both Carolyn and Bob look at me like I've just spoken Finnish or something. 'Yes,' Bob says. 'A fair bit of trouble.'

'You know what I mean,' I say. 'Like, how much trouble?'

'Well, Jack Cohn will be arrested,' he says. 'There'll be a trial, probably some prison time, presuming he's found guilty. No doubt he'll lose his job at Kett. I'd be amazed if he was ever able to teach again.'

'What about Bonnie?'

'Oh, no, *she* won't be in any trouble,' Carolyn says. 'Her parents just want her home safe. We all do. She's the victim in this.'

I frown. 'But she's chosen to go, hasn't she?'

'She's a minor,' Bob says. 'So no, she hasn't. She might think she has, but the law says otherwise.'

My head is starting to hurt. What they're saying is so completely different to what I've heard from Bonnie, and I just don't know what to do with that. She says she's happy, that she wants this. Does it even matter what the law says? I know what she'd say to this. I know what Bob would say. But I have no idea what the answer actually is.

'So what's actually in the papers?' I ask. I can worry about that stuff later. 'What do the police know?'

Bob gives me the run-down while Carolyn sips her tea and looks worried. My biggest takeaway from the explanation is really that the police know nothing much at all. Bob keeps using the word 'disappeared', emphasizing that the trail runs cold after Portsmouth, and that the police are concentrating their efforts on the immediate area, particularly the port. I think about Wales and say nothing.

'Abandoning the car has to be a red herring,' Bob says. 'To throw the police off the real destination. They'll have wasted a lot of time checking all the ferries and boats. Why else drive all the way there when Dover's practically on our doorstep?'

'How would they have got anywhere else without a car?' Carolyn asks.

I cram my bacon sandwich into my mouth and chew, busying myself with the copy of the *Observer*.

'They could have got on a bus,' Bob says. 'I'm sure they could have got far enough away before the alert got out. Think about how long it must have been between getting to Portsmouth and the police starting to look for them. Nearly twelve hours, at least? Plenty of time to get away.'

'Away where?' Carolyn says, shaking her head. 'We live on an island. There are only so many places you can go. And they must have known people would be looking for them.'

Bob doesn't have an answer for this. Instead he says, 'Maybe we're being too generous with how much sense and logic has actually been applied here,' which draws a reluctant smile from Carolyn. He turns back to me. 'Anyway, as you may have gathered, the police don't have much to go on in terms of logistics. But it's not just about the wheres and the whats; the whys are just as important, and that's what a lot of the focus is on. They want to know exactly what's been going on between your Bonnie and Jack Cohn, because that may give them a clearer idea of what his intentions are, where they're going, that kind of thing.'

'How are they going to find out?' I ask. If I didn't know, then no one knew, so who can they ask?

'Well, they'll be going through anything Bonnie's parents can find in her bedroom. Her laptop, for one thing – which they accessed yesterday, and was how they found out about the relationship – and anything else she may have written down about it, any letters or anything. And last night the police raided Mr Cohn's flat.'

My mind instantly conjures up an image from some detective show I must have watched once: police hammering on doors, lots of yelling. I didn't know that was the kind of thing that really happened. 'Did they find anything?'

'Oh, yes. Lots.'

'Is it bad?' I ask, watching Bob's face carefully, trying to read between the adult lines on his face.

'It's not good,' Carolyn says.

'What does that mean?'

Carolyn and Bob glance at each other. 'Well, it confirms everything we feared based on what was found on Bonnie's laptop,' Carolyn says. 'It seems like at least part of this whole mess had been planned. And they've been –' she hesitates – 'together?' She says it like a question, but I don't know who she's asking. 'Yes, I suppose that's the word. *Together*. For a while.'

'A while?' I repeat. 'How long is a while?'

'At least a couple of months.'

This shouldn't be a surprise, not after last night, but somehow it is. That's a long time to keep a secret like this from your best friend. Somewhere inside me, buried for now by the shock and worry and confusion, I can feel something like hurt stirring. All this time, she's just been lying to me?

'The main thing it shows, from a legal point of view . . .' Bob begins, and I look up in time to see Carolyn shake her head at him. He stops.

'What?' I demand.

'Eden will be able to read all of this herself when the papers get a hold of it,' Bob says, his jaw tight. 'It's better that we talk about it with her, isn't it?'

Carolyn rubs her forehead. 'Is it?'

Bob lets out a sigh and leans forward. 'What's clear from the evidence they've gathered is that the relationship was sexual, which has significant legal repercussions.'

'Oh,' I say. It's all I can manage. The weird thing is, I can't figure out if my response to this sentence is 'Well, duh' or 'What the fuck?!' even though it can clearly only be one or the other. On the one hand, I mean, of course they've had sex. They've run away together, for God's sake. But on the other hand . . . *they've had SEX?! Bonnie and MR COHN?!*

This is all too bloody much to take. I didn't even know she'd had sex at all. How could she have kept that kind of information from me? We'd always said we'd tell each other. Couldn't she have found some way to tell me, even if she didn't say who it was with?

And . . . wait . . .

'Evidence?' I say. 'Like . . . what kind of evidence?'

'Pictures,' Carolyn says. 'There were some pictures.'

'Pictures?'

'Of Bonnie.'

'Pictures of Bonnie?'

'Sexual pictures.'

'Sexual pictures of Bonnie?'

'Eden,' Bob says.

'What?' My voice comes out louder than I'd intended, but I don't care. 'You can't tell me something like this and expect me not to react.'

This is the moment Daisy, still in her pyjamas, chooses to come charging down the stairs, demanding – in this order – money for the bus, breakfast, her favourite jeans and an update on Bonnie.

'Everyone's talking about it,' she tells me, gleeful, through a mouthful of toast after Carolyn has persuaded her to sit down. 'My phone's, like, on fire. Everyone's going *mental*. I can't wait to go to school tomorrow.'

'Ah, a silver lining,' Bob says, deadpan.

'My friends think it's so romantic.'

That stops me. 'They think *what*?'

'Running away to be together because they're so in love and society doesn't *understand*!' Her eyes are wide and excited, her voice breathless. 'It's like a film or something. And Mr Cohn is so sexy.'

'Oh my God, you're twelve, don't say words like "sexy",' I say. 'And anyway, he's not sexy. He's kind-of-good-looking-for-a-teacher. That's not the same.'

'Whatever. Tell me everything you know,' she commands. 'When did they start shagging?'

'Daisy!' Bob and Carolyn gasp in unison.

'Oh my God, I'm not eight,' Daisy says, rolling her eyes. 'And it's not like I said fu—'

'I don't know anything,' I interrupt before she can get herself grounded. 'So you can tell all your little friends to mind their own.'

Daisy looks at me for a moment, blinking slowly. The sudden calm is very unnerving. Finally she says, 'Aren't you meant to be best friends?'

'What's that supposed to mean?' I ask, even though I know what she means.

'If she really didn't tell you *anything*, what kind of a best friend is that?'

There's a silence. Daisy, Bob and Carolyn are all looking at me, waiting for me to respond to what is clearly a pretty good question.

And I don't have an answer. Not for them; not even for me.

'I'm going to go revise,' I say.

*

What I actually do is call Connor. I haven't been able to talk to him properly since I left his house yesterday afternoon except for a few texts, and those were before the story hit the news. I hadn't been able to face seeing him in the evening because I was still trying to get to grips with what was happening. Not that I'm in a much better state now.

'Whoa, holy shit!' is how he greets me.

'I know,' I say.

'Holy *shit*,' he repeats. 'So the "secret Jack" was actually Mr Cohn? That is un-freaking-real. Did you know?'

'Of course I didn't know!' I snap, rattled.

'Has she messaged you or anything?'

'No.' The lie slips out before I can think about it, already an automatic response after talking to the police and my family. I hadn't really thought about whether I would tell Connor the truth, but now the decision is made for me, and so I just go with it. 'I can't believe any of this is happening. It's all so weird.'

'Have you been on Facebook today? Everyone's talking about it.'

'Ugh, Facebook.'

'I know it's annoying, but it's where literally everyone is right now. Don't you want to know what they're saying?'

'Not even a little bit.'

He laughs. 'They're all waiting for you to come online and give some kind of update. They figure that if anyone knows what's going on, it's you.'

'Is that why *you're* speaking to me?' I ask. 'To get an update?'

'Yes,' Connor says. I can hear that he's smiling. 'Why else would I want to talk to my girlfriend?'

I'm suddenly very, very glad that my boyfriend is sixteen and an actual boy instead of a nearly-thirty-year-old man. The ordinariness of our relationship is one of my favourite things about it.

Even though we didn't get together until Year 10, I had always known Connor in that vague way you know everyone in your year at school without actually knowing him. I knew he was the spindly ginger kid that Dean Harris – school bully, absolute dickhead – liked to pick on. But we weren't in the same form or in any of the same sets until the start of Year 10, when we were put in the same class for Design & Tech. We ended up on the same table and became friendly in that easy way that happens sometimes, with the right people. It was still during the time when I thought his quietness was shyness and his refusal to stand up to boys like Dean Harris was weakness, though, so I didn't know him at all, even though I thought I did.

Anyway, we'd been friendly acquaintances for a few months when a whole bunch of us from Year 10 were sprawled over several tables in the canteen at lunchtime. A bunch of the boys, including Connor, were playing some weird teen-hybrid version of poker – think liquorice wheels and jelly beans instead of actual cash – and Dean started in on Connor, giving him a hard time.

I can't remember exactly what he said, but it involved calling him 'ginger pubes' about five times. Connor was basically just ignoring him, eyes on the cards, and it was driving me crazy. So I leaned over and said – my voice can be pretty loud when I'm on Kett grounds, because it's how you survive – 'Why are you so obsessed with Connor's pubic hair, Dean?'

And everyone around us cracked up so loudly that Dean couldn't have got a comeback in even if he was smart enough to think of one. I'll never forget how Connor looked at me: a kind of bemused surprise, like he was seeing me for the first time; but also like he was *really* seeing me, in a way that maybe other people didn't.

The weekend after that, there was a party at someone's house, and I went, and there was Connor, who I'd never seen at one of the

Kett-crowd house parties before, wearing a light blue shirt like an adult, leaning against the wall and smiling at me. I said to him, 'I've never seen you at a party before,' and he told me that it was because of me, that he was there for me, and he kissed me and I kissed him, and that's how love starts when you're fifteen.

'Daisy thinks it's all so romantic,' I say.

'Yeah, so do a bunch of girls from Kett.'

I frown at the phone. Is that the normal thing to think? Is there something wrong with me for thinking it's all just a bit gross? 'Do *you* think it's romantic?'

I hear a spluttered laugh. 'No. I think it's weird. I mean, I'm not so surprised about Mr Cohn. If I had to guess which teacher it was, I'd guess him. But I'd never've thought Bonnie would be the other half.'

'How come?'

'Because she's so—'

'No, not her. I know why that's a surprise. I mean, how come you would've guessed Mr Cohn?'

'Oh, cos he's so smarmy, you know? Always talking to the girls instead of the guys. Being too friendly and stuff. Plus, all that extra time he was alone with Bonnie was weird, right? Maybe we should have noticed earlier.'

'You mean the flute lessons?' Mr Cohn had been giving Bonnie extra private tutoring for her upcoming exams for months.

'Well, they obviously weren't actually flute lessons, were they?'

'Oh my God,' I say. 'Thanks for that.'

He laughs. 'You're going to hear a lot worse, I reckon. Mum says the papers are going to go to town on this story.'

'There's some stuff that's not in the papers yet,' I say. I sink down on to the carpet and lean my head back against the wall. 'Carolyn spoke to Bonnie's mum this morning.'

'Oh yeah? Like what?'

'Like they found pictures of Bonnie on Mr Cohn's laptop.'

'Pictures like . . . *those* kinds of pictures?'

'Yeah. Those kinds of pictures.'

Connor is silent for a moment, digesting this. 'Shit,' he says finally.

'Yeah.'

'Shit,' he says again. 'Bonnie Wiston-Stanley. Who knew?'

We talk for a little while more before he has to go, and then I have no other excuse to procrastinate from revision any longer. I make a blanket fort for myself in the living room, parked in front of the TV with my revision materials displayed in front of me, and stay there for the next few hours, every now and then glancing down at one of the books. I'm hoping that just having the information near my eyeballs will help somehow. You never know, it might be a thing that happens. Science doesn't know everything, does it?

I've got used to the rolling coverage now, seeing the stories rotate with the same recorded voiceovers and interviews played over and over. When the story isn't about Bonnie, I watch the red ticker tape scroll across the screen. *Police appeal for help in search for missing schoolgirl Bonnie Wiston-Stanley and teacher Jack Cohn.* Bonnie and Mr Cohn's disappearance was the top story this morning but has now been relegated to second, partly because they haven't had any fresh information since 8 a.m., and also because some old politician I haven't even heard of died, and they keep showing footage of other old politicians saying how great he was.

The Bonnie and Jack story comes around again, and I pull my knees up to my chin, watching as Bonnie's picture comes up on screen, the same one that was smiling out at me from the papers this morning.

God, that's a terrible picture of Bonnie. She'd hate it. Bonnie's mother must have given it out as part of a press release or something. Which is mean, because of all the pictures she could have chosen to represent Bonnie to the wider world, this is not a good one. It's Bonnie's school picture from a few months ago, the one where she had a little fairy ring of spots on her right cheek, and her ponytail was a bit crooked. She's not even smiling properly. Mothers are mean.

But at least it gives me an opportunity to be helpful. I find a picture I know Bonnie likes – one I took of her over half-term at the nature reserve. She's relaxed and smiling, much more like the Bonnie we all know and love – and print off one version and copy another on to a USB stick.

'Can you drive me to Bonnie's?' I ask Carolyn, who is sitting at the kitchen table, sifting through piles of papers. She and Bob have their own business, McKinley Landscaping and Garden Design, which is good because it means she mostly works from home, but less good because she basically never stops, even at weekends.

She starts, immediately alert. 'Did you hear something from her?' She turns to me. 'Did she call?'

I shake my head, shrugging. 'No, I just wanted to talk to her mum.'

Carolyn hesitates, then nods. 'Good idea. We should see if there's anything more we could be doing to help. I'll come with you.' She grabs her keys from the counter and we leave straight away.

Bonnie's house is only five minutes away by car, and it's a route I've both walked and been driven on more times than I can count, but when I arrive everything looks different, mostly because there are journalists camped out across the entire front lawn, as if Bonnie's house has been replaced by a house from a crime show, or something. Is this story really that interesting? Isn't there anything else going on? Don't they know that Bonnie will obviously be back any minute, and this is all a huge fuss over nothing?

'Oh dear,' Carolyn says, looking at the journalists. The road is packed full of cars and there's nowhere for her to park, so she's stopped in the middle of the road, tapping her fingers against the wheel, considering. 'Maybe we should try again later?'

'We're here now,' I say, already undoing my seatbelt. 'I'll just run in.'

Carolyn frowns. 'I'm not sure about this, Eden. What if they try and speak to you?'

'I'll just ignore them,' I say. 'I won't be long. You can just wait here. I'll be in and out.'

Her frown deepens. 'I'd thought I might speak to Matilda. At the very least, let her know she has my support if she needs it.'

'I'll tell her that,' I say, reaching for the door handle.

'Eden,' Carolyn begins. I can tell some kind of a spiel is coming so I open the door and hotfoot it out of the car. 'Eden!' she calls after me, surprise and exasperation mingling in her voice.

'Back in a sec!' I yell – I have to yell because I've already closed the door – and squeeze through an ITV news van and a car to get on to the pavement.

The men – they really are all men – turn to look at me as I walk across the driveway and on to the path towards the front door. I hear one of them mutter, 'That must be one of the friends,' before he raises his voice and addresses me directly. 'Hello, love! Is Bonnie a friend of yours?'

'Do you know where she is?' another chimes in.

'Has she called you?'

'Has Jack Cohn ever tried it on with you?'

This one I can't ignore. I'm startled into stopping on the pavement, almost tripping over my own feet. I give the man who asked this question the look it deserves (*Dude, really?*), which is apparently a mistake because suddenly all these cameras are flashing, the sound of shutters clicking is filling the air, and I panic and sprint through the front door, which has opened to reveal Bonnie's dad, face practically puce, already beginning to yell at the reporters.

'Clive!' Bonnie's mother yells from somewhere else in the house. 'I told you! Don't give them any more ammunition, for God's sake.'

Bonnie's dad slams the door, swearing under his breath about *fucking vultures*, and turns to face me.

'Hi, Mr Wiston-Stanley,' I say awkwardly. Even though Bonnie and I have been best friends for eight years, I don't think I've ever had a proper conversation with him. He's not really the buddy type of dad. More like the stand-at-a-distance-and-frown kind of dad.

'You listen to me, Eden,' Bonnie's dad says, pointing a finger at me. 'You listen. You don't give them a second of your time, you hear?'

'Um, OK,' I say.

'Clive!' Bonnie's mother barks, appearing at the top of the stairs and stomping down them to reach us. 'What did I say about swearing at the journalists?'

'Hi, Mrs Wiston-Stanley,' I say.

'Oh, Eden,' she says, not looking thrilled about my presence. 'You didn't speak to the reporters, did you?'

God, these people are obsessed. What do they think the journalists are actually going to do?

'No,' I say. 'Um, have you heard anything?'

She shakes her head, the sudden hope on her face almost painful. 'Have you?'

'Oh, no,' I say quickly. Maybe a little too quickly, because her face tightens in suspicion, so I add, 'I brought a new photo.'

There's a moment of silence. Finally, she says, 'A new . . . photo?'

'The one in all the articles is crap,' I say, producing the picture I'd printed and holding it out towards her, the USB stick balancing on top. 'Bonnie'd hate it. This one is much better.'

Bonnie's mother looks at my outstretched hand, a look of utter bafflement on her face. Helpfully I add, 'To go on, like, the news and stuff?'

Behind me, there's a knock on the door. 'Don't answer that!' Mrs Wiston-Stanley snaps.

'It's probably Carolyn,' I say, just as a muffled voice sounds through the letter box.

'It's just me, Matilda!'

'Open the door, Clive,' Mrs Wiston-Stanley says. She still hasn't taken the picture or the USB stick from me, and I'm just standing there, a little awkwardly now. 'Eden,' she says, her voice steady in a way that seems to take a lot of effort, 'do you think this is the kind of thing I'd be worrying about right now?'

'Well, no –' I begin, meaning to say that it would be what *Bonnie* would be worrying about, and isn't that just as important? But she interrupts me.

'Because I've got an awful lot going on right now. I have a missing daughter and journalists cutting up my lawn and the last thing I need – *the last thing I need* – is to worry about how *pretty* Bonnie looks in the photos the *police* are handing out.'

'You don't need to worry about it,' I say, staying polite, like Bonnie would have done. 'I've already taken care of it. It's this one, see?'

Mrs Wiston-Stanley snatches the picture out of my hand, the USB stick clattering to the floor. She looks about ready to explode. 'I think you should reconsider your priorities, Eden.'

I glance at Carolyn, who is standing like a quiet sentry behind me. 'I'm just thinking about what Bonnie would want.'

'What *Bonnie* would want?' Mrs Wiston-Stanley shrieks, her

voice suddenly shrill. Oh dear. 'What Bonnie would want? Forgive me, but I'm not in a position to *care* what Bonnie would want, not when she's run away like this, no word, no warning, no phone calls. Like we mean nothing! Her *parents*!'

I take a little step back, bumping up against Carolyn. I feel the light touch of her hand on my arm. 'Matilda,' she says, soft. 'Why don't I make you some tea?'

'*Tea?!*' Bonnie's mum repeats, still sharp but with markedly less bite than when she was talking to me.

'Yes,' Carolyn says. 'How about you, Clive? Could you do with some tea?'

We have tea. Mrs Wiston-Stanley insists on having the radio on, so it's not exactly a relaxing experience, but she does at least seem to calm down a little. Mr Wiston-Stanley holds his mug with both hands and looks sadly down into its contents, brooding and silent.

'Eden,' Mrs Wiston-Stanley says, her voice steadier now. 'I didn't mean to be so short with you.'

''S'OK,' I say, shrugging.

'It's just that you're Bonnie's best friend,' she says. 'I know how close the two of you are. I just find it quite . . . hard to believe that she hasn't been in contact with you. Or that you didn't know that any of this was going on.'

'You didn't know anything either,' I point out. 'And you're her mother.'

'Eden,' Carolyn says, warning.

'Well, why does everyone keep saying that?' I ask. The stupid thing is, I actually do feel pretty offended that they all think I'm lying to them. Even though I am. But, I remind myself fairly, I really didn't know that anything was going on with Bonnie and Mr Cohn before this weekend. So *that* accusation is definitely unfair. 'Why wouldn't I tell you now if I knew? I want her back, too.'

'Maybe you don't realize how serious this all is,' Mrs Wiston-Stanley says. 'This isn't a film. It's not some grand adventure. It's a crime. It's kidnap.'

Kidnap. I mean, honestly! Mr Cohn! A kidnapper?! Way to overreact, Mrs W-S. But probably best not to say that.

'I know how serious it is,' I say instead. 'I'm not a moron.'

'Eden,' Carolyn says again.

'Can everyone just stop saying my name?' I snap, rattled. 'I know what my name is. Find another word.'

'Rethink your tone, please,' Carolyn says. 'It's not helpful.'

'Well, you should all *rethink your tones* too,' I say. 'It's not fair that you're all taking this out on me. I'm not some Bonnie surrogate you can be all mad at. She's the one who buggered off, not me. I'm just trying to help.'

'With a prettier photo?' Mrs Wiston-Stanley says, snide. Sarcastic bitch.

'Maybe you should rethink your tone,' I say. 'It's not helpful.'

I leave before she throws me out.

5

Carolyn has obviously decided to take the understanding-parent approach because she doesn't lecture me on the way back home like I'd expected. She just drives us in silence until I can't help but mumble, 'I was just trying to help.'

'I know,' she says, and that's the only thing she says on the subject.

When we get home, I go straight outside and find Bob in the vegetable garden, earthing up potatoes. 'Hello, love,' he says when he sees me. 'Where have you been?'

'I went to see Bonnie's parents.'

'Ah.' Bob angles the hoe against the earth and pulls it towards the stems of the potato plants, heaping the earth around them. 'And how did that go?'

I shrug.

Bob smiles. 'I see.'

'Her mum yelled at me.'

'Did she?'

'I was only trying to help.'

'I'm sure she knows that.' This is a typical parent-club thing to say, so I let out an appropriately sceptical *mm-hmm*, which makes him chuckle. 'I wouldn't take it personally. She's having an incredibly tough time right now.'

'Well, so am I.'

Another warm I'm-older-and-I-know-better-but-I'm-not-going-to-tell-you-what-I-know smile.

I add, 'She doesn't have to take it out on me.'

'I'm sure she didn't mean to, Eden. But who knows what she's going through right now? How it must feel to have her daughter missing like this?'

'How would you feel if it was me?'

Bob is silent for a while, working the earth, his face red with exertion. Finally he says, 'I'd feel like I'd failed.'

'*You'd* failed?'

'Yes. I'd feel like I'd let you down, as your . . .' He hesitates, his eyes flicking towards me, then back to the earth. 'As your father figure.'

'*In loco parentis*?' I say, smiling so he knows it's OK. This is a phrase I have heard many times in the course of my life. I don't mind it, because it makes me feel smart, knowing a bit of Latin.

He smiles back. 'Exactly. As your *loco*.' He points his finger towards the side of his head and gives it a silly little spin. Bob has always been so careful with me, so kind. He could never let me down.

'Why, though?' I ask, getting back on track. 'If it was my choice? How would it be *you* letting me down? Not the other way around?'

He hesitates again, grimacing, as if this conversation is as hard on him as heavy gardening. 'Will you give me that look if I tell you that a choice made by a fifteen-year-old in this situation is not the same as a choice made by an adult?'

'Yes. And I'm sixteen.'

He laughs, but it's more like a sigh. 'I know that, Eden. What I mean is, sometimes, when we're young –' I open my mouth to protest and he puts up a finger to halt me – 'we can feel like we're making a choice, when actually we're not. We don't have all the facts, or all the perspective. If there's someone else who knows a bit more than we do, or has authority over us, sometimes they can take advantage of that knowledge, or that power.'

'So . . . you think Bonnie's been manipulated? By Mr Cohn?' I'm dubious. Bonnie's too smart to be manipulated, isn't she?

Another hesitation. 'I think people can do all sorts of things they wouldn't usually do if love is involved. Or, worse, if they *think* love is involved. And in this case, I'd imagine Jack Cohn is justifying this whole thing by telling himself he loves her, and she loves him.'

'But you don't think it does justify it?'

'No.' There is not even a second of hesitation this time. 'Not at all.'

'But what if they *are* in love?'

Something dark crosses Bob's face then. 'Love isn't the word.'

We're both silent for a while. I watch as he concentrates on the potato plants, reaching over every now and then to pluck out a weed.

'What you want for your children,' Bob says, several minutes later, 'as a parent, is to keep them safe. And part of that is preparing them for the world and the kinds of people you can find in it. If it had been you, I'd feel like I hadn't done that properly. That I hadn't prepared you.'

'If it was me, you could just blame it on everything before you adopted me,' I point out.

I meant it mostly as a joke, but Bob frowns. 'Part of being your parent is taking on all of that, too,' he says. 'I couldn't blame anything on "before". I think that would actually make it worse. It would be like I'd let you down twice.'

'You think a lot about the whole letting-down thing,' I say.

He laughs, properly this time. 'Well, that's parenting.'

I generally try not to tell people that I'm adopted, partly because it's none of their business, but mostly because of the way people react, like it's a novelty instead of my actual life. They always want to know things like the *why* and the *before*, even though that is clearly none of their business either. People seem to think there's something inherently interesting about adoption. Maybe because there are so many films about orphans getting adopted by rich people and having amazing lives. (Thanks, *Oliver!* Thanks, *Annie*!) The reality is messier, of course. And there's usually less money involved. And more social workers. There's nothing glamorous about it, not at all.

'So what was it actually like?' Bonnie used to ask, in that way she does when she thinks she's learning something Important and she should listen Very Hard.

It was social workers perched on our tatty sofa, smiling at me with tired eyes. It was an endless carousel of strange bedrooms, and adults I didn't know calling me 'Edie' and trying to make me eat food I couldn't manage. It was being carried away from my ragged, crying mother and then returned to her after she'd been neatened up, looking like she'd been put through a human car wash, but still ragged and still crying. It was dirty clothes and hunger and chest infections from the damp in the walls. It was me and Mum against the world – her and me. And being her precious baby, but not precious enough. Never quite enough. It was the way she held me before I got taken away again. The way she held me when they gave me back.

'I don't really remember it,' I said to Bonnie. 'I was super young.'

My mum isn't a bad person – she wasn't abusive or anything, it wasn't like that – but me and Daisy were pretty much neglected for most of the time we lived with her. She just couldn't look after children, really. Some people can't and it's not their fault. She's an addict, and she couldn't even take care of herself, that's the truth. She was twenty-one when she had me, and she was all on her own, no parents or anything. And my dad – whoever he is – didn't exactly stick around to help out.

I've never met my dad, and I don't know anything about him except that his first name is Luiz and he's from Brazil. That's literally it. I don't know how he and my mother met, or whether they were together for longer than a night. I don't even know what he looks like. And I can't ask my mother, obviously. But who knows? Maybe one day, when I'm an adult myself, she'll have got clean – it could happen, right? – and we'll have a relationship, and then we can talk about it. She'll tell me how his smile was both cheeky and kind, how he drank Corona, how when she sees my face, she remembers him.

Or maybe that won't ever happen, and that's fine too. I have Bob, who grew me a rose garden and taught me about snapdragon seed pods, which look like little skulls. Carolyn, who brings entire gardens to life with just a pencil and paper. There's blood, and then there's family. They're not always the same thing.

6

It's not until after dinner that I finally hear from Bonnie. I'm half asleep with my Biology revision guide on my face when my phone buzzes by my head and I lunge for it.

Ivy

HI! How's everything going?

Me

HI!!! It's all VERY WEIRD. You know your face is all over the news, right?

OMG, yes. So bizarre.

How are you doing?

Great!

I frown down at the screen, trying to figure out how to reply. How can she be 'great'? How? Doesn't she care that her parents are going out of their minds with worry? Doesn't she understand the trouble she's in?

Me

Really? Aren't you worried?

Ivy

About what's going on at home? Nope. That's just noise.

Me

But . . . Bon, don't you think you should at least call your mum?

No way!

But she's worried?

She KNOWS I'm safe. I told her I am! I messaged her before I dumped my phone. So she shouldn't be worried.

So, what . . . you're just never gonna come home?

Maybe! I can be free forever ☺

Bonnie, be serious.

This is so weird, E. It's like we've switched places. ☺

True. I've never had to tell her to be serious. Usually I'm telling her to *stop* being so serious. But it's not like we've switched places at all – I'm just the same as I was last week. It's more like my best friend has disappeared and been replaced by a total stranger. Or like she's somehow managed to disengage the 'responsible' setting of her character – and maybe the 'empathy' one too, for good measure – and that's changed everything.

How else could she be acting this way? Not just the running-away bit, but the part where she doesn't seem to care about the absolute clunking clusterfuck she's left behind for everyone else to deal with. And the part where she'll have to come back and deal with it herself. Bonnie is smart – she can't be thinking that she really can escape this forever. She knows that life doesn't work that way. Even if she really is in love with Mr Cohn – and euw, I'm sorry, but euw – that doesn't change reality. It doesn't change mothers and GCSEs and having your face plastered all over the national press.

I don't know how to reply to this, so I change the subject.

Me

Where are you actually? Like, where are you staying? Are you camping in the woods or something?

Ivy

Camping in the woods?!? LOL. No.

It's not that weird! Somewhere with no CCTV, no people?

We're in a little cottage by the sea.

OK but really.

Seriously! Jack's friend owns it as like a holiday rent and we're just staying here until we figure out what to do next.

So someone's helping you?

No, the guy doesn't know we're here. So shhh ☺

Wtf

Ivy

I can't believe you thought I was just squatting in the woods ☺

Me

Yeah, that's the unbelievable bit of all of this.

Haha!

What ARE you going to do next?

The plan is Ireland.

Ireland?!

Yeah! If we can get there without anyone knowing – like pay someone to take us across on their boat, Jack says – then we can properly disappear. Start over ☺

My heart has tightened in my chest and I feel a panicky kind of numbness in my hands. I'm starting to wish that I hadn't asked, that I'm having any other conversation than this, that Bonnie had never even told me she was leaving.

Me

Maybe it's better to not leave the country?

Ivy

Why not?

Because that's so extreme! That's like next-level. Like something you can't come back from, you know?

Eeds, I'm not coming back anyway.

Me

Just good to keep your options open, is what I mean.

Ivy

☺ i love you xx

This seems like a bit of a weird response, but OK. **I love you too,** I reply. I hesitate, then send another message: **Promise me you'll tell me first if you're going to leave properly like that?**

Her response is almost instant: **Promise x**

Me

Are you sure you're OK?

Ivy

Better than OK!

Everyone's worried about you.

Why? They don't need to be. I have Jack. I'm golden.

Have you actually read the stories in the papers?

Not properly! Jack says not to, they're all tabloid trash, they'll just upset me. Are they saying awful things about him? ☹

Um. Yes.

☹☹ He's done this all for me. It's not right if they're making him out to be the bad guy!

Has he? Why?

Ivy

Because I was miserable. He's saved me.

Me

When were you miserable?

My whole life was miserable! Eat, sleep, study, repeat.

I didn't know.

You didn't ask.

So it's my fault?

No! It doesn't matter anyway. I'm happy now. With Jack.

It's so weird you calling him Jack.

Haha! I've been calling him Jack for ages, way before you knew ☺

For how long?

98 days. And about 14 hours ☺ ☺

Shit, Bon. Why didn't you TELL me?

Let's chat later! Got to get some dinner.

Can you go out if you're on the run?

Ivy

Well, not to restaurants or anything. But there's a chip shop! If we go around separately, no one notices. They're looking for a pair. And anyway, I've dyed my hair ☺

Me

WHAT.

It's red!

WHATTTT.

And short.

BONNIE.

Jack says it's sexy ☺

Euw.

That's why I didn't tell you.

Conversations That Took on a Different Meaning after Bonnie Disappeared

The 'Vienna' Edition: four months before

'Have you heard of Billy Joel?' Bonnie asked. We were both lying across her bed, her on her laptop, me with my Maths book, copying her homework.

'The singer guy? Sure. Why?' I had a system. One correct answer – with lots of crossings-out added in for good measure – for every two wrong answers. We were in separate sets for Maths, but there was enough of a crossover to make it worth it.

'Isn't he amazing?'

I shrugged. 'I guess?' My playlists weren't exactly overflowing with Billy Joel tracks.

'Listen to this song,' Bonnie said, shifting closer to me and nudging my shoulder. 'It's called "Vienna".'

The music started, a trilling piano. I recognized Billy Joel's voice from the albums Bob liked to play in the car on long trips to visit his parents in Norfolk. 'Wait, are you saying you *hadn't* heard of Billy Joel before this song?'

'Shh,' she commanded. 'Listen.'

Obediently, I did. When it ended, I said, 'It's pretty.'

Her nose wrinkled. 'It's not pretty. It's *life*. It's so *true*, you know?'

'Uh, sure.'

'Did you listen to the lyrics?'

'Something about slowing down, something about Vienna.'

'It's about not having to be perfect at everything just cos you're young,' she said. 'It's about living your life in the right way. Vienna is, like, a metaphor. Vienna is *life*.'

'OK,' I said.

'Mr Cohn said he thought I should hear it,' she said, a dreamy smile on her face. 'He said it would change my life.'

'Have you got a crush on him again?'

Bonnie's face snapped in annoyance. '"Crush" is such an adolescent word. And no, obviously. For God's sake.'

'So did it?'

'Did it what?'

'Change your life?'

'I don't know yet,' she said. 'Maybe.'

Monday

'STOP FLIRTING WITH ME, SIR!'

LONELY TEACHER 'LOVED YEAR 11S' – TEXTED GIRLS AFTER CLASSES

CREEPY TEACHER Jack Cohn, 29, on the run with a 15-year-old schoolgirl, had flirted with pupils in his classes for YEARS, students tell The Sun.

Cohn persuaded A* student and prefect Bonnie Wiston-Stanley to leave her Kent home last weekend and run away with him as a COUPLE.

'He loved our Year 11 class best and he was always really hands-on,' pupil Michelle Grant, 16, revealed. 'He even gave some of us his mobile number.'

'Mr Cohn acted like he was one of us. He was always up for a laugh,' another girl said. 'I texted him and he replied with kisses. I told him he shouldn't be such a flirt and he sent back a winky face.'

SICK

The perverted teacher sent more than a HUNDRED messages to schoolgirl Bonnie's phone before she said she would disappear with him, a Kent Police source told The Sun. Cohn promised Bonnie that he LOVED her, despite being nearly TWICE her age.

Many of his texts to the underage girl were 'explicit' in nature, while promising that the pair would have a future together.

'He was sick, we all knew it,' explained Lewis Cooper, 15, another of Jack Cohn's students. 'The way he would flirt with the girls and get them to like him. But everyone knew he liked Bonnie most.'

TEARS

Distraught parents Clive and Matilda appeared on telly in tears this week to plead for their girl to get in contact, but there has been no word since the pair disappeared.

Parents have questioned Kett Academy staff over their knowledge of Cohn's tendencies

. . . *Turn to page 4*

7

The official first week of my GCSEs starts with rain. And I don't mean a bit of a drizzle or a passing shower – I mean proper torrential rain pounding against the window, waking me before my alarm. I go down to breakfast to find Carolyn singing a Patty Griffin song at the kitchen sink. When I enter, she grins at me. 'Raaaaaa-aaaaaa–iiiiinnnnnn . . .' she sings.

'Wow,' I say.

'Pop quiz!' she says, pointing dramatically at me as I take a seat at the table. 'What do we call it when the weather is used to show human emotions?'

I blink at her.

'I'll give you a clue!' Only Carolyn can get so enthusiastic about a pop quiz she just made up on a Monday morning. 'Your English teacher would know the answer.'

'Can I just have breakfast?'

'It's *raining,*' Carolyn says encouragingly. 'What might that say about a person's emotional state?'

'That they're miserable?'

'Perhaps! And what would we call that as a literary device?' She smiles expectantly at me, as if she thinks I'm going to suddenly become a different person and know the answer. Actually, not a random different person – it's like she thinks I'm Valerie. Valerie probably loved spontaneous tests at the breakfast table when she was my age.

'I don't know, Carolyn.'

'Come on, Eden! I'll give you another clue. It's a type of literary *fallacy*.'

'That definitely sounds like the kind of knowledge that will be relevant to my life.'

I see her smile flicker slightly, but she doesn't falter. Carolyn is the most unflappable person I know, which is probably why she was so successful as a foster carer.

'Dramatic fallacy?' I guess eventually.

'Close!' She's triumphant, pleased with herself, setting a cereal box in front of me. 'You're thinking of dramatic licence, which is also a literacy device. Using the weather is *pathetic* fallacy. See if you can get that into your English exam if you can. It'll look very impressive.'

'OK,' I say. My English exam isn't for another week and a half, and no doubt I will have forgotten about this conversation by then, but the suggestion has made her happy, so I don't say so.

'Hurry up with your breakfast,' Carolyn says, glancing at the wall clock. 'Isn't the revision session at nine thirty?'

'Yeah, but I'm not going,' I say. The sessions are optional, and the last thing I want to do right now is go into school – a place I basically hate even on a good day – and have to face my classmates and my teachers. All anyone will want to talk about is Bonnie.

'Yes, you are,' Carolyn says simply. 'So hurry up with your breakfast, OK?'

'Carolyn!'

'We agreed you would go to every one of these sessions,' she reminds me.

'That was before!'

'The situation with Bonnie is already taking up enough of your headspace and time,' she says. 'God knows what an effect it's already had on you. You're not going to spend another day sitting in front of BBC News.'

'But—'

'This isn't up for discussion. I promise I will call you immediately if there's a breakthrough in the case. But that's all, Eden. You are going to school today.'

I shove a spoonful of Weetabix into my mouth and scowl, but that's all I can do. Part of being unflappable is being impossible to argue with, and I can tell that there'll be no changing Carolyn's mind on this.

So I send a quick text to Connor. **Coming to Kett today?** and he replies almost instantly. I picture him at his kitchen table, eating cereal while he makes tea for his mother and gran. **Nope. Going w/ Mum to hospital at 11 for check-up after the fall on Friday. Will revise at home instead.**

I send a sad face, hoping he'll realize I mean it for his mum and not for me (even though I do kind of mean it for me too) and tell him to call me later so we can meet up.

'Didn't you get any papers this morning?' I ask.

'No,' Carolyn says. 'And that's for your own good. There's nothing in there worth reading. I promise.'

'I'll just look on the way to school,' I say. 'So you might as well've just got them.'

Carolyn rolls her eyes. 'You can lead a horse to water,' she says.

'What?'

'Finish your breakfast. I'll drive you to school.'

I know that the decision to come into school was a mistake as soon as I walk through the gates. For one thing, there are journalists hanging around on the grass, some of them with cameras, and just the sight of them makes me nauseous. For another, Molly Kale and Livia Vasin practically leap on me before I get halfway across the car park.

'Oh my God, Eden!'

'What the hell's going on with Bonnie?'

'Mr *Cohn*?!'

And the like.

I try to shake them off, but they only multiply as we make our way through the main building and down into the science block where our revision session is being held. By the time I get there, I can't even count the number of my classmates that are surrounding me.

'I don't know anything!' I keep saying, but it's not making any difference. The door to the classroom is locked, so I've got no choice but to stand there and let everyone bark questions at me.

'Do you think she'll be back before Wednesday?' someone asks.

'Of course she will,' I say. 'Bonnie wouldn't miss our exams.' The sea of faces before me all look doubtful, which makes my stomach twist with an anxiety I don't want to feel. 'Look, just fuck off, all of you, OK?'

'Eden McKinley,' a stern voice says, and I groan. Mrs Berwick, our Head of Year and Biology teacher, is walking towards us, pulling a key from her pocket to open the door. The sea of students parts to let her through. 'That's not the sort of language I want to be hearing on school grounds.'

'Sorry, miss,' I mutter. I hate Mrs Berwick, and Mrs Berwick hates me. We have an understanding on this.

'Inside, everyone,' Mrs Berwick says, opening the door. 'Let's try to calm some of this hysteria, shall we?'

That's all she says on the subject for the rest of the session, which takes an hour and a half and is, somehow, even more boring than actual Biology lessons used to be. I doodle vines up and down the length of my notebook, thinking about Bonnie and where she is, what she's doing, at this very moment. I wonder what the day-to-day is like when you're on the run. I imagine it like a film montage of laughing, kissing, eating strawberries and sex (except the figures in my head are a generic couple and not the Bonnie and Mr Cohn I know, like my brain still can't quite compute this scenario), but that can't be it all the time, can it? There must be boring moments too. Or maybe not. How would I know?

'I think that will do for today,' Mrs Berwick says, and I look around at everyone starting to pack up their stuff. 'I'm hoping to see most of you back here tomorrow afternoon,' she continues. She's smiling her cold smile, and I wonder, not for the first time, whether she thinks it makes her look friendly instead of evil. 'I know these sessions aren't compulsory, but they *are* important. You'll be grateful come results day.'

I doubt that, somehow, but I don't have much of a choice about attending the session or not. Carolyn made it pretty clear that for me these sessions *are* compulsory, even with everything that's going on with Bonnie. So I know I'll be back here tomorrow for a last-ditch attempt to learn all the stuff that didn't go into my head the first hundred times around, even though all of this seems to matter even less to me now than it did last week. And it barely mattered then, either. I'm just not an academic person. And you know what? That's fine. I don't need A grades to work with soil and plant flowers and create an entire garden, but I've spent the last five years having all my education concentrated on getting better grades. What a joke. What a total waste of everyone's time. I've never got an A in my entire life. If you ask me, school and teachers have completely warped priorities.

'Hey, Eden,' a voice says from beside me. I glance up to see Alfie Higgs leaning right over, his elbows on my desk, as the room rustles with people packing up to leave.

I look at him, instantly suspicious. Alfie and I aren't exactly friends. 'Hi . . . ?'

'Charlie and me wanna know,' he says, gesturing behind him at Charlie Ruthers, who grins. Charlie and I went out for about five minutes in Year 9. His kissing was traumatizing.

'Know what?' I can guess what.

'Do you think they did it in this classroom?'

'Oh, get lost,' I snap, but it's too late. The very horrible mental image of Mr Cohn and Bonnie *doing things* right on the desk Alfie's leaning on is already parading through my head in full, horrifying technicolour.

'Did she call him *sir*?' Alfie somehow manages to choke this out through his guffaws, and even though I hate him so much I could slap his stupid face, I'm struck dumb, just sitting there, face flaming with rage and embarrassment. Damn Alfie. Damn Bonnie.

And then Charlie leers over the table and says, 'Can't believe the nerd queen was actually getting laid when we all thought you were the easy one.'

Alfie lifts an appreciative hand for a high-five, and the two of them laugh like the pathetic little knobs they are. I want to tell them to fuck off, but the words have sliced into me and I don't quite trust myself to speak.

I'm rescued by Mrs Berwick, of all people. 'Eden, could I speak to you for a minute?' she asks.

'Bye, guys,' I say, shoving my notepad into my bag and legging it to the front of the room, leaving them cackling behind me. My skin is still prickling with that mix of fury and humiliation that comes with guys being guys to girls like me. Girls that have a reputation. A reputation that, in my case, is entirely unearned. I mean, I'm not a virgin (and anyway that's a social construct, blah blah blah), but that's only because Connor and I tried having sex just after we first got together (basically because we thought we were supposed to) and it was so crap (I'm not even sure if it even counts as sex) that we agreed we wouldn't try it again until we were both super ready, and that's just never come up since. I know that it will one day, probably very soon, and I'm even quite excited about it, but there's no rush. In the meantime, there's other stuff. And Connor's really, really great at the other stuff.

Clearly, everyone thinks we're at it like rabbits. I got my totally baseless reputation as an easy shag somewhere around Year 9, which shows what a joke the whole thing is. (One blurry boob picture, and I'm labelled for life.) I wonder sometimes about the other girls who got labelled that way. Are they secretly not having sex, either? Is the whole thing an elaborate con?

The really stupid thing is that as crap as it is for me, it's good for Connor, who gets to enjoy the backslappy bullshit that boys seem to think is a requirement for the sexually active from the same guys who used to bully him for being weedy. It's all such a *joke*.

So I can try and pretend I don't care what anyone says about me, but let's be real: I still want to cry when a clown like Charlie Ruthers announces to the room that I'm easy. I practically run to the teacher I hate to get away from him.

In fact, I've never been so enthusiastic about going to talk to Mrs Berwick, and she looks a little startled by my eagerness.

'Hello,' she says, clearly trying to cover herself but actually making things weirder. 'How are you, Eden?'

'Fine,' I say.

'I wanted to check in with you,' she says, 'to make sure you're coping with everything that's going on with Bonnie Wiston-Stanley and –' she hesitates ever so slightly, but I see it – 'and Mr Cohn.'

What a bizarre question. What does she think? That I'm suddenly going to forget five years' worth of being one of the certified Kett lost causes and confide in her or something? Even if I wasn't coping – *which I am* – why the hell would I talk to *Mrs Berwick* about it?

'I'm coping fine,' I say.

'We're all concerned,' she says. 'The staff and myself, I mean. Concerned that this . . . spectacle could be disruptive at such a crucial time in all of your lives.'

'OK,' I say. 'Well. I'm fine.'

'There's already been a fair amount of press intrusion,' she continues. 'Journalists trying to gain access to the school, digging for any kind of information to pad out their stories. They're banned from school grounds, of course, but with the internet a physical ban is only half the battle.' I'm starting to wonder if she's really having a conversation with me or just herself when she asks, 'Have you had any of that kind of trouble? Any journalists trying to contact you on Facebook? Twitter? Instasnap, or whatever it's called?'

I shake my head and shrug at the same time. This is just a reflex, but it confuses her and she frowns. 'No,' I add helpfully.

'Nothing?' she says, her voice and expression dubious. 'Other students have already told me that journalists have tried to reach out to them through their social accounts. It's quite surprising that they wouldn't try to reach you, as Bonnie's best friend.'

Oh God, this was so easily escapable – well done, Eden. I should have just said that I'd had a couple of messages, but I'd ignored them, or something. I don't want to have to go into why no one's tried to contact me, but I can tell Mrs Berwick has locked on to this now, may even be getting suspicious, so I resign myself. 'I don't use my real name on social media,' I say, adding mentally, *not any more*.

'Oh.' She looks first surprised, then impressed. Mrs Berwick has never, not in five years at Kett, been impressed with me. 'Well, that's very sensible, Eden.'

'Mmm,' I say, hoping I can leave.

'If only some of our other students had your foresight,' she says. 'And some of the teachers!' She gives a little laugh at this, and then looks at me, as if expecting me to join in with this sudden, unearned camaraderie. I blink at her. 'Well,' she says finally. 'You just let me know if they manage to track you down, OK? We'll take care of it.'

'OK,' I say, even though the very last place I'd go for help is Kett.

The thing is, there was nothing sensible – or impressive – about me adopting pseudonyms on all of my social media accounts. It wasn't foresight; it was necessity.

I walk out of the classroom and down the empty hall, pulling out my phone and bringing up the Facebook app.

Heather White. My fake name to hide my real life. All of my privacy settings are on, hiding not just my activity and photos, but also my friends and connections. Anything that could lead someone to me. A specific someone, that is. My mother.

'Real-life subterfuge,' Connor had said, a long time ago, when I first explained to him why I had a different name on Facebook. 'That's cool.'

'It's *not* cool,' I'd snapped, and he'd faltered and apologized – he's the kind of person who apologizes immediately even when he doesn't know what he's apologizing for – and I'd tried to take it back and be relaxed and normal again, but I couldn't, not really. The thing is, nothing gets me as crotchety and brittle as having to talk about my mother with other people. It's just too bloody complicated to be able to explain.

It's not about missing her, that's what you have to understand. It's not about wanting to see her. It's not even about whether she wants to see me. It's about boundaries. Boundaries she has a history of bulldozing right over, given half the chance.

I haven't seen my mother since I was thirteen, which was the first and last time Daisy and I'd had an unsupervised visit since we'd first been fostered by the McKinleys five years before. The visit had ended in failure because my mother is an addict, not because she's a bad person – I feel like I should make that clear, too. So I know, rationally, that she didn't *mean* to abandon Daisy and me at a random McDonald's in Margate while she disappeared with my money and my phone. Just like she didn't mean to forget to feed us when we lived with her, or wash our clothes, or pay the electricity bill. *Some things,* she said on the phone to me after that last awful visit, *just fade out when you need a hit. It's an illness.* She'd been sobbing, like her whole damn heart was broken, and I'd been silent. *You understand, don't you, Eden? You know I don't mean it. I'll be better next time.* But when I'd hung up, I'd told Carolyn and Marisa – my social worker – that I didn't want to see her for a while. And they agreed, and they spoke to Mum, and she agreed too. Understood it was for the best. But she still kept trying to contact me, trying to get to me, even when she'd promised to let some time pass, and so eventually I had to make a choice. And that's when Eden Rose McKinley faded from the internet, and Heather White was born.

I stare at my fake profile for a while, thinking about that last visit, that same horrible churning feeling in my stomach when I remember Daisy's face as she tried so hard to stay optimistic. She was *nine*. She'd worn her best dress.

A text comes in from Connor, and I click on it, glad for a distraction. **Check Twitter!**

It's nearly time for the end of the normal class period, so I go on a little detour to the art block where Daisy's locker is, because I have a sudden need to see my little sister in all her bolshy, present-day glory. I lean against her locker and open Twitter on my phone while I wait for her to appear. Connor knows I'm not much of a Twitter person, so I'm assuming it must have something to do with Bonnie.

I start to type her name into the search bar and it autofills with a hashtag: #BringBackBonnie. No way. They've made Bonnie a *hashtag*? Who came up with *that*?

I click on it, feeling a weird kind of smile/grimace hybrid on my face. This is so, so weird. The hashtag is, apparently, the current top trend in the UK. And it's full of this kind of thing:

> @treacletoes99
> omg imagine if this was u n mr johns @amieleslie wud be sooo romantic!! #bringbackbonnie
> @wesleyfred4ever
> So scary :'(praying for her #bringbackbonnie
> @lcfc77
> Beautiful girl, get her home safe! Teacher deserves to hang #bringbackbonnie
> @rainbowm00n
> Seeing #bringbackbonnie like she didn't bring this on herself smh

I take a few screenshots and send them to Bonnie, adding a quick **LOOK WHAT YOU DID**, and that's when a voice sounds in my ear.

'Eden!'

It's Daisy, of course, and even though I'm standing at her locker I jump like she's the last person I'm expecting to see. She gives me a *what-the-hell-is-wrong-with-you?* look, which would be a lot more intimidating if she hadn't learned it from me.

'Hi,' I say, pasting on a smile and shoving my phone into my pocket.

'What're you doing here?' she asks bluntly.

'Saying hi, obviously,' I say. And then, just because I can, I put my arm around her neck and pull her in for a headlock/hug.

'Get off!' she yells, shaking me off. Her face is puce. 'God, don't you have somewhere else to be?'

'Aw, Daze,' I say, grinning. 'Why would I want to be anywhere else when I could be here with you?'

She glares at me, trying to smooth down her hair from where I'd mussed it up.

'Why's your skirt so rolled up?' I ask her, reaching out to adjust it. 'It's way too high.'

She jerks away from me, slapping at my outstretched hand. 'Because I want it like that!'

'It's too short,' I point out, surprised.

'You always had yours short,' she replies. 'This is how everyone wears them.'

'I didn't have it that short when I was twelve,' I say, trying not to show how horrified I am. Daisy is twelve. Twelve! The skirt is barely touching her *thighs*.

She raises one eyebrow at me. 'Whatever,' she says. 'I'm going now.'

'Hug for your big sister first?' I ask.

I'm teasing, and it's worth it for the look of utter disgust that appears at the mere suggestion of displaying sisterly affection in school.

'Hi, Eden,' a soft voice says from behind me. I glance around and it's Rowan, Bonnie's little sister, spinning the dial on her locker.

'Oh, hey,' I say.

'Anyway, bye,' Daisy says, rolling her eyes and giving me a sarcastic wave. She and Rowan don't even acknowledge each other, even though they're in the same form and their sisters are best friends.

Rowan gives me a shy smile as she pushes her books into her locker. Her skirt, I notice, is the appropriate length for a twelve-year-old. This makes sense, because Rowan is a smaller, skinnier, shyer version of her older sister. Following the rules is in her DNA.

'How are you?' I ask. I wouldn't usually talk to Rowan without Bonnie around, but she looks all lonely and sad and I can't help myself. 'You doing OK?'

Rowan does a little half-shrug thing and looks away from me, her chin wobbling a little, and I realize she's about to cry the moment before the tears spill.

'Oh shit!' I'm so unprepared for this that I wait too long to step forward and hug her, which makes everything even more awkward. 'Don't cry, Row. It's OK.'

'It's not,' she whispers. She whispers it so quietly she has to repeat herself before I understand.

'Bonnie'll come home,' I promise, trying to give her shoulder a reassuring rub. 'Real soon, OK?'

Rowan shakes her head. 'She won't,' she says, and then she starts properly crying, complete with squeaky gasps and shuddering sobs.

'OK, let's get you out of here,' I say, putting my arm around her and leading her out of the doors and away from the gawping stares of the other students. I find us a bench and we sit down. 'Now,' I say, channelling my inner Carolyn, all patient and calm, 'what do you mean, she won't?'

'She told me,' Rowan says, her voice hoarse and low, shoulders hunching. 'She said that if . . . that if I . . . She said she'd go and never come back.'

I wait for a moment, hoping she'll offer more of an explanation, but she just wipes at her eyes with the sleeve of her blazer and lets out another choking sob.

'That if you what, Row?' I ask, as gently as I can.

Rowan drops her hands to her lap, threading her fingers together and squeezing them so hard they turn white.

'You can tell me,' I say into the silence.

When she speaks, her voice is so quiet I almost can't make the words out. 'I'll get into trouble.'

'It's just me,' I say. 'I won't tell anyone, not if you don't want me to. And whatever it is, I'm sure it's not really as bad as you think.'

She looks at me. 'No?'

'No way,' I say. 'I know trouble, Row. And it's not you.' In the instant before I say these words, I'm thinking that it's a true, reassuring thing to say, but when I hear them in the space between us, I realize it's not. Because I would have said the same thing about Bonnie, and I would have been wrong.

She's thinking this too, I can tell, but she doesn't say it. What she says instead half breaks my heart. 'It's my fault.'

'What's your fault?'

'Bonnie leaving. It was because of me.'

'Oh, Row,' I say. 'Of course it wasn't.'

'It was,' she insists, tears brimming and then spilling again.

'Why would you think that?'

'Because . . .' There's another long pause, which she eventually breaks in a breathless torrent. 'Because I told her I was going to tell, and she said if I did she'd run away and never come back.'

She doesn't mean . . . 'Wait, Row . . . Told her you were going to tell who? About what?'

She turns to look at me, her teary brown eyes wide and Bambi-like. 'About her and Mr Cohn. Tell my mum and dad, I mean.'

For a moment, I can't speak. 'You knew about her and Mr Cohn?'

'Well, yeah . . .' Understanding is starting to dawn in her eyes. 'You . . . um. You didn't?'

It's obvious that she'd assumed I knew, too. And why wouldn't she? Bonnie and I are best friends. We're meant to be best friends.

'She . . . she *told* you?' I ask, stupidly. But none of this makes any sense.

'Sort of. Not really. I kind of . . .' Rowan's cheeks have started to turn pink. 'I kind of found out. It was so obvious something was going on, you know?' Nope. Not to me. 'She was so . . . different. And she'd stay late after school and ask me to cover for her, so I knew something was up. A couple of weeks ago I saw him – Mr Cohn, I mean – drop her off at our house after school before my parents got home. And she stayed in the car for a while, you know? It was so obvious. And so when she got in I asked her straight out and she told me everything.'

Everything. There's an 'everything'.

'What did she actually say? Did she tell you that they were planning to run off?'

'God, no! Just that they were in love. And I was like, euw, obviously, but she was really happy, like a different person, and that was kind of nice for a bit, you know? She said they were working things out. I don't know what I thought that meant, but I agreed to keep it all quiet for a while because it was all so weird and I didn't know what to do. But then it started to get *proper* weird . . . like, he came into our house after school? While I was there?' The words are spilling like they've been waiting for their chance, the agitation in her voice making every sentence a question. 'And so I told Bonnie, this is all kinds of wrong, and I'm just going to tell Mum and Dad if you don't stop.' She takes a deep breath. 'And she completely freaked out, said I was ruining everything, ruining her life, ruining Mr Cohn's life, and she'd never forgive me if I told – stuff like that. And I said I didn't care, and I just didn't want to be involved. And that's when she said the thing about running away and not coming back. And I said . . .' She pauses, her breath hitching again. 'I said, "*Go on then!*"'

At these final words, she lets out a little anguished wail and buries her face in her hands.

'Row, it's OK,' I say, trying to make my voice soft and reassuring, like Carolyn or Valerie would. 'Look, when did this happen?'

'Thursday.'

OK, so it makes a little bit more sense why she'd think it was her fault now. There's no way that conversation and Bonnie's disappearance aren't connected. But I'm not a monster – I know that's the last thing I should say.

'Bonnie leaving is all on her, not you,' I say. 'It doesn't matter what you did or didn't say before she left.'

Rowan peeks out at me from between her fingers, doubtful.

'Honest,' I say.

'But I lied,' she says, her voice still hoarse and quiet. 'The police asked me, and my mum and dad asked me, and I just said I didn't know anything, and that was a *lie*. But if I told them the truth they'd know I'd been lying before.' Her chin is starting to wobble again. 'So I don't know what to do.'

Bloody Bonnie. It's one thing to make *me* lie – it comes easy, and it doesn't really bother me that much. But Rowan? Rule-following, anxious little Rowan? That's just *mean*.

'I don't think they'll mind about the lying before,' I say, even though that's almost definitely not true. 'Don't worry about that. If you want to tell them, do it. But, Row—?'

The bell rings with a loud, jarring screech and we both jump. Rowan's eyes widen and she looks around, suddenly skittish. 'I've got to get to English,' she says.

'Wait just one sec,' I say, taking hold of her blazer sleeve. 'Do you know where Bonnie is now? Have you spoken to her since she left?'

She shakes her head, and I don't know whether to be relieved or not. 'No. Have you?'

'No,' I say. 'Let me know if she contacts you, OK?'

'I will,' she says. I watch her sweep her books into her arms and hurry off down the path away from me. She looks so small.

Poor Rowan, carrying that kind of secret around with everything going on.

When she's gone, I pull out my phone and send a quick text to 'Ivy': **Call me asap. I need to talk to you – it's about Rowan!**

I wait a couple of minutes for her to reply, opening Twitter again and scrolling through the hashtag to read the 140-character opinions of total strangers. Whoever thought up this hashtag thing clearly didn't think it through. It's only being used for speculation and judgement, like all of Twitter. A clickbait website is already using the hashtag to run a mini-debate on whether it's ever OK to have a fling with your teacher. I wonder who suggested the safer words 'a fling' over the likely more accurate 'sex'.

I let out a sigh that sounds loud in the silence of the school and lock my phone again. There's nothing for me on Twitter, and nothing for me here at school, either. No Bonnie, no Connor. I sling my bag over my shoulder and head for the exit.

8

It wasn't always just me and Bonnie. Like any twosome, we'd experimented over the years with extras and alternatives, even drifting away from each other at one point in favour of other people, though not for very long. The fact is that Bonnie and I are pretty different people, and though this has always been a good thing in our friendship, it's also meant there's not really room for anyone else. We work because we balance each other out.

When we were in Year 7, Bonnie got friendly with a couple of girls who were much more of a natural fit for her: academic, well-behaved, quiet types. She tried to make us into a kind of foursome, but it just never happened. They seemed, if anything, a bit confused by me and why Bonnie liked me so much. And they were just too bland for me, too polished, too *nice*. When we tried to hang out all together, I was so obviously the odd-one-out it was painful. I thought I might lose Bonnie, for a while, especially as there were girls who were more of a natural fit for *me* too, but it didn't happen. She stopped trying to make us all be friends and returned to my side.

And then, when we were in Year 9, I'd found a group of friends who were more like me. Or at least, the me I felt like I was expected to be, and tried to be, for a while. But that didn't last, and ever since it's just been Bonnie and me, plus Connor for the last year or so. And that's how I like it. Don't get me wrong, she's not my *only* friend. I've got plenty of non-best friends, the casual kind I'll hang out with at parties or whose pictures I'll like on Instagram. But they don't know anything real about me, and they don't know me;

I don't trust them with my secrets or my heart. And for good reason, it turns out – they haven't checked in to make sure I'm OK, what with Bonnie being missing; they've just sent a stream of OMG DID YOU KNOW? texts that I ignored completely. Some friends.

I might be talking a lot about all the things that are different about Bonnie and me, but of course there are things we have in common, too. We both love horror films, especially the psychological ones that totally mess with your head. We both think the person who thought of adding chilli to chocolate is an actual genius. We both think getting drunk is overrated, and have a low tolerance for other people's annoying habits. We watch the Eurovision Song Contest together every year – usually at my house – and we always get overly invested in whichever country we've each picked out of a hat. We both love Harry Potter – her, the books; me, the films. We both took the Sorting Hat test last year to see what house we'd be in, because Bonnie said it was an important part of understanding our own identity. And then she got Slytherin and got cross and said the whole thing was just a story and it didn't mean anything. I got Gryffindor.

People talk about friendship like it's only about shared loves, but it's not. It's also about finding the same things annoying and getting excited about the same silly, irrelevant things. It's the person you can share a joke with, sure. But it's also the person you can subtly roll your eyes at when someone else is talking too loudly. The person who makes the fun things better and the boring things more bearable. That's Bonnie for me.

The thing is, Bonnie and I aren't friends *despite* our differences; we're best friends *because* of them. I need Bonnie's steadiness and level head to ground me, and she needs my occasional recklessness and wild spirit to lift her. Together, we're in balance. That's how it's always been. Through secondary school, my influence protected her from the bullies who would otherwise have preyed on her mercilessly. Her influence protected *me* from the teachers, who still didn't like me, but at least tolerated me in a way they didn't the other girls like me who just hung around with each other. The bullies looked at Bonnie and thought, *She must be all right, if Eden likes her*. And the teachers looked at me and thought, *She must have something, if Bonnie likes her.*

This probably makes it sound all a bit like a you-scratch-my-back kind of deal we made, like it was a calculated decision to make school bearable, but that's not how it was at all. I love Bonnie. I'm picky about people at the best of times, but when it comes to my inner circle, the people I let into my heart, I'm ruthless. Bonnie is fiercely loyal to the core, and in an active way. So she won't just quietly tell me she's on my side if someone's giving me a hard time; she'll tell them, too. Loudly. She's sharp and funny, but generous with it, using it to lighten the mood of a room rather than bring anyone down.

Bonnie is like the sunshine of my life, and I don't mean that in a soppy, shut-up-Eden-you-cheeseball kind of way (though maybe I do a tiny bit). It's more than just that she makes my life brighter; it's that I can *count on her* to be there, rain or shine, every single day. I know I can be a cold, grey, bitter person, sometimes. With Bonnie, *I'm* brighter. I don't even know who I'd be without her, but I do know that this isn't how I want to find out. Left suddenly solo with no warning or preparation, pushed to the side in favour of this new, surprise twosome.

Maybe, while she was all these things to me, I wasn't enough for her. The thought makes me feel heavy. She chose to run away, and I didn't have the slightest idea that was even a possibility. What does that say about our friendship? What does it say about *me*? And who is there for me to talk to about all of this if she's gone?

With these questions in my head, I don't feel like going straight home. What's waiting for me, anyway, except revision and more rolling news? I go on a detour through the park and into the play area, sitting at the bottom of the slide and taking out my phone to wait for Bonnie to call. I just need to talk to her properly. I need to hear her voice.

After a few minutes, I press the call icon for 'Ivy' and watch the screen connect. No answer. I call again. No answer.

'For God's sake, Bonnie!' I snap into the empty air. I tap the message icon and type: **Where are you? Call me!!**

I decide I'll wait fifteen minutes for her before I give up and go home. After seven, my screen lights up. It's Ivy.

'Take your damn time!' I say in greeting.

'Sorry!' she says. 'Jack and I were at the beach.' Of course they bloody were. 'What's going on with Rowan?'

'She's hanging on by a thread!' This is maybe a bit of an exaggeration, but Bonnie doesn't need to know that. 'She thinks you leaving is all her fault!'

There's a moment of silence. Then Bonnie's voice sounds in my ear again, more cautious this time. 'Why does she think that?'

'You know why she thinks that,' I snap, trying to control my annoyance. Why is she still being so cagey with me? Aren't I supposed to be her confidante in all this? The fact that I'm the one she's choosing to be in contact with is really the only thing that's making her previous lies bearable, and even that is depending on me not thinking about it too much.

'She told you about the fight we had?'

'Well, I didn't guess, did I?'

Another silence.

'What were you thinking, telling her?' I ask. What I mean is: *Why did you tell her and not me?*

'She found out,' Bonnie says. 'I didn't mean to tell her. No one was meant to know. That's what made what Jack and I have . . . ours.'

'Was it Mr Cohn who told you to keep it a secret?'

'He didn't need to tell me; it was obvious.'

'Wasn't that a bit of a warning sign, Bon? If something needs to be kept a secret, it's probably a bad thing?'

'Lots of relationships have to be kept secret,' she replies. 'When people are in love, that's the most important thing, that's why. Romeo and Juliet had to keep it a secret.'

'Do you want to try an example where they both don't end up *dead*?'

'You're missing the point!'

'*I'm* missing the point?'

'Look, just calm down, OK?' Bonnie says, sounding suddenly so much like the Bonnie I remember that my throat closes up. 'No one's ending up dead. That's part of the problem with this whole thing, you know. Everyone's being so overdramatic.'

I close my eyes and let out a small laugh to release some tension. 'I think the problem is you're being *under*-dramatic. You ran off with your teacher. That's literally headline news.'

'We wouldn't have needed to run off if we'd been allowed to be together,' she replies. 'There's such a taboo around age gaps in our society. It's so prudish.'

'Bonnie, this isn't like you being twenty-five and him being thirty-eight, or something. You're underage. It's literally illegal.'

'So?' she says, which is such a baffling response I don't even know how to process it. 'Besides, even if I was a few months older, it's not technically allowed until I'm eighteen, because he's my teacher. Why should I wait that long, when I know I love him, and he loves me?'

I don't know how to reply to that either. I try, 'Because he could get arrested?'

'Yeah, hence the running away,' she says, like I'm being stupid on purpose.

God, there's no arguing with her, is there? 'Couldn't you at least have waited until after your GCSEs?'

'Don't bring up those,' she says. 'Some stupid little exams. They don't *matter*.'

'But . . .' I still don't know what to say. 'But, Bonnie . . . They've always mattered to you.' I feel like I'm reminding her that she wears glasses or something. Bonnie being studious and academic is just a thing; it's who she is. Or was?

'Yeah, and what good did it do me? Worrying all the time? Never getting to do anything fun? None of it ever being good enough for my parents?' This all comes out in a bit of a torrent. 'Other girls at school laughing at me and calling me a nerd? *You* used to tell me I needed to chill out. *You* said I worked too hard and it was all so pointless. Well, you were right.'

'I never said it was pointless!' I protest. 'I said it didn't matter to *me*, and it doesn't, but you want things that are different from what I want. You were working towards something.'

'Well, I'm not any more. Now I have Jack.'

'And, what? That's your life plan?'

'Why can't it be?'

'Because you're fifteen?'

'Love is love, Eden. However old you are.'

I swear I almost hang up on her. 'Can you be Serious Bonnie for just one minute?' I ask. 'What about when you need to get a job? You think you can just be on the run forever?'

'I already told you this. No, not forever. Just until everything calms down. When they all realize we really do love each other and no one has to get arrested.'

'And how long will that be?'

'I don't know, Eden! As long as it takes, OK?'

'And what about me? What about Rowan? What about your parents?'

Bonnie doesn't answer.

'You're being so selfish.' The words fall out of my mouth, unintentional but burning with truth. There's a long, weighted silence.

'Maybe I am,' she says finally. Her voice is cold. 'But maybe I'm allowed to be. Maybe it's not the worst thing in the world to get what I want for once.'

'You're ruining your life. You know that, right? You know that's what you're doing here?'

There's a short laugh at the other end of the phone, humourless and entirely un-Bonnie-like. 'Now who's being dramatic?' she says.

9

When I get home, I go straight through the side entrance and head for my section of the garden. I don't even bother to change my clothes, just tie my hair up into a ponytail and grab my outdoor gloves from the shed, pulling them over my hands. I can't be around people right now. I can't bear the thought of Carolyn asking about the revision session. I don't want to think about what Joe Journalist at the *Guardian* thinks of Mr Cohn's motives. I just want the earth under my fingers and things I can understand.

When Bob and Carolyn first adopted Daisy and me, they gave us each a small part of the garden to make our own. Daisy lost interest almost straight away, but I fell in love. My section has grown over the years, first taking over Daisy's plot, and then growing ever further as I learned how to garden properly, experimenting with different types of flowers and plants, fruits and vegetables. My very favourite is my cherry tree, which I bought as a bare root when I was thirteen with the allowance I'd been saving for months. It's growing into a thing of beauty, if I do say so myself, and it's not even producing fruit yet.

People are always surprised when they find out I like gardening. I don't know if that's because they assume things about me, or they assume things about gardeners, but either way I like seeing the faces they make when I tell them. The first time Connor came round to my house and I showed him my garden, he looked at me like he was waiting for the punchline. 'Don't take this the wrong way,' he said, in that nervous voice he used a lot right at the beginning of our relationship, 'but you just don't seem like the kind of person who likes flowers.'

The truth – and I told him this at the time – is that it's more than about just liking flowers. 'Everyone needs a place of their own in this world,' Bob says, and my garden is mine.

I know that the garden is a therapy thing. I know that my adoptive parents have done a lot of research over the years, back when they were fostering and then when they decided to adopt us. *How to care for damaged kids*, or something. *Hints and tips for raising a second-hand child*. Something like this, my garden, is practically textbook. Give them a space that is just theirs: *a sense of ownership*. Give them something to take care of: *a sense of responsibility*. Give them something to grow: *a sense of accomplishment*.

I don't mind. I'm not complaining. I'm glad Carolyn and Bob read those books, that they are the kind of people who try. And I'm glad I have my garden. This patch of land is mine – the first thing that truly *was* mine, except maybe my name, and I lost half of that when I got adopted. It is beautiful, and it is mine.

I didn't know a single thing about gardening before Carolyn and Bob. It's funny how your life's passion can just be there waiting for you before you even know. Sometimes, when I can't sleep and my head goes on its wild tangents, I think about how easily I could have not known, not realized. If I hadn't been fostered and then adopted by two professional gardeners, how would I ever have found out how the soil feels when it gives underneath my fingers? Who else would have thought to show me how to nurture the earth? Daisy and I could have been fostered by anyone; so much of it is about timing, and Carolyn and Bob just happened to have a room at a time when we needed one.

I got lucky; I know that. I'm so aware of that. I thought everyone had thoughts like this, about the almosts and the could-have-beens and the lucky chances. The lives that aren't lived alongside all the ones that are. But when I asked Bonnie, she looked at me with such genuine confusion, I realized that for her, family was just a given, a fact of life, and she'd never thought, *What if I'd been born into a different family? What if I'd grown up in Scotland or New York? What if I'd had a brother instead of a sister?*

I never asked anyone else, even Connor. Maybe it's just a thing that adopted kids do. Or maybe it's just me.

But I still think about it. All those passions that never were, just because life went one way instead of another. How many would-have-been violinists grew up in homes without music, or, more likely, where there wasn't any money for instruments? I think about the ballerina who never danced, never wore the shoes, never even had a lesson. The lives some people never get to lead.

These are the kinds of things I think about when it's just me and my garden. I stay for a good couple of hours, losing myself among my flower beds. My mind empties and my nerves stop jangling. I take a few slow breaths, the familiar earth soft beneath my knees, before I pull myself up and head slowly back towards the house.

I take a late lunch of toasted cheese sandwiches and Quavers up to my room and settle down with the cat, who stretches across my thighs, claws digging into my skin, and purrs.

I open my laptop and click on to a few news sites to see how up to date they are. The *Daily Mail* is running with a huge CCTV picture of Bonnie and Mr Cohn at the Tesco garage from right after they disappeared, along with the headline *WHERE ARE THEY?* – which seems a little unimaginative to me. The BBC has a timeline of their known movements from Friday evening through to Saturday afternoon, which only reminds me that the trail has gone cold. The *Guardian* has a comment article about whether 'we' (who is this 'we' in opinion articles, I always wonder?) put too much pressure on 'young women'. It talks about the 'sexualization of girls', the 'abundance of porn', the 'inherent competitiveness of a social media world' and the 'ever-present pressure to meet the expectations of even the most loving, supportive parents'.

And then, this:

> By all accounts, Bonnie Wiston-Stanley is the model pupil and daughter: high-achieving and responsible; well-mannered and polite, with not a detention to her name in all her years of schooling. What this cannot tell us is what was going on behind the smile, and the danger is that we don't even try to find out. We equate intelligence and academic success with happiness, even though we surely know such equivalences are futile. How many high-achieving young people go on to experience high levels of anxiety and depression? How many, colloquially, go 'a bit off the rails'?
>
> Perhaps Bonnie Wiston-Stanley, with all her intelligence, saw this coming. Perhaps she saw an escape in her handsome, charming teacher, offering her love and acceptance, irrespective of her test scores and university prospects. This is surely a tantalizing thing at any age, but how must it feel for a fifteen-year-old? A fifteen-year-old who has only learned to value herself through exam results?
>
> We all deserve the opportunity to expand ourselves, to spread our wings and see how it feels to fly. We all need that time to do something wrong because it feels right, to face the consequences of a decision made in passion, to learn what it means to fail. I hope when Bonnie does return, after what she will likely come to remember as her wild phase, that there is sympathy, and we don't forget how young fifteen really is.

I read the article three times, trying to figure out how I feel about it. I keep coming back to that word 'sympathy'. It seems to me like people are already being pretty sympathetic to Bonnie. All this stuff about a wild phase, about spreading her wings . . . Aren't they just fancy ways of saying fucking up? Why is it that when girls like Bonnie have a 'wild phase', people try to understand it? But girls who aren't like Bonnie, girls who don't get the A grades, don't have the 'loving, supportive parents' and have many detentions to their names, get written off?

Take me. I'd tried having a wild phase of my own, mostly because that seemed to be what was expected of girls like me – troubled girls, whatever the hell that meant – but it hadn't stuck. It wasn't satisfying, basically. It didn't make me feel good. The kind of things I did, things that were meant to make me feel free, actually made me feel lost.

Carolyn and Bob had been well prepared. I think they'd been planning for it since they decided to adopt my nine-year-old self. *One day*, they must have thought, *she's going to be a troubled teen tearaway. We should prepare*. So when it happened, a couple of years ago now, when I started staying out, answering back, smoking and drinking, they were ready. They chose the room-to-breathe, unconditional-love approach. And I don't just mean they told me they loved me even when I swore at them, or whatever. I mean things like this:

Picture me, fourteen years old, stoned and trippy, tiptoeing through the back door to find Carolyn sitting in the kitchen, nightgown on and a smile on her face. 'Hello, darling,' she said. And then she made me hot chocolate and warmed up a cinnamon bun. I am not kidding. Do you know hard it is to keep up some kind of bad-girl act when you're drinking hot chocolate with your adoptive mother in the kitchen with the lights dimmed low? Especially when she starts telling you the story about how she got stuck once trying to climb back through her childhood bedroom window, and had to call for help? And then you snort on your hot chocolate, and the cinnamon bun is cosy and warm, and she says, 'I like how you've done your eye make-up,' and it makes you love her, despite everything that had made you want to leave.

Being wild is all about boundaries, right? You either have none, and so being wild is all you know, or you have them, and you resist them. You rebel. With Carolyn and Bob, I had boundaries, but, it turned out, nothing to rebel against. It would be like trying to punch a bean bag; the blows just get soaked up and it's still so comfortable, warm and snug. So the thrill of night-time wanderings wore off, and the friends I shared cars and joints and adventures with just didn't know me like Bonnie did, and joyriding was terrifying, and so I just stopped. The whole thing only lasted a few months.

So yeah, I get it about the whole 'wild phase' thing. And I know that even good girls like Bonnie have their moments . . . but this? This is beyond wild, right? This is major, potentially life-ruining stuff. This is front page of the freaking *Sun*. This is trending on Twitter. This is *running away with your teacher*.

I scroll down the page to look at the comments, and immediately regret it. *Why are you wasting space on some teenage slapper and her paedo boyfriend*? asks one of the politer ones. I shudder and close my entire browser as if this will somehow cleanse my laptop – and me – of the below-the-line dirt of the internet.

Daisy gets home from school after four and comes straight into my room, curling up next to me on my bed.

'What's up, chuck?' I ask.

'Got a detention.'

'Oh, Daze. What for?'

'I asked Mr Hale if he'd picked which one of us he was going to run off with yet.'

It feels good to laugh as hard as I do. 'Worth it, then?'

At my reaction, the sulk vanishes and she grins. 'Everyone else thought it was funny. 'Cept Rowan, but she's a square anyway.'

'Hey, be nice to Rowan!' I say. 'Imagine how you'd feel if I took off.'

I'm saved from having to hear her answer to this by footsteps in the hall, followed by my door opening. I look up, expecting to see Carolyn, but it's a different smiling face that appears.

'Valerie!' Daisy shrieks, leaping up for a hug.

'Daisy!' Valerie replies, wrapping her arms around her and squeezing. Over Daisy's head, she grins at me. 'Hi!'

'What are you doing here?' I ask, a little more bluntly than I'd intended.

'Seeing you,' Valerie says cheerfully.

'Why?'

'Because everything must feel so crazy and I figured you could use a friendly face.' She stretches out her grin deliberately so it takes up her whole face, then points at it. 'See? Friendly face.'

'Are you staying?' Daisy asks hopefully. She's still cuddled up close, her arm around Valerie's skinny waist, and I'm struck by something that might be jealousy if I think about it too hard. Daisy reverts back into cute-little-sister mode around Valerie. Me, I get total-pain, talking-back, super-snarky Daisy. Great.

'Yep,' Valerie says. 'My exams start next week, so I'll have to head back on Sunday, but I can revise here instead of York.' She grins at me and gives my knee a poke. 'We can revise together, right, Eeds? Share the exam hell.'

'Do you even need to revise?' I ask, only half kidding.

'Like a demon,' Valerie says. 'Final-year exams, man. You think GCSEs are tough? Mine are all three hours long. Three hours! It's like they're trying to kill us. Whoever survives gets a degree.' She smiles. 'How about you? How are you feeling about yours?' I mime choking to death, and she laughs. 'When's the first one?'

'Wednesday. Biology. Then Chemistry on Thursday.'

'Ooh, the sciences!' Valerie says with a grin. 'Those are the best ones. What time? We could get lunch before and I could help you cram.'

'They're both morning exams,' I say.

'Breakfast then,' she amends, her cheerfulness unwavering.

'I don't know,' I say, trying to think of a good reason why not, except the fact that Valerie and her A-grade perfection is not the kind of thing I want shoved in my face just before an exam, which is the kind of true thing you can't say out loud. 'There's a lot going on.'

'All the more reason to let your big sister drive you around and buy you food,' Valerie points out. 'Come on, Eeds. I came all the way from York to be here for you.'

'You *drove*?' It's like a four-and-a-half-hour drive from York to Larking. Usually she gets the train. 'Why?'

'To be here for you,' she says again, like it's obvious. 'And I brought the car because of the aforementioned driving-around-and-buying-you-food thing.' Who uses the word 'aforementioned' in an actual sentence? This is why Valerie and I will never be as close as she wants us to be.

'Fine. OK,' I say. I can't exactly say no when she's driven for that long, can I? I'm not that horrible. I can think of an excuse later.

'Great,' Valerie says. 'Hey, Daze, want to help me make dinner? I'm doing fajitas.'

I feel a buzz under my leg, which is where my phone ended up when Daisy jumped on my bed. It's probably Bonnie, so I stop myself reaching straight for it.

'Can I do the fun bit?' Daisy asks, meaning stealing scraps of cheese while Valerie cooks and not helping with any of the prep or clean-up.

'Sure,' Valerie says, too easy on her as usual. 'Want to come, Eeds?'

I shake my head and point at my textbook. 'I'm revising.'

If Valerie was like me, she'd shrug and leave at this point. But, because she's Valerie, she lingers. 'Aw, come on,' she coaxes. 'Everyone should know how to cook fajitas.'

'I can cook fajitas,' I say, which is kind of true. They come in one of those ready-to-make kits, right? I feel my phone give another buzz against my leg and I bite down on the inside of my cheek to stop myself grabbing it.

'But—' Valerie starts.

'I'll see you later,' I interrupt. 'Make them properly spicy, yeah?'

Valerie looks at me for a moment, then sighs a little and shrugs. 'OK, fine. Come on, Daze.'

When they've gone, I pull out my phone from under my leg and unlock it.

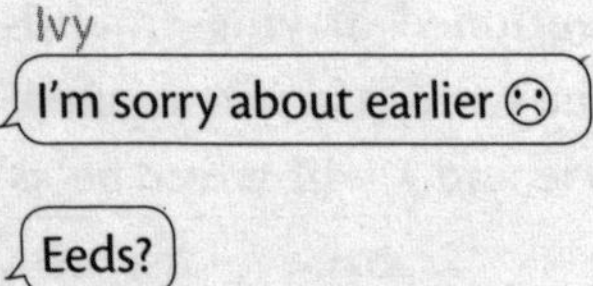

I stare at the messages, trying to figure out how to reply. Bonnie and I don't argue much, not really. And when we do, they're short, sharp snarling matches that flare up and burn out too quickly to cause any real damage. The argument we had earlier was more passive-aggressive and somehow deeper, which is not like either of us, and now I don't know what to do.

My fingers are still poised over my phone when another message comes through.

Ivy

This is such a weird situation and I'm trying to deal with it but I don't really know how.

Me

I'm just worried about you, Bon.

I know. I'm sorry.
ilu xxx

ilu2 xxx

I really AM fine though. Jack is just so amazing, you have no idea. I love him so much. And he loves me. This is all worth it, I promise.

You get why that sounds so weird to me, right?

Haha yes of course! He's just Mr Cohn to you. You don't know him like I do.

Probably for the best.

☺ Right!

Are you HAPPY, Bon? Really?

Yes! Look, I'll show you! One sec . . .

An instant later, a photo appears, and I'm so stunned I almost drop my phone. It's a selfie of Bonnie and Mr Cohn, cheeks pressed together, beaming into the camera, like they're just another ordinary couple and not actual fugitives with a fourteen-year age gap between them. I'd forgotten that she'd cut and dyed her hair, and the sight of her is a shock. She looks like a different person. Bright and dazzling. I can't stop looking at her.

Mr Cohn – I just can't call him Jack – looks just the same as I remember him, except the glasses have gone and he's wearing a baseball cap. I try to see him like Bonnie does, but I can't. He doesn't look like a teacher any more, but he's still, undeniably, an adult. A grown man.

Ivy

Well??? Aren't we the CUTEST?!

God, what am I meant to say to that? Agreeing is probably the only option, but I don't really want to encourage her. I take option C: make a joke.

Me

No, me and Connor are the CUTEST. But that's a cute pic.

Ivy

That'll do ☺

Don't you think you should talk to Rowan?

If I do, she'll tell. I can't trust her.

😐 But she's your sister.

I know. But this is more important right now.

Me

Is it?

Ivy

It has to be. You and me, though – we're OK?

Yes.

<3 You're the only one I miss.

Really?

Really.

Conversations That Took on a New Meaning after Bonnie Disappeared

The 'Veggie-Connor' Edition: one month before

'You love Connor, right?'

'Yeah, of course.'

'How much?'

'What do you mean, how much?'

'Like, what would you give up for him?'

Bonnie and I were sitting on a picnic bench on the edge of the playing field, watching Connor play football with some of his guy friends. As we watched, Connor glanced over at us, grinned and waved. I waved back, feeling the smile on my face.

'Why would I need to give up anything for him?' I asked Bonnie.

'If you had to, I mean. Like, if it turned out he was really allergic to peanuts. Would you stop eating peanuts?'

'Yeah, of course.'

'What if he wanted to be a vegetarian? Would you become one too?'

I made a face. 'I don't think that's the same as the peanut thing.'

'What if he wanted you to, I mean. If he asked you to give up meat. Would you?'

'No, probably not,' I said. 'He'd have to really convince me. And let me make an exception for bacon sandwiches. And Christmas dinner.'

Bonnie was looking at me like I was deliberately missing the point. 'But if you love him, wouldn't you want to support him?'

'Sure. I wouldn't eat ribs in front of veggie-Connor. Doesn't mean I couldn't eat them when he wasn't around.'

'I think if *I* loved someone,' she said, clearly deciding to make the point herself as I kept missing it, 'I'd give up anything to be with him. I think that's true love.'

'What do you know about true love?' I asked.

She smiled and shrugged. 'Enough,' she said.

Tuesday

Bonnie Cops Bungle Swoop on Runaway Teacher and Missing Schoolgirl, as it Emerges the Pair Left HOURS Before Police Acted on New Info

- Cops act too late to catch up with vulnerable 15-year-old Bonnie Wiston-Stanley
- Music teacher Jack Cohn still on the run
- Love letters passed to police reveal teacher groomed pupil for 'romantic getaway'

Police arrived hours too late to tackle disgraced music teacher Jack Cohn, who remains on the run with schoolgirl Bonnie Wiston-Stanley, 15.

'Solid information' on the pair's location passed to detectives yesterday afternoon could have seen police finally catch up with the couple, sources say. But instead of immediately acting on the information, police waited until late in the evening before bothering to show.

Cops were left red-faced when they raided a property in the seaside town of Tenby, Wales, which was believed to be the hiding place of the runaways – only to find it empty. The holiday home's owner, a former friend of Cohn, yesterday tipped off police to the fact the pair may be there. The friend, who could not be reached for comment, is not believed to be involved.

Police now admit they are 'back to square one' in their search to catch up with the couple, as damning new evidence of Cohn's plans comes to light.

Letters written by Cohn reveal dozens of messages to

his pupil, which date back to at least February this year. The teacher had previously suggested a 'romantic getaway' for the pair after 15-year-old Bonnie Wiston-Stanley confided in him how she felt pressured by her upcoming GCSEs. The months of messages lay bare Cohn's desire to groom the girl and convince the straight-A student of his interest in a romantic relationship with her.

As Head of Music, Cohn first met the pupil in her first year at Kett Academy, aged just 11, and became her form tutor the following year. Now in Year 11, Wiston-Stanley is one of just three students taking Music GCSE – and it is during this period that fellow students suggest the pair 'grew close'.

The letters show how Cohn took advantage of this trust and asked Bonnie to text him 'any time' she felt stressed by preparation for her upcoming exams, and invited her to 'just say if there's anything I can do to make you feel better'.

10

Carolyn wakes me up on Tuesday morning with a cup of tea and a plate of jammy toast. This is so unusual I immediately assume that Bonnie has been found and/or something terrible has happened, so I sit bolt upright in bed – Carolyn starts in surprise and the tea sloshes out over the mug, dripping on to my bedsheets – and demand, 'What is it?'

'Oh dear,' Carolyn says, frowning. 'I'll have to wash those.'

'Is it Bonnie?' I ask. My voice is managing to be both shrill and crackly with sleep. 'Tell me!'

'Calm down,' Carolyn says. 'Everything's fine. I didn't mean to scare you.'

'I can get my own breakfast!' I say. I mean by this that I know there's a reason she's woken me up early, and I want to know what it is, but my mind hasn't quite woken up properly so it just comes out like I'm snapping at her, and she looks hurt. 'Sorry,' I add.

'Shuffle over,' Carolyn says, setting my cup of tea on my bedside cabinet. I shift across the bed a little, leaving a space for her to sit down. She settles down next to me and pats my shoulder. 'Have some toast.'

'Is it Bonnie?' I ask again. She just looks at me, so I roll my eyes, grab a piece of toast and shove it in my mouth.

'Yes and no,' she says as I begin to chew. 'There's some good news, some so-so news and some bad news. Which would you like first?'

I swallow. 'Chronological order.' This is what Bob always says to this kind of question.

She smiles. 'Good choice. OK, now, I don't want you to worry, but there was a very significant lead in the case last night. The police were tipped off.'

I feel my eyes widen.

'Don't get too excited – this is the so-so news. There was a raid at the property where the police believed Bonnie and Mr Cohn were, but they weren't there.'

My breath comes out in a short, sharp burst. Is it relief or disappointment? I don't even know.

'Did they have the wrong place?' I ask.

Carolyn shakes her head. 'No, it was obvious that they'd been there, and that they'd only recently left.'

'So how come they weren't there?'

'I don't know. Something spooked them, presumably. Maybe they got a heads-up somehow that the police were on their way. But anyway, even though they weren't caught, this is a very significant step in the case. Knowing where they've been can help us know where they're going.'

'OK.' I take another bite of toast, relaxing a little.

'The good news is, you don't have to go to that revision session at school today,' Carolyn says. 'The bad news is that the police are coming here this morning to talk to you.'

I choke on the toast, crumbs catching in my throat. 'What?' I manage.

'Ten a.m.,' she adds. 'I thought I'd get you up now to give you time to prepare.'

'Why?' I ask, still coughing.

'I'm sure they'll have a list of questions to ask you.'

'Like what?'

'Well, if they're anything like me, they'll be curious to know why you aren't wondering where this bust took place.'

For a moment, I don't understand what she means. And then

I realize in a rush of panic that I try very hard to keep from my face: I haven't asked anything about where they'd almost been caught.

'I thought you didn't know!' I say. 'Otherwise why didn't you say straight away?'

Carolyn's expression is completely unreadable.

'Go on, tell me then,' I say. 'Where?'

'Wales,' Carolyn says slowly.

Shit. I have royally fucked up. She looks so suspicious. But in a Carolyn way, because she's trying to hide how suspicious she is. Quick, Eden. Save this.

'Why would they go there?' I ask.

'I don't know, Eden.' She doesn't need to say the next bit: *But I think you do.*

We look at each other for a moment, neither of us speaking. I have no idea how to fix this.

Finally, she begins, 'Eden—'

I interrupt. 'How could they not get them?'

'What?'

'How could they get so close and fuck it up?'

'Eden, language.'

'What are they even doing?' I demand, feeling myself getting actually worked up even though this outburst is meant to be just for show. 'They find out exactly where they are and still miss them?! They could be anywhere now! Anywhere! They're back to square one!'

'It's not quite square one—'

'Why would they go to Wales, anyway? What's in sodding *Wales*?' The show is all real now. My voice is getting squeaky again, my breath catching in my throat.

'Have some tea,' Carolyn says with a sigh, passing me my cup. 'I really don't know, love. But that's likely to be the kind of question the police will be asking you, so have a think about the answer, will you?'

I nod, gulping my tea. Oh God, I don't want to talk to the police. What the hell are they going to ask me? What the hell am I going to say?

I wait until I'm sure I'm alone – in the bathroom with the door locked – before I text Bonnie. I'm not subtle about it. WHAT HAPPENED LAST NIGHT?!?!? WHERE ARE YOU???

I sit on the edge of the bath, nibbling on my thumbnail, waiting for her to reply. For some reason, I feel really nervous. What if she thinks *I* shopped her to the police? What if she doesn't ever talk to me again? Keeping her secrets is stressful enough, but being on the outside of them is unthinkable.

Barely a minute after I send the message, my phone lights up with an incoming call and I jolt with relief. 'Hello?'

'Hi! It's me!' Bonnie's voice is bouncy and cheerful, which is completely not what I was expecting. 'What's with all the caps? I can read lower case just fine, you know.' When she says this, she laughs, like it's an ordinary conversation on an ordinary day.

'What *happened*?' I demand, trying to keep my voice quiet.

'The police almost got us,' she says.

'Yeah, I know that bit. But what happened to you? And how did they find out?'

I hear her sigh on the other end of the phone, like this is already an old, boring story. 'Well, we were staying in this cottage in Tenby, right? It's a holiday home that Jack's friend owns, and Jack had stayed there before, so he knew the key-code. It wasn't booked out, so it seemed like the perfect place to lie low for a bit while we figured out what to do next.'

'Okaaay . . .' I say.

'Like, there was no reason why anyone would suspect we were

there. But Jack's friend must have got suspicious or something, because he rang the house. We didn't pick up or anything – we're not stupid – but Jack says no one else would have the landline for the property. That was yesterday morning. Anyway, Jack got spooked, said if Rob thought there was even a chance we were there, he'd tell the police, because he's that kind of guy. So we left.'

'Just like that?'

'Yeah, Jack doesn't like to hang around when he makes a decision. Lucky, otherwise we'd probably be caught by now.'

Lucky. I make a face at the bathroom tiles. 'Where are you now?'

'Somewhere in Yorkshire.'

I pause, waiting for more, but she doesn't elaborate. 'Somewhere in Yorkshire?' I repeat.

'Yeah, I don't know exactly where. It's green, very quiet. Super pretty.'

'Why Yorkshire?'

'We wanted to get as far away as possible, as quickly as possible,' she says. 'We drove all the way here and then slept in the car last night. They don't even know how we're getting around, right? So distance is key.'

Distance is key? I think but don't say. This is so clearly a Mr Cohn phrase that it makes me wonder how much of anything she says is actually coming from her.

'And it's so pretty here!' she adds, her voice picking up again. 'Jack's going to find us somewhere to stay today.'

'How?' I ask, the question coming out more like a demand. 'Do you even have money?'

'Yeah, of course. Just cash, though, so we have to be careful.'

I don't understand how she can be so laid back about all of this. Bonnie, who's never been laid back about anything. 'Have you given up on Ireland?'

'Oh, that. No, it's just on hold for now. We might head to

Scotland in a bit. Jack says it's easy to get lost in the Highlands.'

'You could just come home,' I say, trying for casual and missing.

There's a pause. 'I haven't gone through all of this just to give up,' she says. 'I thought you understood all this? That I'm happy?'

'I do,' I say quickly. I don't. 'I just miss you.'

Another brief pause, and then she's back, cheerful again. 'I miss you too! Hey, how are you, anyway? How's Larking?'

'I'm OK,' I say, because the truth is, I don't actually know how to answer a question like that at the moment. 'And Larking is just Larking. Bon, the police are coming here this morning to talk to me.'

'What?!' Her voice is suddenly panicked. '*Why?* I thought they spoke to you already?'

'I don't know, do I? Probably something about Wales.'

'You're not going to tell them anything, are you?' I can hear the paranoia in her voice, like *Oh, shit, probably shouldn't have mentioned Yorkshire*. She's probably wishing she'd saved this conversation for later in the day.

'No, Bon, of course not. I promised, didn't I?'

'Yeah. OK, sorry.' She's silent for a moment, and then I hear her sigh. 'God, I really miss you.'

'I miss *you*,' I say. 'Everything's so crazy here, and I keep thinking I want to talk about it with you, and then I remember that the crazy bit *is* you.'

She laughs a little. 'Right. I've never been the centre of anything before.'

'Well, you really went for it.'

'Yep. Go heavy or go home.'

'There's so much I want to talk to you about. Properly, I mean. Not all secretive.'

'We'll talk properly soon, OK? We've just got to wait for all the crazy to blow over.'

'What makes you think it even will blow over?'

'It has to eventually.'

'You think your family is just going to stop looking for you?'

'No, but I'll be sixteen soon, and by then all the press people will have got bored and stopped covering it. I can deal with Mum and Dad then.'

'*Bonnie!*' I can't believe this. 'You're going to wait until *July* to talk to your parents?'

'If I have to, yeah. Don't you get it yet, Eeds? I love Jack. I'll do anything to be with him.'

I put my fingers to my forehead and press down, trying to sort out my thoughts into something coherent that will make her realize what she's doing. What comes out is: 'Bon, this is *crazy*.'

'Love is crazy. Look, I should go. I'll speak to you later, OK?'

'OK.'

'Good luck with the police. Love you.'

'Love you too.'

I sit there for a few minutes on the edge of the bath after we've both hung up, thinking. I still can't quite make the link between this Bonnie and the Bonnie I've known for eight years. The meticulous, responsible girl with this lovestruck, reckless runaway. Has she had both versions of herself inside of her all this time and I just didn't know?

It's the not-talking-to-her-parents-until-July thing that's really getting to me. How can she do something like that? How can she act like her parents don't matter to her? How can she not care about giving up her family like this? Doesn't she realize how *lucky* she is to have had it? The security and safety of family? No questions in the back of her head about belonging, about blood vs choice. None of the confusion of having and loving another mother when your 'real' one is still living and breathing somewhere else. No feelings of responsibility for her little sister's life and happiness, because that's what parents are for.

Everything I've ever lost has been chosen for me. I never had a say.

And she's *chosen* to throw it all away, like it's nothing. The thought comes into my head, unbidden and a shock: *I will never forgive her for this*. The thought frightens me and I push it away. That is a thing that can't be.

It's getting close to 10 a.m., so I slide my phone back into my pocket and go to the sink to wash my face. 'I don't know where Bonnie is,' I whisper to my reflection. 'I don't know where Bonnie is.'

11

The two police officers I find waiting for me in the kitchen when I go downstairs are the same ones who spoke to me on Saturday, one man and one woman. They are sitting at the table while Carolyn fusses about tea or coffee and do you want biscuits too and isn't it a lovely day. She's nervous, and it's catching. I sit down opposite them both and cross my hands in my lap so they won't see if they start to shake.

DC Delmonte – 'Milk and no sugar, thank you, Mrs McKinley; a custard cream would be lovely' – does most of the talking, while DC Doyle – 'Just a black coffee for me, please' – takes notes.

'Let's get straight into it, shall we?' DC Delmonte says to me, nodding as he speaks. 'When did you last speak to Bonnie?'

I swallow. 'Um, last Friday?'

DC Delmonte glances up at me. 'You're not sure?'

'Huh?'

'You said it like a question,' he says.

'Oh. Well. No, I'm sure. It was last Friday.'

'And how did you speak to her? Was it a phone call? In person? Were you Snapchatting?'

I wonder if he even knows what Snapchat is. 'It was over the phone,' I say. 'The last time. I saw her earlier in the day, at a revision session at school.'

'How did she sound on the phone?'

'Fine. Just normal Bonnie.'

Once again DC Doyle is staying silent, just scribbling away as DC Delmonte and I talk.

'What did you talk about?'

'I don't remember.'

'Did she mention Jack at all?'

'Yeah, I think so.' This seems safe to be honest about. 'I think she told me she was seeing him that evening. But I'm not sure, that could just be a different conversation that we had some other time.'

'What time did you speak to her?'

I shrug. 'Early evening? Like, six?'

'And the Jack she spoke about. Did you know that he was your teacher?'

I shake my head.

'What did she tell you about him?'

'Not much. She was all secretive about it.'

He nods, then abruptly changes tack. 'How long have you and Bonnie been friends?'

'Eight years,' I say promptly.

'And how close is your relationship?'

'Er . . . well, she's my best friend.'

'Do you see her every day? Spend your social time together? Tell each other everything?'

I nod, cautiously.

'You share all your secrets?'

I catch on just in time. 'Well, I thought we did.' At this, Carolyn gives me a sad smile.

'Did she ever tell you that she was seeing Mr Cohn?'

I shake my head.

'Any hint at all?'

Another head-shake.

'What about her behaviour? Has she been acting differently recently? Ever talked about wanting to run away?'

'Well,' I say, trying to figure out the best way to reply, 'I haven't seen as much of her over the last few weeks. But it's exam time. I thought she was revising.'

'And what about running away? Did she ever say anything to you?'

'Not really.'

'Not really?'

'I mean, no.'

'How do you feel about Bonnie running away with Mr Cohn?'

Is that a trick question? Not *What do you know about it?* or even *What do you think about it?* But *How do you feel?*

How *do* I feel?

'Angry,' I say, surprising myself.

'Angry?' he prompts.

'It's selfish,' I say. I feel my hands screw into fists at my lap. 'And stupid. And gross.'

'What makes you say "selfish"?'

'Everyone's worried. And she's just off having fun like it doesn't matter.'

'What makes you think she's having fun?'

I close my mouth and bite down on my lips from the inside. Suddenly everything looks like a trap.

'Well, it's not like he kidnapped her, is it?' I say.

'Actually, legally, it *is* abduction.'

'Well, then legally that's stupid.'

Carolyn gives me a look, but I just glare back. I feel hot and weirdly itchy, like I'm sitting under a spotlight.

'When did you last speak to Bonnie?' DC Delmonte asks.

'Friday,' I say tightly. The repeated question is a trick, and I know it is, and it makes me hate him. 'Like I said.'

'Ah, yes, sorry about that.' He gives me a smile I don't buy for a second. 'What was your relationship like with Mr Cohn?'

I make a face involuntarily and I see a slight smile twitch on DC Doyle's face.

'I didn't have one.'

'Well, what did you think of him?'

'He was just a teacher.'

'Was he ever inappropriate with you in any way?'

'No.'

'Ever make any remarks that may have been a little . . . over the line?'

I think about the newspaper article I read yesterday morning. Those idiot, big-mouth girls in the paper. *Stop Flirting With Me, Sir!* For God's sake. No one believed that bullshit, did they?

'No.'

'Did he ever initiate contact with you on Facebook?'

'No.' I could add that I have watertight privacy controls on my Facebook, but I don't like this man, so I don't.

'Did you like him?'

I shrug. 'He's a teacher.'

'Meaning yes?'

Did this guy ever go to school? 'Meaning no.'

DC Delmonte chuckles a little, like *Haha, these crazy teens and their silly opinions*. 'Why do you think they chose to go to Wales?'

I lift my shoulders again. 'Dunno.'

'Was Tenby special in some way to Bonnie?'

'Not really. I never heard her mention it.'

'No? Did she ever mention anywhere in particular?'

I shake my head, wondering what it is he thinks I'm going to say. Bonnie and Mr Cohn are runaways, not holidaymakers. What difference does it make if a place is special to Bonnie or not?

'You don't have any idea at all where they might go next?'

'Why would I? You know more about it than I do.'

'Mmm,' DC Delmonte says, impenetrable. 'Your GCSEs are starting this week, aren't they?'

He obviously knows this is true, so I don't know why he's phrasing it as a question. 'Yeah?'

'How was Bonnie feeling about them?'

I have a sudden flash of Bonnie sitting at the dining-room table at her house, two highlighter pens in one hand and another between her teeth, putting together her revision schedule, two whole months ago. 'How'd you mean?'

'Was she maybe a bit stressed? A bit overworked?'

'I guess.'

'Did she ever talk to you about that?'

Another flash of memory surfaces: a moment I'd forgotten. Bonnie, eyes earnest and searching, asking me, 'Eden, do you think I'm wasting my life caring about the wrong things? Am I doing my life all wrong?' What had I even said? I can't remember. Why can't I remember?

'No.' I don't even know if I'm lying.

'OK, just one last question, Eden, if I may. Do you *want* Bonnie to come home?'

I frown. 'What do you mean? Of course I do.'

He looks at me for a moment, then nods. 'All right, that's all from us for now, I think.' I wonder how he knows DC Doyle doesn't have any questions without even asking her.

They start gathering up their things, and Carolyn gets to her feet, smiling in relief. 'Are you any closer to finding them?' she asks.

'We're following some significant leads,' DC Delmonte says. 'It's just a matter of time.'

After they leave, Carolyn gives me a little hug, and I let her. 'That wasn't so awful, was it?' she says, sounding even more relieved than I am.

'They must really have no clue if they're talking to me,' I say.

'Don't be so negative. They know what they're doing.'

'If they knew what they were doing, they would've found her by now,' I reply.

Carolyn picks up the kettle and clicks the lid open, holding it under the tap to fill it. 'I'm not sure things are ever that simple.'

'Their questions were so weird.'

'Tea?' she asks, a very obvious attempt to avoid agreeing or disagreeing.

'Didn't you think?' I persist. 'All that stuff about wanting her to come back or not? Like, what difference does that make? And why wouldn't I?'

'Well, they know what they're doing,' Carolyn says again. 'It seems to me like they're trying to understand *why* Bonnie would leave – and leave now – as much as trying to find out where she is.'

'And they think that's something to do with our exams?'

'It seemed so, didn't it? That would make sense.'

I frown. 'That makes *no* sense. It's Bonnie. She lives for exams.'

'I know, and maybe that's the problem. That poor girl has been almost obsessively academic for as long as you've known her. Always working herself up into a state about end-of-year exams and insignificant bits of homework.'

'I thought you admired that about her,' I say. 'I thought you wanted me to be more like her.'

Carolyn looks at me in genuine surprise. 'Why on earth would you think that?' The kettle clicks off and she reaches for it. 'You and Bonnie are very different people. I'm glad she's been such a good friend to you over the years, and that she's been a . . .' She trails off, considering. 'A *steadying* influence on you. But I've never wanted you to be more like her. I'd have been worried about you if you'd started acting like school was all that mattered in your life. Do you remember your mocks, before Christmas? How Bonnie was? I remember feeling worried about her then. I almost called her mother.' She hesitates, then frowns. 'Maybe I should have done.'

'I doubt it would have made much of a difference,' I say.

Carolyn stares out of the window for a moment, then sighs and starts pouring out the kettle into two cups. 'Maybe not,' she says. She's silent for a while, letting the tea brew, before she speaks again. 'Have you spoken with your sister about all this?'

'Daisy?'

I see her smile as she spoons sugar into my cup. 'No, Valerie.'

'Oh. No.'

'Maybe you should. She's very insightful, you know, and she understands academic pressure. It might help.'

I shrug. I can't imagine having a heart-to-heart with Valerie, especially about all of this, but it doesn't seem necessary to say so. 'Maybe,' I say.

Our mock exams, which were meant to prepare us for our GCSEs, had happened last November. 'Think of them like a trial run,' Mrs Berwick had said. 'You'll have an idea of what it feels like to undergo the proper examination process, and we'll get a sense of how you're likely to perform.' She gave us one of her pointed glares before she added, 'And so will your parents.'

In other words, they didn't actually matter.

Unless your name was Bonnie Wiston-Stanley.

Bonnie threw herself into exam mode like it was the real thing and her entire life depended on her success. She drew up revision timetables and taped them to her bedroom walls. She walked around translating everything she said into French, a look of constant worry on her face.

'Will you chill your damn boots?' I asked, repeatedly. 'You already know you're going to do well. Give it a rest.'

But she didn't. One night, during dinner at my house, Carolyn asked her gently if she was getting enough sleep.

'It's fine,' Bonnie said, as if we couldn't all see the dark circles under her eyes. 'I'm on top of it.'

But she wasn't. Once, she fell asleep during a special assembly about drugs and would have got thrown into detention if I hadn't woken her up before Mr Hale noticed.

'I think you're working way too hard,' I said.

She laughed. 'No offence, Eeds, but to you turning up for a lesson is working too hard.'

'Seriously,' I said.

'It's fine; it's just a few more months,' she said confidently. 'Yeah, OK, it's a bit stressful right now, but it'll be over by, like, June.'

'Yeah, and then you have your A levels,' I pointed out.

For a moment, I saw actual fear on Bonnie's face. She faltered, frowned, and then smiled, shrugging. The moment was gone. 'It won't be like this. Four subjects instead of ten. That's totally different. And they're ones I've actually picked for myself. I'll be fine.' I must have looked unsure, because she laughed. 'I can't wait!' she insisted.

It was around this time that she started having panic attacks – just small ones at first. They'd happen on the way to school or inside it, and usually in between lessons rather than during them. I'd turn around and she'd have disappeared and I'd find her in the nearest toilets, wheezing over the sink.

It can't just have been me who noticed. But still no one else said, *Bonnie, you're working yourself too hard*.

Except, that's not true, is it? Someone did notice. Mr Cohn did. What was that song he played her? Something about slowing down, about not burning out? Something about Vienna?

I find the song on Spotify and play it over and over, listening until the lyrics are embedded in my mind. I imagine Mr Cohn playing it for her. I imagine what it would have meant for her, to hear words like this from someone like Mr Cohn. And for the first time, a part of me begins to understand.

12

It feels like a long time since I've properly seen Connor, especially with everything that's been going on, so I suggest meeting at the nature reserve after lunch.

When I arrive he's already sitting on top of the main gate. There's a folded-up blanket on his lap – Connor is the kind of person who thinks to do things like bring blankets – and he grins at me as I approach.

'Hi!' He jumps off the gate and kisses me hello.

God, it's so nice to see him. Sweet, uncomplicated Connor. My proof that I can make good decisions, good life choices, here in front of me, taking my hand on a Tuesday afternoon.

'How's your mum?' I ask.

He smiles. 'Doing good! The doctor said the bones should heal up without any problems because they were clean breaks. She's on some strong painkillers this week, so she's in a super-good mood.' He laughs, which I take as a cue to smile.

'That's good,' I say.

'Yep, it is. She told me to tell you that she's thinking of you and Bonnie.'

'Aw,' I say, touched. 'That's so sweet.'

Connor takes my hand and we walk through the main gate into the nature reserve, taking our usual route through the woods and past the stream to get to the field of heather. When we first started going out and we didn't want our parents to know, we'd come to the nature reserve together and spend the whole day kissing and talking. (Mostly kissing.) We even came here once when it was raining, because we thought it would be really romantic to kiss in the rain. (It wasn't. I got mud all over my jeans, and Connor got a cold.)

Today is dry and sunny. We find a spot on the heath, and Connor shakes open the blanket for us, settling it on the grass. We curl into each other and kiss for a while under the sun, and it's all so perfect I actually forget about Bonnie and secrets and exams. Kissing Connor is like its own kind of magic.

But, sadly, we can't stay like that forever, mainly because the magic is starting to turn into something else, something that can't happen on a blanket in the middle of the public nature reserve, so we break apart, all breathy and pink. He lies back on his elbows and I settle my head on his chest, listening to his heartbeat slow to its usual steady beat.

'So how *did* it go this morning?' Connor asks. 'With the police?'

I shrug. 'It was OK. Kind of stressful.'

'Why?'

Because I know where she is and I can't tell them. Or you. 'Have you ever spoken to the police?'

He laughs. 'No, of course not.'

'Well, there you go. Just take my word for it.'

'What kind of questions did they ask?'

'*Do you know where she is? Did you know about her and Mr Cohn?* Stuff like that.'

'And what did you say?'

Oh God, I don't want to lie to Connor, but I can't tell him the truth. The best I can do is fudge it. 'I basically said I had no idea they were together until they were gone, like everyone else.'

Connor shakes his head. 'It's so crazy that she didn't tell you.'

This I can agree with. 'I know, right?'

'And you really didn't have any idea?'

'No! I mean, who knew Bonnie was such a good liar, you know?'

'You're taking it a lot better than I thought you would,' he says.

I frown. 'What do you mean?'

'I just thought you'd be more upset. You know, about all the lies? I can barely believe she's done all this, and she's not even my best friend.'

I'm not sure how to reply, so I just sit there for a bit, watching a bird swoop towards the lake on the other side of the reserve. 'Being upset won't do much good right now, will it?'

'People don't get upset to do good, though, do they? They get upset because they're upset.'

And sometimes people bury the upset because it's just too much. If I let myself think about what it means that Bonnie has lied like this to me, about something so huge, and for so long, how could I ever deal with that? If nothing else, that kind of heartache can wait.

'I think . . .' I trail off. 'I think maybe I'm just saving it. For when she gets back. Does that make sense?'

My phone buzzes and I look distractedly down at it. *Ivy*. **How did it go?!?!** A four-word text, hours after the fact, to make up for an actual police interrogation.

I make the fatal mistake of letting out the tiniest, softest tut of annoyance. And Connor looks over at me, curious. Shit. Aiming for nonchalant, I shove my phone into my bag.

His eyebrows go up, questioning.

'It's nothing,' I say.

Connor's face wrinkles in confusion. 'No it's not,' he says, correctly. 'Who was the message from?'

'Oh, just . . .' I have forgotten the names of every single person in my life except Bonnie. 'Daisy. It's Daisy. Being annoying.'

'No,' he says again, slowly. 'If it was Daisy, you'd just reply.'

There's a silence. 'I don't feel like I replying,' I say.

'Eden,' Connor says.

I sit up and grab a handful of heather, starting to shred it into my lap so I have something to do with my hands, trying to string out the time before I have to tell him for as long as I can.

'*Eden*,' Connor says again, with more urgency this time. 'Who was the message from?'

I mutter, in my very smallest voice, 'Bonnie.'

'What?'

'*Bonnie!*'

(A weird truth: it feels really good to say it.)

Connor's eyes go all wide, like I've really shocked him, even though I thought he'd already guessed from my terrible lying. 'You . . .' he begins, then stops. 'She . . .' he tries. 'That was *Bonnie*?'

'She wanted to know how it went with the police,' I say, as if this is any kind of an answer to the question on his face.

'Eden,' he says, very slowly.

I can feel my face turning red, even as I will myself to stay cool. I open my mouth, but I don't know what to say.

'You're in contact with Bonnie?' he says finally, spelling it out.

I nod.

'Do you know where she is?'

I hesitate for a moment too long, which is an answer in itself. 'No . . . ?'

'Holy *shit*!' he explodes. 'Eden, what the fuck?'

'OK, fine – they're in Yorkshire.'

'Eden!' His whole face is one big shock emoji. His mouth is in an actual O-shape. 'Are you shitting me?'

I am obviously not shitting him.

'How long have you known?'

'Since Saturday.'

'And you haven't told anyone? Even the police?'

I shake my head.

'You have to tell them.' He says this like it's the most obvious thing in the world.

'Er, no I don't.'

His eyebrows raise, an incredulous look on his face. 'Jesus, Eden. Are you being serious right now?'

OK, so I knew Connor wouldn't be immediately on-board with the whole keep-this-secret thing, but this reaction is so unexpected it makes me defensive.

'I promised Bonnie,' I say.

'Then that was a stupid promise,' he says, like it's as simple as that. 'Why did you agree to that?'

'Well, I didn't know in advance!' I snap, irritated.

'So? As soon as you found out it was Mr Cohn, you should've been like, *Oh shit, better tell the police.*'

'No,' I say, shaking my head. 'Just no. She asked me to keep quiet and to trust her, and so I have to do that. That's what being a friend is.'

'Even when they're completely screwing up?'

'Especially when.'

Connor lets out a groan and runs his hand over the back of his head.

'Look, think about it this way: if I'd gone off by myself for a while, and not told Carolyn or anyone, and I asked you not to tell them where I was, would you tell them? If you knew I needed this, and that I was completely safe?'

Connor frowns. 'But it wouldn't just be about you if Carolyn and everyone was worrying about you, would it?'

'I'd tell them I was safe.'

Connor shakes his head. 'I feel like we're just having two different conversations here, Eden.'

'Look, fine, whatever, OK?' I don't even know what I'm trying to say, and he looks appropriately baffled. 'Forget I told you.'

He laughs. 'OK, sure.'

'Seriously.'

We look at each other.

'Are you at least telling her she should be coming home?' he asks finally. 'Or calling her parents?'

'Yes, obviously.' Have I actually said that? Yes, I must have. 'Besides, I really think she's going to be back tomorrow.'

Connor's whole face scrunches in surprise. 'What? Really? Why?'

'The exam. Our GCSEs.'

There's a pause. I can tell by his expression that he doesn't think this is likely. 'You think she's just going to . . . come back?'

'I know it sounds crazy, but this is *Bonnie*. I just can't believe she'd miss these exams.'

'Eden, you seriously think she'll have run off with our *teacher* and then just be like, *Whoops! Better pop back for that Biology exam!*'

'It could happen.' The fact that he thinks this is so ridiculous makes me want it to be true even more.

'You think she's just going to turn up?'

'Sure. She'll just come walking into the gym, ready for the exam. A surprise, but a low-key surprise, you know? That would be so like Bonnie.'

'Would it?' Connor looks baffled. 'In what world would that be a "low-key" surprise?'

'Seriously, do *you* think she'd miss these exams?'

Connor is quiet for a while, looking at me. When he speaks, his voice is careful, like he's worried how I'll react. 'It doesn't matter what I think. Not when the facts are that she's *gone*, Eden. It's not like she's just shut herself in her room and told everyone she's not going to take her exams. She's run away. You don't just come back from that.'

For a moment, I can't speak. 'You think she's not going to come back at all?'

'That's not what I meant. I just mean that when she does come back, whenever that is, and whether it's because she wants to or because the police catch up with them, it's going to be for a bigger reason than one exam. Do you have any idea *why* she went?'

I shrug. 'Love?'

'OK, yeah – but why now?'

'Dunno.'

'Haven't you asked her?'

'Sure. She just says she wants to be with Mr Cohn.'

'Maybe she's pregnant,' he suggests.

A jolt of horror hits me right in the chest. '*What?*'

'Would make sense, wouldn't it?'

'No! You watch too many films.'

'Right, so you thinking Bonnie's just going to turn up for the exam tomorrow makes total sense, but me wondering if she's pregnant is too stupid to consider.'

'Can we talk about something else now?'

Connor takes in a deep breath and then lets it out slowly. 'Look, I really think you should tell someone.'

'Yeah, I get it.'

'Really, Eeds. Just talk to Carolyn, or something. You can make sure the police know without Bonnie ever needing to find out it was you who told.'

'*I'd* know. Why is that so hard for you to get?'

He puts both his hands up. 'OK, OK. I'm sorry.' He chances a smile at me. 'Hey. C'mere.' He opens his arms to me and I hesitate, part of me wanting to hold on to my annoyance for a little longer, but I can't resist his face. I move across the blanket and sink into his lap, pressing my face against the inside of his shoulder as he wraps his arms around me and squeezes. A proper Connor hug. I feel him press a kiss against the top of my head. 'How does she sound when you talk to her?' he asks after a while.

'Cheerful.'

'Really?'

'Yeah. It's weird. Like, she knows what's going on over here, but she's still all happy about being with Mr Cohn.' It's such a relief to be able to talk about this with someone who isn't Bonnie.

'She's probably in denial.'

'You reckon?'

'Sure. Mr Cohn'll go to prison for this, Mum says. Prison! And anyway, you've got to be pretty heavy in denial to be able to cut yourself off from your family, right?' I can tell he's realized what he's said the instant after he says it because his whole body jerks. 'Uh . . . I mean . . . Shit. Sorry, I didn't mean—'

'Yeah, I know.'

'Obviously it's different when you've been adopted,' he says. I can tell by his voice that his face is that shiny red it gets when he's embarrassed. 'I'm not saying you, um, cut yourself off or anything . . .'

'Right.'

'And there were circumstances there, anyway.' He's rambling now. 'So, obviously, you're not. Um. In denial.'

I give his knee a pat. 'You can stop now.'

'Oh God, thank you.'

'Maybe she *is* in denial,' I say. It would make sense. 'How long does denial last?'

I feel him shrug. 'Dunno. I guess it depends on the circumstances?'

What exactly *are* the circumstances here? I try and count the things that Bonnie could be in denial about. The fact that her boyfriend is old enough to be her dad. The effect this is having on her family. The novelty value of the runaway life.

'Would you run away with me?' I ask. I mean it as a joke, but he doesn't laugh and say yes, like I expect.

'Nope,' he says.

'Oh great,' I say, shifting away from him. 'Thanks.'

He laughs. 'Seriously. I wouldn't ask you to do that for me, and I know you wouldn't expect it of me either. Giving up everything. You wouldn't want me to leave my mum, would you?'

I shake my head immediately. I don't even need to think about it.

'And I'd never try to make you leave Daisy. That would hurt you, and hurt her, and the rest of your family.'

'What if you didn't have a choice? What if you had to leave, and you wanted me to come with you?'

'Well, of course I'd *want* you to come with me.' He's careful now, choosing his words. 'But . . . I guess I just think it would still be selfish to put that on you. I'd just never ask you to. I think that's what love *is*. It's caring about the person's entire life, not just the bit with the two of you in it.'

I sit up on my knees and put my arms around his neck, looking down at his sweet, freckly face. My Connor. 'You're kind of the best, you know that?'

He smiles. 'Was that the right answer, then?'

'A hundred per cent. Full marks. A star.' I lean down to kiss him, feeling his arms curl around my back, pulling me close.

I spend another hour or so with Connor before he has to go back home. I like the idea of having some time completely to myself after the frenzy of today (and yesterday . . . and the day before . . .) so I don't go straight home. I meander into town and stop off at Chrissy's, which serves the best hot chocolate in Kent.

There's a queue, as always, and I'm standing in it, minding my own business, thinking about how much difference it would make to put cream into hot chocolate instead of milk, when my brain suddenly tunes in to the conversation that's going on directly behind me.

'There's obviously something deeply wrong at the school,' one woman is saying. She has a thick Welsh accent, heavy with disapproval. 'That this could even happen. It's not right, now, is it?'

'No, it isn't,' her companion agrees, less Welsh but equally judgemental. 'And she seems like such a *nice* girl, not like some of those awful kids from Kett Academy. What's a nice girl like that doing, causing so much trouble?'

I make a face at that word. *Nice*. It's even worse than *good*. Here's the thing about Bonnie – she's brilliant in a lot of ways: she's funny, smart and loyal, the best person to have on your team for pretty much anything, but she's not always . . . totally . . . *nice*. She has it in her to be mean to Rowan, snide about her parents, impatient with people who can't keep up with her.

She has an edge to her, that's what I'm saying. Maybe everything I've said about her being a good girl, with all her academic achievements and being Head Prefect, you're thinking of her as one of the nice girls, too. Sweet and soft. The kind who sits at the bedside of old ladies to listen to their stories all day.

Nope.

I mean, she'd sit at the bed of old ladies, and she really would listen to their stories, and they'd all love her and call her 'dear' and insist she has another biscuit or whatever. But she'd be making sure she was getting some kind of credit for it. She'd be sweet-talking the managers just in case she needed a reference from them one day. That's Bonnie. *Good*, sure. But smart. A few sharper shades down the line from *nice*.

I almost want to turn around and tell them. Luckily for all of us, I've reached the front of the queue. I order my hot chocolate politely, like a good girl, but I can't quite resist making eye contact with one of the women when I turn to leave. And making a face. Just so they know that I'm one of 'those awful kids' from Kett, and that I heard them.

The funny thing is, even though Bonnie is supposedly the nice one, if she was here she would have said something. She'd have been so polite about it, practically angelic, but she would have found a way to stick up for me if she thought I was being slighted, even indirectly. She's protective like that. Once, our History teacher Mr Hale said – in front of everyone – that if all students were like me he'd have stopped teaching years ago, and Bonnie said, 'Variety's the spice of life, sir,' so cheerfully and brightly that he didn't even realize she was being sarcastic and *agreed* with her.

Outside, I sit on one of the benches by the river and wait for my hot chocolate to get cool enough to drink, pulling out my phone to message Bonnie. I've decided I might as well ask.

Me
Bon, are you pregnant?

For once, she replies immediately.

Ivy
WTF no! WHY?

Me
OK good – just checking.

???????

I thought maybe that's why you left.

Oh. Well no (OBVIOUSLY). Did the police say something about it?

No.

Ivy

Do you think they know where we are?

Me

No, they seem totally clueless.

GOOD! That means we can relax a bit ☺

There's still time to get back in time for Biology tomorrow.

Lol OK I'll bear that in mind. Xxx

By the time I get home it's after four, and next morning's exam feels an awful lot closer than it did before I left. I take my Biology revision guide into the living room and lie on the sofa, trying to concentrate on ecosystems and food chains, but I only manage ten minutes before Daisy comes in crying, a large patch of skin along her wrist and elbow shredded and bloody, demanding care.

I clean up the wound and bandage her arm, only half listening as she wails about misjudging the leap over a bench, and heat up a cup of Ribena, which she drinks curled up in my lap like a five-year-old, hiccuping.

And then Carolyn and Valerie come in from their trip to the supermarket, laden with bags to unload, and Carolyn wants to know everything about Daisy's elbow and the bench and whether I remembered to clean the wound properly before I bandaged it, which obviously I did, and we're unpacking and talking and Valerie's bought me a Good Luck card for my exams, and then Bob's back, and he wants to know about the elbow and the bench, and also how did it go with the police this morning, and Daisy suddenly remembers that the police were interviewing kids at school all day, and we all want to know about that.

And then it's dinner-time, and then it's dark, and then it's nine o'clock and I haven't done any more revision, and I know as much about biology as I did this morning, which isn't much.

Valerie offers to test me, but I say no because there doesn't seem to be much point now it's so late, and anyway I don't really want her to know how bad I am at science, not when she's so perfect at it.

I retreat to my room and get comfortable under the covers of my bed, thinking about how this day and night would have gone if everything was normal. Bonnie would have wanted to spend the evening on her own, getting ready, but she'd have made time for me in the day. She'd have tested me without making me feel stupid, helped me with the parts I still have a chance in, and made me feel better about the bits I don't. I would have teased her about being so smart and how obsessed she is with academics.

I miss her. I miss the Bonnie I knew.

I turn on the BBC News channel in time to catch an interview with a former police detective about the case. He's talking slowly, patronizingly, about how we live in a surveillance society and it's 'impossible, just impossible' to stay hidden. Except they *have* stayed hidden, haven't they? It's been four days. If it was that easy, why didn't they get them straight away? The BBC woman points that out, and I smile, but the detective just repeats himself, almost word for word, and the interview ends. Useful.

I go online and do a quick sweep of the news sites and Twitter to see if I've missed any actual updates on the case while I was out and occupied, and find a long think-piece in the *Telegraph* about what this 'debacle' says about the relationship between students and their teachers in 'the age of social media', which features three paragraphs detailing the journalist's own schoolgirl crush and mentions Bonnie by name twice.

Why isn't it enough for any of these newspapers or radio

stations to just report the facts of the case? What's with all the commentary and guesswork? Why do they have to keep talking about how she's a schoolgirl all the time? Once is enough, you'd think. But no. It comes up a *lot*. It's everywhere. *Schoolgirl* Bonnie Wiston-Stanley. Schoolgirl, schoolgirl, schoolgirl. Like that's the only thing about her that matters – her age. I don't really want to think too much about why that is. As gross and weird as it is to think of Bonnie and Mr Cohn being 'in love' or whatever, it's a million times worse to think about him going after her even though – or worse, *because* – she's underage. Like, that's a whole different level of sleazy wrong. Thinking about it makes me feel ill, so I try very, very hard not to.

The other buzzword is 'good', just like it has been since Bonnie first went missing. It's as if all the editors and journalists from all the different papers got together and agreed that this would be their angle: Bonnie is a good girl who doesn't do things like this. They all seem to find this *so* fascinating. Why someone like Bonnie would behave this way, as if it would be less surprising if it were a different kind of girl, whatever the hell that even means.

It makes me feel weird, reading it all like that. Bonnie's 'goodness', I mean. Because I'm not an idiot; I know what it means. It doesn't just mean 'good' as in makes her bed in the morning, is polite to old ladies, goes to church. It also means that she is white and middle class. No one has to tell me this for me to get it. You don't have to be in the top sets to understand how the world works.

What would the papers have said if it hadn't been Bonnie, but one of the girls from the council estate I'd grown up in? What would they have said if it was me? *What can you expect with an upbringing like that?* they'd say. They'd call it a failure of social services. They'd bring up the stats on failed adoption cases, talk about how many kids of addicts leave school without qualifications or end up in prison. No one would say I was 'good'. No one would even bother to ask if I was.

Or let's be honest here. They probably wouldn't talk about it at all if it was me. I wouldn't get half the press coverage. Me, with my bitchy resting-face and my indeterminate-but-not-quite-white-enough race, scowling from the front pages? No way. I'm not front-page material – not like Bonnie, with her braces-straight white teeth, combed hair and placid smile.

Nothing about realizing any of this is fun. It makes my stomach hurt. And it makes me think of Bonnie in a way I never have before. It makes me resent her. She gets to do something so stupid and yet everyone is still on her side? She gets to be the darling of the front pages? How is that fair? How is any of this fair?

I know that all that matters right now is getting Bonnie home. I know that it's a good thing there's so much press coverage of the story and her face, that more people being aware of her and Mr Cohn means a greater chance of finding them. But did it all have to happen in a way that makes me feel so cold?

Here's what I'm really worried about: when Bonnie comes back and the story fades from the minds of strangers and the newspapers stack up in recycling bins, what will happen to us? Will I be able to look at Bonnie and see my best friend, or will she always be that frozen image from the front pages? How can anything ever be the same?

Conversations That Took on a New Meaning after Bonnie Disappeared

The 'Missed Out' Edition: three months before

'Do you think I've missed out?'

'Missed out? On what?'

The two of us were in Topshop, trying to find her an outfit for her cousin's wedding. I was looking through the racks while she stood beside me, chewing on her thumbnail. Bonnie can do a lot of things, but she's completely incapable of shopping alone.

'On . . . you know. Teen stuff?'

'Oh, teen stuff,' I said, rolling my eyes, none the wiser.

'I've nearly finished Year Eleven and I've never even got a detention. Is that weird?'

'Yep.' I pulled out a bright yellow crop top and held it up, grinning at her.

'Eeds,' she whined, for my response or the suggestion, I wasn't sure.

I shoved the top back on to the rail and moved over to a new display, her trailing me like Daisy in a supermarket. 'Are you asking me if I think you've missed out by not getting detentions?'

'Not just detentions. I mean the whole lot. I've never done anything that's not exactly what I'm supposed to do. I've never even handed in homework late.'

'So what?'

'Well, isn't that bad?'

'To be good?'

'To not have experienced being . . . less good.'

'What're you basing this on?' I asked, pausing in my search and focusing my attention on her. 'You're freaking out because you've never got detention? Cos I don't see why that's bad.'

'I'm not freaking out; I'm just curious.' This was true – she wasn't freaking out at all. She was totally calm.

'You're responsible, Bon,' I said. 'You're one of the good ones. You worked hard to be that way. You might as well appreciate it.'

She didn't say anything, her eyes serious even as her mouth smiled.

'I don't know what it is you think you're missing.'

'Life experiences!' she said. 'Getting drunk in a park. Staying out all night. I don't know . . . Being grounded!'

I laughed. 'Those aren't *experiences*; they're just crappy mistakes. They don't sound that great to me.'

'Yeah, but at least you've done them.'

'Oh, is that what this is about?' Bonnie and I never really talked about the few months I'd gone ever so slightly off the rails. I'd always assumed that was because the whole idea freaked her out. 'I wouldn't call that teen stuff, anyway,' I said. 'More like stupid stuff in general.'

'You know what I mean.'

'Bon, I really don't.'

'I just . . .' There was a long pause. 'I've never done anything crazy.'

'That's good.'

'Is it?'

'Where's this come from, anyway?' I asked.

'Oh, it's just something someone said to me,' she said vaguely.

'Someone told you you're missing out on teen stuff? Who?'

'Not like that. More like, maybe I should test my own boundaries a bit more, you know? Push myself instead of always playing it safe and doing the right thing. Be braver. More bold.'

'Sure,' I said, shrugging. 'That sounds like good advice.'

'So you think I should?'

'Push yourself? Sure,' I said again. 'Go for it.'

Well done, me.

Wednesday

School Ignored Runaway Teacher's Ex-Girlfriend When She Warned of Inappropriate Behaviour with Pupil

Disgraced teacher Jack Cohn could have been stopped in his tracks – before absconding with 15-year-old schoolgirl Bonnie Wiston-Stanley – if school authorities had listened to a warning from Cohn's former partner.

That's the firm belief of Rebekka Bridges, 27, Cohn's ex-girlfriend of three years, who has spoken exclusively to *The Mirror* of her anger at her former lover, and hinted that the opportunity to intervene was missed by Kent comprehensive Kett Academy.

Bridges, a fellow teacher, met Jack Cohn when both attended the same training course five years ago, when he 'seemed very normal'.

'He was sweet and shy at first,' Bridges recalls. 'But mostly kind. I remember him offering to help me with my work as an attempt to get to know me better.'

Their relationship ended 'amicably' a year ago, Bridges says, and since then the pair have remained on good terms – until two months ago.

'Jack and I had arranged to meet for coffee on a weekend – and when I arrived he was saying goodbye to a girl who was clearly of school age,' Bridges reveals. 'I questioned him about it, but he shrugged it off as a pupil who had happened to see him in town.'

Bridges thought little more of it until they met next, a month later, when Cohn was 'completely distracted' by messaging someone on his phone.

'I asked him about it – I have moved on and I was honestly pleased that it seemed like he had too – but he declined to go into detail. That was fine – Jack had often been a private person.

'But then while showing me a document on his phone, I saw a

text message come through from an unregistered number saying, quite clearly, "Can't wait to see you in class tomorrow xxxx."

'He was clearly embarrassed and tried to make out like the message had been a joke. Then he suddenly changed his story and said it was another member of staff who he had started a relationship with.'

Bridges contacted Cohn's school the following morning to report her suspicions, but could not confirm the pupil's identity.

The school appears to have taken no action – and Cohn continued to teach the girl he would flee with just weeks later.

Bridges is a popular English teacher at the nearby Normandy High School and says she has stayed in contact with Cohn after growing close to his family.

'I know Jack's parents Graham and Dorothy well – both are lovely people and neither deserve what Jack is now putting them through. I spoke to them this week and both of them share my view he has acted appallingly. He has abused the bond of trust that is expected between teachers and their pupils.

'I never expected he would ever do anything like this.'

13

On Wednesday morning, I wake up with a heavy weight in my stomach. I lie on my back for a while, staring at the ceiling, listening to Daisy's chirpy voice from the hall. She's going on about some ingredients she's taking to Food Tech to make a trifle, something about sponge fingers and jam. Food Tech is one of the only subjects Daisy likes at school, and Carolyn is going in hard, trying to fan the flames, hoping to turn her into a budding chef.

'Are you allowed to put sherry in it?' Bob asks. His voice is more distant, like he's calling from the bathroom.

'Bob!' Carolyn exclaims, and I smile.

I pull out my phone and open BBC News, but there haven't been any breakthroughs while I've been sleeping. I do a quick search of Bonnie's name on Twitter and find a lot of links to the same article from the *Daily Mirror*, an interview with Mr Cohn's ex-girlfriend, Rebekka. I scroll through the article, feeling a frown scrunching up my face. I read the paragraph about her calling Kett three disbelieving times until there's a knock at my door and Carolyn's voice telling me to get up.

When I go downstairs, showered and dressed but no more prepared for my coming exam, Daisy is still in the kitchen, taking her time over a bowl of cereal.

'Hi!' she says, bouncing up.

'Daze, you're going to be late for school,' I say, realizing how much like Carolyn I sound and almost wanting to take it back.

'What a tragedy,' Daisy says, but she sits back down.

Bob is sitting at the kitchen table, reading the paper and sipping coffee. 'How are you feeling?' he asks me with a smile.

'So weird,' I say. 'Do you think Kett will get in trouble for not doing anything about it?'

Bob rolls his eyes. 'I meant about your exam.'

'Oh, that. Fine. Do you think Rebekka is telling the truth?'

Bob sighs, like *Aren't Eden's priorities so backwards?* 'Who's Rebekka?' he asks.

Carolyn walks into the kitchen, notices Daisy and looks in horror at the clock on the wall. 'Why are you still here?' she demands. 'You're going to be so late.'

'Not if you drive me,' Daisy says.

'Mr Cohn's ex,' I say. 'She sold her story to the *Daily Mirror*.'

'Daisy, I'm leaving in three minutes,' Carolyn says. 'If you're not down here ready to go in two, then you'll just have to be late.'

'She says she told Kett that she thought Mr Cohn was getting close to a student,' I finish. Daisy crams the final spoonful of cereal into her mouth and bolts from the kitchen, leaving the bowl on the table.

'Oh dear,' Bob says. 'That won't go down well.'

'Is this the Rebekka story?' Carolyn asks, already in motion, picking up the bowl and opening the dishwasher. 'Smart woman.'

'You think?' I say, surprised. 'Isn't selling your story a really cheap thing to do?'

'That depends on your point of view,' Bob says. Valerie comes into the kitchen as he says this, and he smiles at her. 'Morning, love.'

'It's a sensible way to control the narrative,' Carolyn says, eyes on the clock. 'Daisy! I'm walking out the door!' She leans over to drop a kiss on my cheek. 'I have a meeting with a client, so I have to go now,' she says, tying her hair up into a ponytail as she speaks. 'I'll be here when you get back after the exam, though, and you can tell me all about it. But I'm sorry I can't take you to school.'

'That's OK, Connor's coming and we're going to walk together,' I say. The exam is due to start at 9.15 a.m., and I'm meant to get to the gym for 9 a.m. If I really wanted to, I could get a lift with Carolyn and Daisy and get there early, but I try to spend as little time on Kett grounds as possible.

'What?' Valerie says, startled, from where she's pouring coffee from the pot into a mug. 'I was going to take you, wasn't I?'

Bob and Carolyn both look at me, and I squash down the automatic guilt, shrugging. 'No, Connor's coming.'

Daisy comes back into the kitchen, her backpack hanging off one arm, stepping into her shoes as she goes. 'Good luck!' she says breathlessly, hugging me. 'Hope it's not too shitty.'

'Daisy,' Bob says warningly, but I'm smiling as I hug her back.

Valerie closes the fridge, empty-handed. 'I could drive you and Connor,' she suggests.

'We can walk,' I say. 'It's not far.'

'But—'

'Let them walk, Valerie, love,' Bob says gently.

She looks from me to him, the hurt on her face unmistakable, then shrugs, turning away from us both. 'Fine.'

Bob glances at me, raising his eyebrows slightly, and I know I should say something to ease the sting in the air, but at that moment there's a knock on the door, and *thank God for that*.

Connor is on the doorstep, his hair still rumpled, and a smile lights up his face when I open the door.

'Good morning, Connor,' Bob says from behind me.

'Hi,' Connor says. 'I've just come to pick up Eden.'

'You mean you're not here to see me?' Bob asks, all innocence.

Connor blinks at him, and I laugh as I lace up my brogues and stand to pull my bag over my shoulder. 'See you later, Bob.'

'Good luck, Edie, love,' he says. He only breaks out 'Edie' on very special occasions. 'You'll be smashing.'

'Did you see the article with Mr Cohn's ex?' I ask as we head down the road.

'Let's not talk about anything to do with that right now,' Connor says. 'Get into exam-mode.'

'But—'

'Seriously, you have to try to not think about it for the next, like, two hours. All that shit will still be going on *after* the exam.'

My stomach gives a nauseating little churn. God, I hate exams. Sitting in a silent hall and having to face the fact that I know sweet fuck-all about biology is right up there with the worst ways to spend an hour.

When we get to the school, my stomach drops. I hear Connor mutter, 'Oh shit.' The place is swarming with journalists. It's nothing like the handful that were there on Monday; this is more a full-on siege on the school. There's even a camera crew, complete with a woman I recognize from the local news. 'Er . . .' Connor says. 'What were you saying about an article with Mr C's ex?'

'She told the papers that she'd warned the school and they didn't do anything,' I summarize.

'Oh,' he says again. He makes a face. 'Oh shit.'

We brace ourselves and head for the gates. Mr Petrakis, our Deputy Head, and Mr Townsend, the Maths teacher, are trying to create a clear pathway for the students coming in for the exam, and that seems hard enough. I wonder what it was like a little earlier for the start of the normal school day.

Connor puts an arm around my shoulder and steers me through the gates and into the car park. I hear some of the journalists calling my actual name, which makes me feel panicky and exposed.

I think about Bonnie, hidden and safe and cocooned in her little love nest with Mr Cohn, and for a second I actually hate her.

As we walk towards the school, a crazy part of me seriously considers turning around and screaming 'SHE'S IN YORKSHIRE!'

I don't.

Maybe I should have.

But you know the really stupid thing? I mean the *really* stupid thing? There's still a part of me that is expecting to see her. I actually look for her in the crowd of my classmates that is gathering outside the gym where we'll be taking the exam. I look for the curve of her high ponytail – wilfully forgetting that she's cut her hair short – and the curve of her cheeks in profile. I know her face so well, I'd know it in an instant, but still I look, so carefully, so stupidly, at everyone I see.

Because I don't think I ever really believed that she would miss this. The first of the exams she'd been preparing for since she was ten years old. The first step in the sequence that would make up the rest of her life.

But she's not here.

She's not here.

We file into the gym together, everyone strangely quiet, and take our seats at our individual desks.

'Good morning, everyone,' Mrs Berwick says, smiling at us from the front of the room. 'We've just got a few minutes to go.' She glances behind her at the clock on the wall, which confirms it's almost 9.15.

My head whispers, *There's still time*.

The exam papers are waiting face down on the desks. We're allowed to turn them over to write our names and candidate numbers, and I fill in the boxes slowly, my heart drumming, one eye on the door. 'MCKINLEY', I write. 'EDEN ROSE'. The paper has a big fat F on it and, even though I know it stands for

'Foundation', it feels like a bad omen.

I think about the journalists, no doubt still gathered outside the school gates. All the noise that's going on outside this cold, silent room.

Two rows across, Connor is looking over at me. Our eyes meet and he smiles.

The second hand edges closer to 9.15.

The door hasn't opened, and there is no Bonnie.

'Good luck, everyone,' Mrs Berwick says, her voice softer than I've ever heard it. 'You may begin.'

14

The exam goes very, very badly. I answer the first question on food webs and then the follow-up question after it, but the third, fourth and fifth questions are beyond me. I waste time panicking on number six, staring at the two diagrams that apparently have something to do with the circulatory system, waiting for sense to come, but it doesn't.

I close my eyes and conjure an image into my head of Bonnie and me, not even two weeks ago, revising in her bedroom. She'd tried to explain double circulation to me. It had made sense when she explained it.

What was it she'd said?

'Do you ever think about running away?'

No. No, Eden. Concentrate.

'Pulmonary is the one for the lungs, see the diagram with the sideways arrows? Think, like, "pulmonary" has an L in it, OK?' She'd exaggerated the word, sticking out her tongue on the L. 'Pu*llll*monary.'

L for 'lungs'. I look at the diagrams, the sideways arrows. I write in the answers to the four questions in the section, but my hand is trembling slightly and my chest feels so tight it's painful.

I move on to the next question. I can't answer it. Next question. Guess. Next question. God, I'm so stupid. Can't even answer questions on a Foundation Biology paper.

'You're not stupid, Eden; don't say that.'

Shut up, Bonnie. You're not even here.

All around me my classmates are scribbling away, looks of

intense concentration on their faces. Everyone, even the friends I'd joked around with during class instead of working, is fully in exam mode. I can see the back of Connor's head bent over his paper. I try and think of his smiling face.

Half an hour passes and my heart is fluttering with panic. It's not just that I'm not going to do well on this paper. I might not even *pass*. I'm thinking of myself on results day, looking at my letter, seeing a big fat F next to Biology. F for 'Foundation'. F for 'Failure'. I imagine Bonnie giving me a hug, telling me it doesn't matter.

Will Bonnie even be back by then?

Will she have any results to collect?

Stop thinking about Bonnie.

A question comes up about compost, and it's finally something I know. I answer four questions in a row – correctly, I'm pretty sure – and the relief must be too much for my frazzled, panicking brain because to my absolute horror I realize there are tears spilling from eyes and trailing down my cheeks. I am *crying*. In *school*. Two years ago I fell down half a flight of stairs going into the canteen and broke my ankle, and I swear not a single tear escaped.

But now I'm crying in the middle of the gym and apparently there's nothing I can do about it, because I don't stop for the rest of the exam. I cry through all the questions I can't answer and all the questions I can. I cry through the extra time I get allotted because of my dyslexia. I cry while the papers are collected, while everyone starts to file out row by row. I cry when Mrs Berwick touches my arm as she walks past me.

When I walk out of the gym, I don't stop to talk to anyone, obviously. I go straight to the toilets, lock myself in a cubicle and wait for fifteen minutes, which I'm sure will be enough for even the nosiest of my classmates to get bored of waiting for me.

When I venture out, I see Connor sitting alone on the bench by the door, a paperback open in his hand, brow furrowed in concentration. I go to sit next to him and he reaches out an arm to me without a word. I lean into him and he hugs me, warm and close, and I feel the tension in my chest relax, my shoulders loosen.

'Ah, Eden.' It's Mrs Berwick, appearing around the corner.

'Ah, shit,' I mutter.

'Hi, Mrs Berwick,' Connor says loudly.

'Are you feeling OK, Eden?' Mrs Berwick asks me. 'You seemed very upset during the exam.'

'I'm fine,' I say, a clear lie.

'If you're about to leave,' she says, 'I suggest going across the playing field instead of the car park. We've opened the gate at the back so students can avoid the journalists.'

'Thanks, miss,' Connor says. He squeezes my wrist. 'Let's go.'

'Is it true, what Mr Cohn's ex-girlfriend said?' I ask.

Mrs Berwick's whole face tightens. I watch her press her lips together, but she doesn't answer me. It *is* true. And I bet she was the one who made the call about not following it up.

'So you could have stopped this?' I press. 'All of you. You could have stopped him.'

'This isn't appropriate, Eden,' Mrs Berwick says.

'Who cares about what's appropriate?' I demand, my voice coming out all shrill. I can't bloody believe this place. 'They're *gone*.'

Connor has taken hold of my arm and is steering me towards the exit. 'Bye, Mrs Berwick,' he calls.

When we're outside, I shake him off irritably. 'For God's sake, Connor. You're such a suck-up.'

'Why bother yelling at Mrs Berwick?' he asks. 'You think that's going to bring Bonnie back?' I glare at him and he grins, crossing his two forefingers against each other in the air. 'Hashtag!'

I try not to laugh. 'You suck.'

'Made you smile, though,' he points out, pleased with himself.

We head across the playing field together and out the open back gate, which feels very weird to me. This is meant to be the secret smoking spot, not an authorized exit. It's where you go if you're bunking off a lesson or something. In all my years at Kett, including all the times it's been me hiding out here, I've never seen the gate open. Everything is wrong.

'Do you have to go straight home?' I ask Connor as we walk out into the street.

Connor nods. 'Yeah, sorry. I can walk you partway, though?'

This is better than nothing, so I take the hand he's holding out to me and let him lead the way.

'Do you want to talk about the exam?' Connor asks.

'Nope.'

'Was it, um . . . why you were crying? Or was that a Bonnie thing?'

I lift my shoulders in a shrug, because I don't even know what the answer is. Probably a bit of both.

'I've never seen you cry before,' he says.

The words are such a surprise that I find myself shaking my head. 'That's not true,' I say. 'You must've.' We've been together for over a year. There's no way he hasn't seen me cry in that whole time. That would be weird, right?

'No, really,' he says. 'I would've remembered.'

I frown at a passing cat. How can I not have cried in front of my boyfriend? What's wrong with me? 'I'm not much of a crier,' I say finally, which is true. In fact, now I think about it, I can't remember the last time I cried at something. Oh wait, yes I can. It was in March. Daisy was ill with some kind of virus and it had made her all droopy and sad, and we watched *A Little Princess* together. You just try and watch a film like that with the little sister you got adopted with while she's cuddled up close, sniffling on to your

T-shirt, and *not* cry. It's impossible.

'Are you feeling better now?' Connor asks. 'I feel like I should be doing something to make you feel better.'

I smile. 'You *are*. Anyway, I'm fine. Really. Totally fine. See?' I point at my face. 'No more crying.'

When I let myself into the house, I hear Carolyn come hurrying through the kitchen to greet me. I close the door behind me and turn in time to see that she's all smiles.

'How did it go?' she asks.

And I burst into tears.

'Oh, Eden!' she gasps, horrified. She reaches for me, taking hold of both my hands. 'What's wrong, darling?'

There are a lot of responses I could give to this question, considering I just failed my first GCSE and I actually care even though I always thought I didn't and my best friend is shacking up with her music teacher and I'm the only one who knows where they are.

What I say, through sobs, is: 'Bonnie wasn't there.'

'Oh no,' Carolyn says, a soft murmur. 'Did you think she would be?'

I shake my head and nod at the same time, because I know it's stupid and senseless, but somewhere in me I really *had* been thinking that she'd be there, because the Bonnie I know wouldn't miss her GCSEs. But she has, and that means I don't really know her at all, and maybe I never did. And that *hurts*.

'Let's go and sit in the living room,' Carolyn says, guiding me.

'I'll make some tea,' Valerie says. When did she turn up? I blink through my tears and see that she's standing behind Carolyn, a sympathetic half-smile on her face.

'I don't want tea,' I growl, dashing the tears from my eyes with my sleeve.

'Gin?' Valerie offers.

'Valerie!' Carolyn scolds.

In the living room, Carolyn sits me on the sofa and fusses with a blanket, and I somehow manage to feel both smothered by her attention and needy for more of it. She sits next to me and takes my hand. 'Let's get the exam out of the way first. How did it go?'

'Awful,' I say. 'I don't want to talk about it.'

'That's fine; I understand. But just tell me, was it actually awful, or do you think you might be making it worse in your head?'

'I didn't even answer half the questions.'

I hear a very soft 'Oh' and I look over in time to see Carolyn paste an encouraging smile over her worried face. 'It's just one exam,' she says, most likely talking to herself as much as to me. 'You've got a lot going on, and it's just one exam.'

There's a silence. 'I'm sorry,' I say.

'Oh, no, Eden, you don't need to be sorry.' She squeezes my hand, tight and sudden. 'I'm not going to love you any less because you didn't get an A on one Biology exam.'

She says this as Valerie walks into the room, carefully holding on to three mugs of tea. Valerie, who got As in every single one of her exams. I see something unreadable flash across her face. Our eyes meet, and then she looks away.

'Do you want to talk about Bonnie?' Carolyn asks, reaching out with a smile to take one of the mugs.

I shrug, but it's half-hearted. 'What's there to say?'

'Tell me why you're so upset,' she says. 'Let's start there.'

Valerie sinks down on to the carpet beside the sofa, curling her legs up underneath her.

'I don't understand how she can be doing this,' I say finally. I can feel fresh tears starting to build at the corners of my eyes. 'How she can ruin her life like this. I'm trying to understand why she'd run off with Mr Cohn –' at his name, my voice breaks a little, and the tears blink down on to my cheeks – 'when that's such a crazy thing to do and he's so *old* and she's so . . . She's meant to be the sensible one.'

'It's a lot to try and understand,' Carolyn says. 'I don't think any of us understand, not really.'

'But why didn't she *tell* me?' I ask. My voice is hoarse through my tears; I hate how raw I sound. And feel.

Carolyn is silent for a while, stroking my hair. 'Most likely she knew it was wrong,' she says finally, 'and telling you would mean having to face that. And I wouldn't discount the possibility that Mr Cohn made sure she kept it all quiet. He has the most to lose, of course. And it's very easy to convince someone besotted to do what you say, even if that means lying to their best friends, or their family.'

I don't say anything, because what I'm thinking is that if Bonnie didn't tell me because she knew it was wrong, why did she decide to tell me she was running away with him? That's surely a lot worse than a secret affair. None of this makes any sense.

'Why did she go now?' I ask. Now I'm talking, all the whirling worries I've been having are coming out. 'Why now? She's been so obsessed with exams and qualifications for so long. Why go just when they're about to start?'

'Probably for that reason,' Valerie says. 'She was under so much pressure that she just broke under it and gave up completely. That happens.'

I frown. 'Bonnie's not the kind of person who gives up.'

'She is now. She's run away, Eeds.'

'Yeah, but *with* Mr Cohn.'

'People don't just run *to* things,' Valerie says. 'It's called running *away* for a reason. I don't think she's chosen Jack Cohn *over* her GCSEs, if that's what you're saying. I think she was escaping them.'

'Why would she need to escape them? She's so smart. It's what she's been working for. It'd be like training for a marathon and then just not running it. It would make no sense.'

'If you really want to understand why she's done this,' Valerie says, 'you should try to have a bit more empathy for her reality. Being so young and being under so much pressure. That's hard.'

'But she *wanted* it,' I say, my voice coming out harsher than I'd intended. 'You're making out like it was all put on her, but it wasn't. She was the one who was obsessed with being top and getting the grades. No one made her be such an overachiever.'

'You think it counts any less when the person is putting pressure on themselves?'

'Well, yeah. I *told* her she should calm down and stop stressing herself out so much. But she never listened to me, and now suddenly she's gone, and I'm meant to feel bad for not seeing it coming?'

'What?' Valerie is shaking her head. 'No one said anything about whether you should feel bad. This isn't about you, Eden.'

'Great, thanks,' I snap. Bloody perfect Valerie and her sodding answer for fucking everything. 'It's more about me than you. Why are you even here?'

'Eden,' Carolyn says, her hand on my wrist.

'I'm here for *you*,' Valerie says. Her face is flushed. 'So don't fucking talk to me like that, OK?'

'Girls.' Carolyn says it like a plea. 'Don't fight.'

I know I should apologize, but I don't want to, so I don't. I bite down on my lip and swallow and look down at the tea Valerie made for me. The silence stretches on. I can feel Carolyn and Valerie making eyes at each other, a whole voiceless conversation going on right over my head.

'I'm going to go out for a bit,' Valerie says finally, getting to her feet. 'See you later.'

Sometimes I'm not a very nice person.

'Do you want some company?' Carolyn asks her.

'No, I'm fine.'

'Thanks for the tea,' I mumble.

Valerie pauses slightly on her way out of the living room. She glances at me. 'No problem,' she says, then leaves.

I stare down at my lap, not wanting to see the look on Carolyn's face, until I hear the front door close, a car door opening, the engine starting. 'Sorry,' I mutter.

'She wants to be closer to you,' Carolyn says, which makes me feel worse because I already know this. 'Maybe you could be a little . . . gentler with her.'

Why would she want to be closer to me when I'm such a bitch? I wonder. I've never made things easy for Valerie, and the fact that she carries on trying regardless just makes it clearer that she's a better person than me. Like that wasn't obvious anyway.

'I'm just worried about Bonnie,' I say.

'I know, love.'

'If she didn't come back for this, what will she come back for?'

'There are an awful lot more reasons to come back to Larking than exams,' Carolyn says. 'Her family. Her home. You.'

'So you think she will come back?' I ask.

'Yes, I do,' she says, surprising me with how fast she responds. 'True, I don't know if that will be of her own volition, but the police will find them eventually.'

'How?'

'Oh, they'll track them down somehow. Bonnie or Mr Cohn will talk to someone they shouldn't, or someone here who knows something will slip up. No one stays hidden forever.'

'Even if they want to?'

'Especially if they want to.'

'OK,' I say. My voice sounds so small. I'm not sure whether the idea of Bonnie being brought back against her will is that much better than her not coming back at all.

'Oh, Eden,' Carolyn says, putting her arm around me again and squeezing me in for a hug. 'I'm sorry this is such a hard time for you. Look, maybe we should go away this weekend. Get you far from this . . . this circus. Clear your head.'

'Go where?' I ask. I don't want to be anywhere else but here at home, not until Bonnie gets back. What if they find her while I'm off somewhere else?

'We could always take a drive to Norfolk, see Bob's parents,' she suggests.

'Mmm,' I say, unenthusiastic. I like Bob's parents, but I can't imagine having to put on my best adopted-granddaughter face right now.

'Maybe have a think about it,' Carolyn says. 'I really think a break could do you good.'

The only break that would do me good, I think but can't say, is one to Yorkshire to see Bonnie, if that's even where she still is. *That* would be a trip worth taking. Something in the back of my mind gives a little *click* at this; the start of an idea. Thought-kindling.

'I'll think about it,' I say.

15

I go up to my room and sit on my bed for a while, turning my phone over in my fingers, trying not to think about Bonnie. Her absence and silence today is, in a weird kind of way, more unsettling than anything that's happened so far this week, and thinking about it makes me feel nauseous. She's not just physically gone any more. Something else feels lost, something I don't understand. Something that might not come back, even if she does. *When* she does.

I flop on to my back and stare at the ceiling, wondering despite myself whether Valerie was right about the whole Bonnie-putting-herself-under-pressure thing. I don't want Valerie to be right about this, but then again, she's right about everything else, so why should this be any different?

And then, of course, my phone buzzes with a message from Bonnie. **Hi! How was the exam? :)**

It's the smiley face that does it. **Do you even care?**

Ivy
?! Of course I care!

Me
The exam was ages ago.

Are you cross? What's the matter?

Nothing. The exam was shit. How's Yorkshire?

Ivy

We're not in Yorkshire any more!

The '. . .' of an incoming message appears onscreen, so I know she's elaborating, but I toss my phone to the other side of the bed and sink, face down, against my sheets. I can't keep up with this any more. I'm not even sure I want to. It's just all so tiring. For a few moments I imagine taking the phone downstairs and presenting the messages to Carolyn. I wouldn't even have to say anything. Show, not tell.

I let out a sigh-groan and sit up, reaching for my phone again. I know I can't do that. Even if I was prepared to betray Bonnie – which I'm not, however annoyed I am – I've lied too much to be able to do it now. If I sell her down the river, I'll get dragged in too.

Ivy

We couldn't find anywhere to stay and anyway we felt a bit exposed. Jack figures we should hide in plain sight. So we're in Glasgow! Jack found us this great place on Craigslist. Takes cash, no questions asked. All good :)

Yeah, sounds all good, I think, rolling my eyes. None of this is surprising me any more, but still – Glasgow?! I thought being on the run was meant to be romantic.

Me

Great.

Ivy

Sorry I didn't message you for a while. Couldn't charge my phone!

Me

That's OK.

Bonnie sends me the zipped-mouth emoji, followed by a smiley face, and it's all I can do not to throw my phone across the room.

God, this time last week we were making rocky-road fudge in her kitchen. She was quizzing me on the Periodic Table and letting me eat a marshmallow for every right answer. Was she planning all this then? Did she already know?

Forget it, I tell myself. Stop thinking about it for one tiny hour. Do some revision.

And then the doorbell rings.

I hear voices drifting up the stairs, one Carolyn's, the other . . . Oh, God. It's Bonnie's mother. What if she's here to see me? What if . . . Wait. What if they've found out where Bonnie is and the police are on their way to get her right now? I start to climb off the bed, then stop, one foot on the floor. That's not very likely, is it? It's not like I'm the first person she'd want to tell.

I'm still in that awkward half-on-half-off-the-bed position when Carolyn comes into my room. 'Matilda's here,' she says. 'She'd like to talk to you.'

'Have they found Bonnie?' I blurt.

She shakes her head. 'No, love.'

So why is she here? It's not like we had a constructive conversation last time we spoke. Oh God. I really don't want to be yelled at right now.

Seeing my face, Carolyn smiles reassuringly. 'It'll be fine,' she says. 'I think it will be good for both of you to talk to each other. Remember, you both love Bonnie. You both want her home.'

She's right, of course, and I hesitate but don't move.

'Come on, Eden,' Carolyn says, more firmly this time. 'She's waiting.'

I clearly don't have much of a choice whether to follow her or not, so I do, slowly. When I go into the kitchen Mrs Wiston-Stanley is sitting at the kitchen table.

'Hello, Eden,' she says, smiling. It's not a full smile, or even really half of one. There's too much sadness on her face to lift it properly, and I feel instantly, horribly, guilty. She's lost a lot of the fierce anger she'd had on Sunday, like it's all drained out of her and all that's left is this sad, strained woman who's just missing her daughter.

The thought whispers: am I on the wrong side of all of this?

'Hi, Mrs Wiston-Stanley,' I say, hearing how it comes out in a mumble. It's hard to even look at her properly.

'Matilda,' she says. 'I've told you that before, Eden. You can call me Matilda.'

I half nod, half shrug, and sink on to one of the kitchen stools.

'How was the exam?' she asks.

I shrug.

'Eden,' Carolyn says, a little warning in her voice. It's gentle, but it's there. 'Now is the time to verbalize.'

I clear my throat, but it doesn't really help. 'It was fine,' I lie.

Matilda's mouth twitches in a would-be smile, and there's an awkward pause. She shifts a little in her seat, leans forward as if to speak, then changes her mind. Finally, she says, her voice crackly with hope, 'Have you heard from Bonnie today?'

I shake my head.

'Oh.' She leans back again and looks away. 'I hoped, what with the exam, that maybe . . .'

'I thought that too,' I say, because I did, and if no one else understands that, she does.

Matilda looks back at me, her face much softer than usual. Oh God. This is worse than the police. Worse than journalists. Worse than Carolyn and Bob's gentle, searching questions. She looks so *broken*.

'I want you to know,' she begins, looking at Carolyn and then back at me, 'that I won't be angry with you. None of us will be. Not if you tell us now.'

My head goes, *Wait, what?* It goes, *Careful.*

'Angry with me?' I manage.

'For not telling the truth earlier,' Matilda says. 'I understand you feel . . . *loyal*. To Bonnie. And that you feel like you should protect her somehow. But it's very wrong to do that. What's more important than anything is that she's safe.'

But she *is* safe. I don't understand. I've tried, but I just don't. If Matilda had said 'home' instead of 'safe', that would make sense. Or even 'found'. But 'safe'? What does 'safe' even mean?

She's watching me, waiting for a response, but I have no idea what to say. I look at Carolyn, who attempts a smile that doesn't quite land. There's a strain on her face she doesn't usually let show, her forehead crinkled in a frown.

The silence drags on, and finally Matilda breaks it. 'I just don't believe that you haven't been in contact with her,' she says. 'I'm sorry, Eden. I wish I could believe you. But I think you're lying to me.'

Carolyn opens her mouth, then closes it again. I swallow, trying to sort through the feelings crowding my head. It's the weirdest mix of guilt and resentment, shame and anger. OK, I'm lying, but why is it such a given for her that I am? Why does she think I'd ever want to open up to her when she's always treated me like I'm untrustworthy?

'Why do you think I'm lying?' I ask.

'Because I know Bonnie,' she says. 'And I know you.'

Both of these statements are so obviously wrong that I have to bite down on my lip to stop myself saying so. Now is not the time to start a fight, I tell myself.

'Bonnie told Rowan,' she adds, surprising me. I wonder when

Rowan caved and confessed. 'If she told Rowan, she told you.'

'She didn't tell me anything,' I say. 'I had no idea about Mr Cohn until the police told me. You were there, remember?'

Matilda lets out a frustrated sigh and looks at Carolyn. 'Can't you help?'

I feel my head whip round to Carolyn, bracing myself against the tide of betrayal. They've talked about this, haven't they? Discussed what a little liar I am. Strategized about how to get me to confess.

Carolyn doesn't even flinch. She just gives me a reassuring nod across the table. 'Go ahead,' she says gently. 'You're doing just fine.'

What does *that* mean? Is she on my side or not? Does she believe me or think I'm lying? I usually like Carolyn in this mode – totally unflappable, calm and reliable – but right now it's really not helping. And I am not reassured.

'I just want to *know*,' Matilda says, shaking her head with what looks like defeat. 'I just want to understand how this could have happened. All of this . . . it's just not my Bonnie. There has to be an explanation.'

'If there is, I don't have it,' I say.

'The thing is, Eden,' she says. 'The thing is . . . I can't help but think this is your influence.'

The words are such a shock it takes me a moment to register them. 'My . . . influence?'

'Well, you're no stranger to trouble, are you?' Matilda has squared her shoulders a little, making her seem suddenly a lot taller than me, even though we're both sitting down. 'I always worried what Bonnie might be convinced to do, with a friend like you.'

'Now, hang on a second—' Carolyn begins, half standing.

But I've found my voice and I am *mad*. 'Bonnie runs off with our fucking teacher and you think it's *my* fault?'

'Eden, don't sw—'

'I think you've had an influence, yes.' Matilda interrupts Carolyn with a look that says, *This is exactly what I mean.* 'Oh, Eden, don't make that face like you're some kind of saint. Don't think I've forgotten the things you've done. Practically arrested at fourteen, for Christ's sake.'

I was never 'practically arrested'. Being brought home by the police and given a stern little lecture in my living room maybe once or twice is not 'practically arrested'. And that was fucking years ago and things are different now and anyway—

'What's that got to do with me and Bonnie?'

Carolyn's face is tense with anxiety. 'Please, can we all just—'

But Matilda ignores her. 'Everything!' She almost spits this at me. 'How can I protect her and guide her and keep her safe when she's around someone like you?'

For one horrifying second I think I'm about to cry, but what comes out is rage. *'I'm still here!'* I yell, all of my frustration exploding out of me. 'I didn't leave, and I didn't know anything, and I didn't tell her to fuck our teacher—'

'Eden!'

'And maybe the problem is the person who thinks that's all OK, not the one she left behind.' The words hang in the air, both Carolyn and Matilda staring at me, so I add, 'We've been best friends since we were eight. That was before everything you're talking about. You don't know her without me. You can't know that this is anything to do with me, or if it's just the way she is. Unless you think I somehow corrupted her when I was *eight*?'

Matilda's chin juts. There's a look on her face that's pure ugliness, the kind of face adults aren't supposed to show to children or even teenagers. I think, *She won't say it,* but then she does. 'Well, we all know what you came from.'

'That's enough.' There's such fury in the words that for a bizarre

moment I think they're mine, but it's Carolyn who's standing, shaking her head. I glance down and see that her hands are clenched into fists. 'How dare you speak to Eden like that? How *dare* you?'

'Carolyn, that girl is—'

'That girl is my daughter, and you need to leave.' Carolyn is trying to hold it together, I can tell. I feel both touched and scared, all at once. 'I told you that you could speak to her, not insult her. I know you're frustrated, and I know you're scared, but that's not Eden's fault.'

'What did I come from?' I ask.

'Eden, stop it!' Carolyn snaps, reaching a hand out towards me. 'Don't make this worse, for God's *sake*.'

But I really want to know 'what' I came from. Does she mean a council estate? Or does she mean my real mother? My living, human, made-some-poor-life-choices mother. She's not a 'what'. Her name is Lina.

'I'm sorry, Carolyn,' Matilda says, because of course she apologizes to her and not to me. 'This is just a hard . . .' Her voice breaks. 'A hard time.'

'You should go,' Carolyn says. I can tell she's still struggling not to lose it. 'We can talk another time.'

Matilda must be able to tell that she's blown it because she doesn't argue, just collects her things and leaves without another word to me.

I follow Carolyn into the hall as she sees Matilda out, then hover awkwardly as she stands there with her back to me, staring at the closed front door.

I begin, 'Thanks for—'

She rounds on me, all that pent-up energy suddenly coming at me. 'Why do you have to do that?' she demands, not quite yelling, but not quite not-yelling, either. Her face is scrunched and red, her eyes shiny with . . . Those aren't tears, are they? 'Why do you have to always try to get a rise out of people?'

I falter, opening my mouth and then closing it again. I don't know what to say, so I just shrug, which by the look on her face is the wrong response.

'Matilda is dealing with an unimaginably stressful situation. Her daughter is *missing*, Eden. It's like you don't understand that.'

'So *you* think I'm stupid, too?'

She closes her eyes for a moment, like I'm just too much to deal with, like she'd rather not even look at me. 'No,' she says, the word ground out from between her teeth. 'I think your lack of empathy is disappointing.'

'Well,' I say. 'I guess that's just what I came from.'

And Carolyn loses it.

'Don't you throw that in my face!' she yells. Actually yells. *Carolyn.* 'I am on your side. I'm trying to do right by you. Why can't you just try and make this easier on me? On all of us?'

Carolyn has never yelled at me before. It turns my insides cold.

I could yell back. I could crumple and cry. I could apologize.

I turn and walk out of the kitchen.

'Don't walk away from me, Eden!' It starts out fierce, but Carolyn's voice breaks on 'from' and it falls apart. I hear the hitch of her breath come out in one defeated exhale.

I go upstairs and into my room, closing my door behind me and climbing up on to my bed. The mattress sinks underneath me, comforting and familiar, and I press my face into the sheets.

My heart, I realize, is going a mile a minute in my chest, and I concentrate on the beats for a while, eyes closed, trying to calm down. God, that was horrible. That was really horrible. I've never seen Carolyn lose it like that. Not with me, not with anyone. Even when I was at my wildest worst, she never lost her calm Carolyn-ness.

I curl myself into a ball on the bed and rest my face against my knees, trying not to cry. But my hands feel all tingly and I can hear that my breath is doing that scratchy thing it does when tears are on their way. I'm thinking of Carolyn alone in the kitchen, of Valerie coming home and asking her what's wrong, making her a cup of tea, listening quietly. Mother–daughter sharing time.

Look what Bonnie has brought into my house and my head. This is her fault. She didn't just run away – she lobbed a great big hand grenade behind her as she went and blew everyone else's lives up. So much for steady. So much for reliable. So much for bloody perfect.

I should have just told them about her messages, about Glasgow, about the whole damn thing. Because that's where this is all going, isn't it? How much longer can I carry on like this?

I don't know how long I lie there before there's a soft knock at my door and I tense but don't move. I hear the door open and footsteps on the carpet, followed by the bed sinking slightly and then the light pressure of a hand on my shoulder.

'I've brought you tea.'

I sit up, brushing my hair out of my eyes, and reach for the cup. Carolyn smiles, but her face is still tense and I can see there's red around her eyes, like she's been crying. I am the worst person alive. But still I just take the tea and sip it so I don't have to talk.

'Listen,' she says. 'I'm sorry I shouted at you. I shouldn't have done that. But you have to understand, this whole situation . . . it's stressful. As a parent, it's very *stressful*. I'm not excusing Matilda for how she spoke to you, but I expect more from you than how you behaved.'

I open my mouth, but she shakes her head.

'I'm trying to convince her that you're trustworthy, Eden. That her prejudgements of you are unfair and baseless. But when her daughter is missing and she asks for your help, you just give her attitude.'

'I don't!'

'It doesn't help anyone. You have to be gentler with people. You can't just choose people you like and push everyone else away.'

'Why not?'

'Because people change, in both directions. Because at some point a person you like will do something you *don't* like and it will pull the rug right out from under your whole world,' she says pointedly. 'And that sort of thing is a lot easier to deal with if you have a wider network around you, instead of just a chosen few. Valerie came all the way down here to be here for you, and you've practically ignored her since she arrived.'

How have we got to *Valerie*?

'I didn't ask her to come,' I mutter, but very quietly, because even I can hear how childish I sound.

'Eden,' she says warningly. 'You're not covering yourself in glory, here.'

I shrug, twisting my hands together and squeezing my fingers.

'I'm going to ask Matilda to apologize to you,' Carolyn says. 'Once she's calmed down. And I'd like you to think about doing the same.'

'She basically called me trash, Carolyn. I'm not fucking apologizing.'

'*Eden*.' My name comes out like a groan.

'Well, I'm not. *And* she's blaming me for Bonnie going. Like it's not bad enough that my best friend's disappeared, I have to get the blame, too?'

'Eden, she's just frustrated. Any mother would be.'

'Well, it's a lot easier to blame me than herself, right?'

'Yes,' Carolyn says, so simply that I start in surprise. 'Yes, it is. It's not right, and it's not fair, but it's easier. Sometimes that's all a person can manage.' She sighs. 'Look, I have to go out to meet a client in about an hour. How about I make you some lunch before I go?'

I know that this is her way of ending the conversation, even though nothing's actually been resolved and I don't know whether she expects me to apologize to Matilda or not, but it's not like I'm invested in carrying on an argument. So I shrug and nod and follow her downstairs.

She makes cheese toasties with brown sauce and tells me about her client's tiered garden until her face has loosened and the stress has drained away. I eat and smile, and neither of us mentions Matilda again.

Somehow, the evening arrives and I haven't done any Chemistry revision. What I have done is messaged Rowan on Facebook – **So you told? Are you OK? xx** – and talked to Connor on the phone. And painted my toenails. And watched a video of Daniel Radcliffe singing the Periodic Table song.

After dinner, Carolyn drives Daisy to her friend's house, and I go to my room to actually try and revise, but the words all tangle together into a meaningless mass of letters and symbols, and I almost feel like crying again. It's so unfair that I have to deal with this on top of everything else.

I try to concentrate for about half an hour before I get up off my bed, tuck my revision guide under my arm and pad across the hall to Valerie's room. The door is closed and I can hear the sound of her talking on the phone, cheerful and chatty. I knock softly and poke my head around the door.

Valerie looks up and sees me, her expression turning neutral but not unfriendly. She lifts a hand to acknowledge me and says into the phone, 'Eden's just come in. I'll call you back later, OK?' She hangs up and drops the phone on her bed. 'Hey, you,' she says to me. 'What's up?'

There's no trace of anger in her. People like Valerie are too good for this world. If I was good, like her, I'd jump on to the bed and give her a hug. I'd say that I was sorry for snarling at her. I'd say all the right things.

Instead, I lift up my revision guide so she can see the cover. 'Could you help me revise?'

Valerie smiles at me. It's just small, nothing like her usual full-body smile and actually more sad than anything else, but it's there. 'Sure,' she says. She pats the space on the bed next to her. 'Come on up.'

Conversations That Took on a New Meaning after Bonnie Disappeared

The 'Perfect' Edition: five months before

'Are you OK?' Bonnie asked, peering at me, concern all over her face.

I put my fingers on her chin and pushed her away. 'Obviously.' She was still looking all anxious, so I laughed. 'Seriously, I'm fine. It's what I expected. No surprises here.' I glanced down at my list of mock exam results again and shook my head. 'Hey. At least I passed most of them, right?'

She frowned. 'Is a D actually a pass?'

'Bonnie!'

'Sorry,' she said quickly.

The expression on her face was starting to get on my nerves. So when I asked, 'How did you do, then?' it came out a bit more harsh than I'd meant.

She shrugged. 'Does it matter?'

I rolled my eyes. 'Come on, just tell me. All A stars?'

'Not all of them,' she said, which I knew meant the rest were just plain old As.

'Smile, then,' I said, trying not to get annoyed. 'That's what you wanted, isn't it? At least own it.'

'I guess.'

'What's the matter?'

'I just thought . . .' She hesitated, glancing at me and then away again. 'I thought I'd feel a bit . . . more. But they're just letters, aren't they?'

I didn't say anything, because what could I say? We both knew that we were on polar opposite sides of the scale when it came to education. Usually it didn't matter, not to us, but in moments like this . . . well, it felt like the elephant in the room we'd always ignored suddenly trumpeting in my ear. Looking at her, with her A*s in her hand and a frown on her face, she felt like someone I didn't know at all.

The silence between us was just starting to shift into awkward when Mrs Berwick walked out of the main building into the courtyard we were sitting in. When she saw Bonnie, she beamed. 'Ah, Bonnie,' she said, ignoring me. 'Congratulations on your fantastic results.'

I watched Bonnie move flawlessly into perfect mode. The Head Prefect with straight As and not a detention to her name. Her shoulders unhunched, her smile bloomed, her chin lifted. 'Thanks, miss.'

'They're only mocks,' I said. 'They're just letters, aren't they?'

Mrs Berwick glared at me. 'Maybe that attitude is why your "letters" are so unimpressive, Miss McKinley.'

I shrugged. 'Maybe I'm just thick, miss.'

'You're not,' Bonnie said immediately.

'Well,' Mrs Berwick said loudly, in the voice she uses when she wants everyone to shut up. 'I'm glad you have the right priorities, Bonnie. We're all very proud of you.'

Bonnie smiled back. The wide, confident, teacher-pleasing smile I hated the most. 'Thanks, miss.'

I waited until Mrs Berwick had walked off before I spoke, but it wasn't long enough for the snap of irritation to leave my voice. 'Don't you ever get tired of being perfect all the time?'

Bonnie, back to her hunched-shoulders, tense-smiling, chin-lowered self, swept her hair behind her ear and looked away from me. 'Yes,' she said.

Thursday

16

I wake up the next morning confused and groggy. I'd been dreaming about being with Bonnie in her sunny garden, the two of us blowing dandelion clocks across the grass, the feel of her arm around my shoulder, the sound of her laughing beside me. It's disorientating to open my eyes to my own bedroom, still dark, even as the first morning light is starting to leak through the curtains.

I try to go back to sleep, but I can't. My brain is too alive. As the room gets lighter I unlock my phone and find a reply waiting from Rowan, sent after I'd fallen asleep. **Yeah, I had to tell,** she's written. **Did it on Mon. Mum showed me the letters Mr C had sent Bon and told me about grooming and stuff and I caved. This is all so messed up. Didn't want any part in it. Mum wasn't even mad I hadn't told her before. See the pics for some of the letters. Hope you're OK. Good luck with the exam. Row x.**

Poor Rowan. I send a quick reply and make a mental note to tell Daisy to be nice to her again before I open the pictures she's sent and squint to read the contents properly.

The letters are . . . intense. One is explicit (it contains a line about Bonnie's mouth that I will never be able to unread), but the others all come across as mostly sweet and romantic, even funny. At least, they would, if I didn't know who'd written them. They're full of song lyrics and lines of poetry, reassurances and compliments, dreams and promises. No wonder Bonnie went and bloody fell in love with him. They're like every letter any girl has ever wished she'd get from a boy. Except Mr Cohn isn't a boy, is he?

> If I was allowed to love you, I'd do it properly. You'd never feel lost or worried or under-appreciated again, not with me.

Seeing the handwriting I recognize from school writing words like this makes me feel first uncomfortable and then full-out weird. He's our teacher, I keep thinking. He's a grown man.

> I see the way you are at school, how you carry it all on your shoulders, how it diminishes your beautiful light. Those friends who don't know you, but think they do. Your parents who expect too much from you, but all the wrong things. You're so much more than all of this. You're special. Bonnie, do you know how special you are? I want to take you away from here. I want to protect you from the world.

But Bonnie didn't need protecting from the world until you changed it by taking her away, I almost say to the screen, right out loud. God, why didn't Bonnie tell me? Why didn't she show me these letters? I would have said . . . What would I have said? It's a bit weird to be that intense, Bon. Maybe tell him to chill out a bit. How old did you say he was? He's not too old for you, is he? He's not committing a crime, is he?

> One day we'll be together, and I can give you everything you want and deserve. No more hiding. I know we have to wait, but I don't

want you to think that means what I feel isn't real. I love you. One day I'll tell the world.

I look back at Rowan's message, then google 'grooming' and click on the top result that comes up.

There's a lot on the page I read that fits Bonnie, from 'personality changes' right down to 'the child or teenager may not understand that they have been groomed', and when I'm done I feel itchy all over, hot and cold. I try and reconcile what I've read with Bonnie insisting that she's happy, that she's in love, that this is all her choice. I bite down on my nails and then the pad of my thumb.

I take out my phone to message Bonnie, but just stare blankly at the screen for a while instead. What am I supposed to say? *Er, Bonnie, do you think you've been groomed?* There's no point, I already know what she'll say. She'll say no, we're in love. And who am I to know the difference?

I wish I could talk to her properly, face to face. WhatsApp and the occasional phone call is part of the problem. Besides, even if I did speak to her about this over the phone, she'd just hang up and speak to Mr Cohn straight after, and he's going to be way more convincing than me.

Oh God, maybe I should just tell everyone where she is. No. I can't. But maybe I should?

But I *promised*. It's *Bonnie*.

'Eden?' There's a rap of knuckles at the door and Carolyn's voice. 'Time to get up, OK?'

'OK,' I call, tossing my phone to the side and closing my laptop. At the very least, I decide, this can all wait until after the exam.

I walk to school alone. There are still journalists hovering near the Kett school gates, but there are definitely fewer of them, and they're not yelling this time. Mr Sudbury, the lower school PE teacher, is leaning against the gatepost like he's keeping guard, which is probably why.

I try to put them out of my mind completely when I walk into the hall, my clear pencil case clutched in my hand, but it doesn't really work. I'm wondering what information they have and don't have, what stories they're trying to write, what will be in the papers tomorrow. I'm thinking about Bonnie waking up in bed with Mr Cohn in Scotland and how completely weird it still is. I'm thinking about grooming. I am not thinking about chemistry.

But then I have to think about chemistry, because the exam's starting and I don't have a choice. I skim through the paper before I write a word, looking for questions that don't make me panic outright. I try and channel Valerie, remembering how she'd sketched out an atom on to a notepad for me the night before. The electrons on the outside, the nucleus in the middle. It helps, just a bit.

But still, the best thing I can say about the exam is that it ends.

When I get outside of the hall, I find Connor waiting for me, leaning against the wall. He doesn't say anything at first, just smiles hopefully and raises his eyebrows, like, *Well?*

'Ugh,' I say.

His face falls. 'Really?'

'Ugh, ugh, ugh. Let's go.'

'Was it at least better than yesterday?'

'Well, I didn't cry, so I guess so. You?'

'I think it was OK,' he says cautiously. 'That whole section on halogens was a bitch, though.'

I make a face as he opens the door for me and I walk out into the sunshine. Deconstructing an exam after it's over is almost as bad as having to go through it the first time around. 'Do you want to go to Costa or something?' I ask, shielding my eyes from the sun and wishing I'd thought to bring my sunglasses.

'I need to get home,' Connor replies, an apologetic twist of a smile on his face. 'Gran's picking me up and I'm going to make a brunchy lunch. Eggs and bacon. I was thinking about it all the way through the exam.' He laughs a little. 'Want to come?'

'Is that OK?'

'Of course!' He takes my hand and starts leading me towards the car park. 'She'll probably be here already. Have you heard from Bonnie today?'

I give him a shove. 'Shh! God, Connor!' I look around frantically, as if a journalist – or worse, Mrs Berwick – might be standing right behind me. Luckily, there's no one. 'Remember how that's a secret?'

Connor rolls his eyes. 'Worst secret ever.'

We've reached his gran's car, so I stick my tongue out at him rather than reply before opening the back door and sliding in.

'Hello, Eden,' his gran says, turning to look at me as Connor gets into the passenger seat. 'How did you find the exam?' She says this in a voice that suggests she knows exactly how I found the exam. Connor's gran is like that. I think the word is 'shrewd'.

'It was OK,' I say.

'And how about you?' she asks Connor. 'All plain sailing?'

Connor wiggles his hand in a so-so gesture. 'Could have been worse.'

'Hmm,' she says. 'Could have been better, though?'

He shrugs. 'Couldn't it always?'

It only takes a few minutes to drive to Connor's house. When we get there, one of their cats, Snufkin, is sprawled out in the middle of the driveway, and he refuses to move even as Connor's gran slams her hand down on the horn. Eventually Connor has to get out, laughing, and physically lift him out of the way.

'Cats,' Connor's gran says, shaking her head as she switches the engine off, 'have got life figured out.'

'They have?' I ask.

'They make their own decisions and won't budge for anybody,' she says. 'It might be annoying, but you have to respect it.'

Connor is still holding Snufkin under one arm when he opens the front door for us and leads the way into the house. He deposits the cat on to the carpet and heads into the kitchen. 'Connor!' I hear his mother, Helen, say. 'My study bug. How was the exam? And Eden!' she adds as I appear behind him, before he can even reply. 'How lovely to see you.' Her smile is wide and genuine. 'Come and sit next to me and tell me how you are.'

'I'm fine,' I say quickly. 'How are *you*?' Her arm is in a sling and I can see the yellowing dark of a bruise on her face. So little time has passed since her fall on Friday. I slide into the chair beside her as Connor opens the fridge and starts collecting ingredients.

'Oh, I'm just fine,' Helen says dismissively. 'Broken bones heal, and I've got lots of pain medication to be getting on with. And my lovely son to make me cups of tea.' As she says this she leans back, beaming, and touches Connor's arm. He rolls his eyes at me but he's smiling, the tips of his ears pinkening. 'But *you* . . .' She gives me a significant look. 'You've been having quite a week.'

'Yeah.' I shrug a little. I don't really know what to say. It's not like any of it is happening to *me*, not really. I'm just on the sidelines. It's Bonnie's drama; Bonnie's mess.

'There was a girl in *my* school who had an affair with our teacher, you know,' she says. 'Big scandal.'

'Really?'

'Mm-hm. We were in the sixth form, so it isn't quite the same situation, and they didn't exactly run away. She left school to go and be with him.'

'Did they stay together?' I ask.

'Oh, no. They were engaged for a while, I think, but they never married. They split up after a couple of years.'

I don't know whether to be disappointed or not. On the one hand, I want Bonnie to be happy, don't I? But on the other, it doesn't seem right if she gets to be rewarded with a great love story for messing up everyone's lives.

'This kind of thing,' Helen says. 'It's not as rare as you might think.'

'It's not?'

'No. Where there are men –' she gives me a rueful smile – 'and there are girls, there's the risk.'

'Unscrupulous men,' Connor's gran amends. 'Seeking out lovelorn girls to dazzle and manipulate.'

I frown. 'That doesn't sound like Mr Cohn.'

'I'm sure he'd be pleased to hear that,' Helen says, and they both laugh.

'But maybe they really did just fall in love,' I say. 'And they just happen to have a big age gap. And it's, like . . . taboo. And that's why they had to leave.'

'Maybe,' Connor's gran says, her voice dry, eyes sharp. 'Maybe this is all about two people in love. Or maybe it's about a *man* taking a *girl* away from her home and her family.'

'A man who should know better,' Helen adds. 'Needless to say.'

'So . . .' I try to gather the conversation together in my head. 'So you're saying this won't last? And Bonnie will come home?'

'We're saying don't worry,' Helen says, patting my hand. 'We're saying this will blow over soon.'

'This too shall pass,' Connor's gran says, in the kind of grand voice that suggests this is a quote that I should probably recognize, but don't.

I look at Connor and he grins at me from where he's scrambling eggs at the hob. I smile uncertainly back, because I'm not sure whether this conversation is helping sort the confusion in my mind or actually making it worse. Helen and Connor's gran are talking in the way adults often do about teenage problems, like they've already seen the future, just because they're older, and are talking with hindsight they haven't actually earned. Yes, they've lived their lives. But they haven't lived mine.

'I just want Bonnie to come home,' I say.

'She will,' Helen says, so confidently, like there's no other option. 'One way or another, she will.'

We stay in the kitchen for a while, talking about non-Bonnie things while we eat, but she's still all I can think about. All of the adults – Connor's mum and gran, my parents, the people on the radio – they're all so sure that Bonnie will be found and returned home, whether she wants it or not. Like it's just as simple and inevitable as that. But if that was true, wouldn't it have happened by now? She's already made it from here to Wales to Yorkshire to Scotland. What's next? What if they really do make it to Ireland? What if they really do disappear?

When we're finished eating, I follow Connor up to his room, my head still fizzing.

'What do you think about what your mum and gran said?' I ask.

'About Bonnie?'

'Yeah.'

'Well, I think they would have said some different stuff if they'd known you knew where she was.'

I know this is true. 'Yeah, yeah. I meant about her coming back, and this all blowing over. Do you think that's true?'

'I don't know. I guess so? You know Bonnie better than I do. What do you think?'

I've been thinking about little else all week, and I still don't have an answer. 'I think Bonnie's stubborn. That's what I keep going back to. And . . . what's the word for when you don't want to admit that you're wrong? Enough so you'll do anything to avoid it?'

'Er . . . proud?'

'I guess. Anyway, that's the thing . . . I just can't see her deciding it on her own, not when she's with Mr Cohn in that weird love-bubble they've got going on. She has to talk to someone about it.'

'Someone?'

'Me.'

'Uh . . .'

'I'm going to go and get her,' I say.

'What? You're what?'

'I know where she is, Connor. I know she's in Scotland.' He opens his mouth, and I know he's going to ask when she went to Scotland, but I hold my hand up to stop him talking. 'I'll go there and get her and bring her back with me.'

He closes his mouth again, looking perplexed, then shakes his head. 'That's your whole plan?'

'It's the important bit.'

'What about the logistics?'

'The what?'

'How are you going to travel? Where are you going to sleep? What are you going to tell Carolyn and Bob?'

I shrug. 'I don't know, train, I guess—'

'You're going to get a train.' He says this as a statement, not a question. A statement he thinks is ridiculous. 'All the way to Scotland.'

His tone is infuriating. 'Connor! Either actually help me out or go away.'

'I am helping you. I'm being practical. How would you even pay for a ticket?'

'With money, genius.'

But Connor's capacity for patience is boundless, so he just grins at my annoyance. 'Money from where?'

I turn away from him, trying to push my mind to tick faster, faster. Where *could* I get that kind of money? I'd have to borrow it, I guess. Maybe Carolyn would—

'Maybe Carolyn would lend it to me,' I say out loud. 'She was the one who said I should get away for the weekend. I could just tell her I'm going . . . I don't know, somewhere else. Margate or somewhere. And just use the money to get to Scotland.'

I feel Connor rest his chin against my shoulder, the tickle of his breath against the back of my neck. 'Maybe, but that's a pretty long way away, Eeds. It's hours on the train up there. And won't Carolyn be suspicious if you asked to borrow that much money just to go to Margate or something?'

Frustration is beginning to burn in my stomach. He's right. Damn.

'So what are my options?' I ask him, finally turning my head to face him. His chin is still on my shoulder and we're face to face, his nose against my cheek.

Connor thinks about it for a while, silent. 'Well, you could always tell Carolyn the truth.'

Instinctively I make a face.

'She'd probably want to help,' he points out.

'But then I'd have to tell her I know where they are,' I say. 'And that I knew all along. If I told her I know, she'd skip the going-to-get-them part and just send the police.'

'Eeds, I know you don't want to hear this, but maybe that's the best—'

'You're right; I don't want to hear it.'

'The end result would be the same, wouldn't it? Bonnie would be home and safe. Isn't that what you want?'

'No, the end result wouldn't be the same. She trusts me. If I tell the police where she is, I'm betraying her. What kind of friend would that make me? I'm not a grass.'

He lets out a noise; part huff, part tut, part groan. 'Don't you think it's got beyond words like "grass"? It's been six days. She's missed two GCSEs.'

'Which is why I'm going to go and get her. But I have to do it like this. Talk to her, convince her. Not *tell on her*, for God's sake. Do you really not get the difference?'

'Sure, I see the difference. But she's made this mess for herself, and you're killing yourself trying to help her and I'm just not sure she deserves it.'

His words are a shock. 'Are you serious?'

'Yes.'

'Connor!'

'Shit, Eden, how can you still feel like you should be defending her after this week? After seeing what it's doing to her parents? She's screwing up everyone's lives and she doesn't even care.'

'She isn't. Why would you say that?'

'You walked out of yesterday's exam crying!' he reminds me, sitting back with wide, frustrated eyes. '*You!* She shouldn't have even told you where she was. She shouldn't have put that on you. What kind of friend does that?'

'She wasn't putting anything on me. She told me because I'm her best friend. That's what best friends do. They tell each other stuff. Especially the bad stuff. Especially the secrets.'

'Oh yeah?' He leans back, and I can tell by his face that he's about to say something I don't want to hear, but before I can stop him . . . 'So why didn't she tell you about Mr Cohn before?'

Oh, that.

'Why didn't she give you a heads-up before disappearing into a whole different country?'

'Wales is hardly a whole different—'

'Why didn't she tell you she was in love with one of our teachers? Having sex with one of our teachers? How long did the papers say it's been going on?'

'Stop it, Connor.'

'Three months? Four?'

'All right, I fucking get it, OK?'

There's a long, heavy silence. I look at him, hearing my own breath coming out slightly haggard. What does he think I'm going to say? That he's right, that what Bonnie's done is so awful that I'm prepared to just . . . cut her loose? Leave her to disappear into Scotland or Ireland or God-knows-where with our freaking teacher, the person we were all meant to trust? Act like she's suddenly nothing to me, like the past eight years of friendship can just be erased by one stupid mistake?

'Do you think I don't know all this?' I ask finally. My voice comes out quiet. 'I know how messed up this all is. But she's still Bonnie. I have to do this. I'm *going* to do this.'

Connor doesn't say anything for a while, his fingers tapping a rhythm against his knee. Finally he nods. 'OK.'

I take a deep breath. 'OK. So what are my other options?'

He sighs. 'Well, if trains are out, you could always get a coach? But that would take such a long time, it might not even be worth it. The other option is a car.'

'I don't drive.'

'I meant a chauffeured car.'

'Who do we know that drives?'

We realize it at the same time. 'Valerie,' we both say.

Valerie.

17

We spend the next hour working out the best way of getting Valerie to agree to drive me to Glasgow. The way Connor sees it, there are three possibilities.

(1) I tell Valerie the truth and hope she won't just go running straight to Carolyn. (She probably will.)
(2) I tell Valerie half of the truth, which is that I want a lift to Glasgow without telling her why, and hope that she won't guess immediately. (She definitely will.)
(3) I lie.

The only possibility, really, is option three, and that's the one I'm going with. Yesterday, Carolyn had suggested I need a weekend away from the circus, and who better to spend that time with than Valerie? Hasn't she been spending the last few days trying to do just that? I won't even need to ask her to drive me all the way there. I'll just say I fancy a weekend in York, her university city, and then worry about the second leg of the journey when we're too far into it for her to change her mind.

'Foolproof,' I say, pleased.

'It's pretty far from foolproof,' Connor replies, always the realist. 'But I don't think we're going to get anything better.'

'What time is it?'

He glances at his watch. 'Half twelve.'

'God, I better get home. If Valerie's there we could even get going this afternoon. It's, what, a few hours from here to York? We can get there tonight and do the Glasgow bit tomorrow morning. God, I hope they don't move on before then.'

'Hey,' Connor says, and I look at him obediently. 'We haven't talked about me.'

'You? What about you?'

'I'll come with you.'

'What? Connor, no, you can't. Not with your mum . . .'

'Mum will understand,' he says. 'She and Gran can be without me for a couple of days.'

'Can they?'

'Yeah, of course. This is important.'

'Are you sure?'

'Yes, Eden. Jesus.' His brow furrows. 'My mum isn't bed-bound or anything, OK? Sometimes you act like you think she can't do anything for herself.'

'But—'

'You think I'd even suggest going away with you if I thought it would mean she wouldn't be OK? I know what I'm doing, for God's sake.'

He's on the defensive, and I don't even know why. It's true I don't really understand much about his mum's condition and what it really means for him to be her carer, but that's because he doesn't ever really talk about it. And that's not my fault, is it? I'm not going to push him to talk about something he doesn't want to talk about. I know too well what that feels like, and it sucks.

Connor's looking at me like he expects an apology, but I'm not the type to offer one unless I actually mean it, so I don't say anything, just look back.

'I was only asking,' I say eventually.

'You asked if I was *sure*,' he says. 'But I don't need you to check me for that. I've been doing this since I was eight years old, for God's sake. If I make an offer to come with you on some rescue-

Bonnie mission, I'm already sure. OK?'

'OK,' I say. I reach out and take his hand, threading my fingers through his and lifting them to my lips for a kiss.

He softens, then smiles. 'So do you want me to come?' he asks.

'Yes,' I say.

When I get home, Valerie is sitting at the dining-room table, working through what looks like an old exam paper. I've come up right behind her, but she's so focused she hasn't even noticed. I give her shoulder a poke.

'Jesus!' she yells, leaping out of the chair and spinning to face me. 'Holy shit, Eden. Are you trying to kill me?'

'Hi,' I say innocently.

'Hi yourself.' She puts a hand to her chest and pats it like she's putting out a fire. 'I think you just took a few years off my life.'

'Is it possible you're overreacting?'

She glares at me. 'Did you actually want something?' She turns back to the table and reaches for the kitchen timer, which had been merrily ticking away for some reason, pausing it with a click. 'Because I'm doing a timed test paper, here. And you kind of just ruined it.'

'I'm sorry,' I say, letting my mouth drop and my eyes widen. 'I just wanted to talk to you about how my GCSE Chemistry exam went, but I didn't mean to—'

'Oh God, of course!' Valerie drops the timer on to the table and pulls me over to sit on the chair she'd been using. 'God, I'm sorry. Of course I want to hear about it. I'm so sorry, Eeds, I just forgot. I had bio-chem brain.'

'I shouldn't have interrupted you when you were studying. We can talk about it later, honestly. When you're not busy.' Me, an emotional manipulator? Never.

'Don't be silly, I want to hear about it!' She grins at me, sitting on the carpet and crossing her arms over her knees. 'Tell me. How did it go?'

'Pretty bad,' I say, shrugging.

'Oh.' Her brow furrows and I can almost read the confusion on her face. But I helped her revise, she is clearly thinking. How can it not go well if you revise? 'Well . . . I'm sure it wasn't as bad as you think.'

'Maybe,' I say. (It was.) 'Everything's so distracting, you know? With Bonnie . . .'

Valerie's eyes cloud with sympathy. 'I bet. Were there journalists at the gates again?'

I nod. 'More than yesterday. And it's all anyone will talk about.'

'When's your next exam?'

'Tuesday.'

'At least you get a bit of a break, then?'

'Yeah . . .' I shrug again. 'I think maybe Carolyn was right about getting away from here this weekend.'

'She's usually right about stuff like that,' Valerie says, smiling. She looks just like Carolyn when she smiles. 'Do you know where you want to go?'

'As far from here as possible,' I say.

'Yeah, that's probably best.'

'Actually . . .' I'm trying to be casual, but I'm pretty sure I'm not pulling it off. 'I was thinking you might be able to help me out.'

Valerie's eyebrows raise slightly. 'Yeah?'

'Yeah. We've never really, um, hung out together properly, have we?' God, I'm already laying it on too thick and I've barely started. 'So I thought maybe now might be a good time?'

Valerie's cautious smile quirks a little. 'Yeah?' she says again. 'You want to spend the weekend with . . . me?'

She doesn't have to look *quite* so surprised, does she? It's not that unlikely. 'Yeah!' I say, injecting as much enthusiasm into my voice as possible. 'I was thinking I could come to York. You could . . . show me around, you know?'

There's a second when Valerie just looks at me, that same searching smile on her face, when I'm convinced that she's already seen right through me. But then a real smile blooms, expanding so much that it takes up most of her face. In fact, she looks so happy – genuinely, sweetly happy – that it makes me feel a bit bad for manipulating her.

'Eden, of *course*,' she says. 'That's an amazing idea! You can come back with me and I'll spend the weekend showing you the city. It's perfect. You've never visited, right? So there's loads to see. You can meet my friends, and I can take you to a bar that will let you in without ID.' She's already pulling out her phone and tapping at the screen with excited little jabs of her fingers. 'You can stay in my bed and I'll sleep on the sofa,' she's saying happily. 'I'll have to give my flatmates a heads-up, but they won't mind, people stay over all the time.'

Well, this was easier than I thought it would be. 'Brilliant!' I don't have to pretend that I'm excited; it's so genuine I actually clap my hands like a seal. 'We'll be away from Larking, and away from all the journalists and rumours and shit.' I drop down on to the carpet and throw myself at Valerie for a hug.

I'm not the huggy kind, you should know. I like to keep my affection selective – usually it's reserved for people like Daisy and Bonnie. And Connor, of course, though it's different with boyfriends. Valerie I've always kept at a bit of a distance, and she's always respected that. But now I've launched myself at her, my arms are around her neck, and even though it's all part of getting her to say yes, I also mean it.

'Aw,' Valerie murmurs into my hair, 'Eden.' She hugs me back, squeezing tight. 'Our own adventure!'

I'm beaming as we break apart. 'How soon can we go?'

She shrugs. 'Tomorrow morning, I guess?'

'Or!' I point my finger in the air. 'We could go, like . . . right now.'

Valerie's face drops. Her eyes squint a little at me. 'Right . . . now?'

'Or in an hour. Or even two hours. But I think we should go today.'

'Why?'

'Because I need to get away. As soon as possible.' I suddenly remember Connor. Shit, I really should have planned my pitch for this trip before I tried to speak to Valerie. 'And . . . hey, could Connor come?'

The look on Valerie's face is now completely unreadable. 'You want to bring Connor?'

'He's stressed out too.'

'You want to bring Connor on our trip where you want us to spend more time together? To my tiny little student house?'

'Yeah.'

We look at each other.

'Why?' she asks, when I don't offer anything else.

'He doesn't get much of a chance to go away,' I say, surprising myself with my quick thinking. 'What with his mum and everything. Just a quick trip like this would be perfect. And he's never been to York either.' I actually have no idea whether Connor has ever been to York. 'It just seems like a great opportunity.'

Valerie is silent for a while. She's watching me, hawkish, as if she's trying to read my mind. 'Eden,' she says finally, her voice soft. 'Eden, are you thinking that Bonnie might be somewhere near York? Are you trying to look for her?'

I shake my head quickly. I can't have Valerie connecting these dots before we've even left Larking. 'No, this isn't about that. I know she isn't in York.'

SHIT. I see the flash in Valerie's eyes and know she's clocked my use of the word 'know'. Shit, shit, shit.

'You do?' she asks, overly casually.

'The papers said,' I say. 'Right? They were in Wales, last anyone heard.'

'Right . . .' she says slowly. 'And so it's a total coincidence that you want to go to a random bit of the country, like, immediately?'

'Yes,' I say. 'And it's not random, is it? It's where you go to uni. It's not like I want you to take me to Wales.'

Valerie takes in a slow, thoughtful breath, her front teeth nibbling her bottom lip, her eyes never leaving me. 'Let me talk to Mum,' she says finally. 'See what she thinks about all this, OK?'

'OK,' I say, trying not to let on how frayed my nerves are getting. 'And if she says yes, when can we go?'

'*If* she says yes,' Valerie says, beginning to stand, 'then we'll pack our stuff and go.'

I want to hug her again, but I restrain myself. When she's left the room I pull out my phone and text Connor: **Stand by!**

18

Valerie is gone for a while, talking to Carolyn behind the closed door of her bedroom, so I don't know what she actually says to get the all-important yes, but she does, and that's all that matters. Carolyn doesn't even question me; doesn't raise her eyebrows at the coincidental timing of my trip proposal, doesn't ask me again whether I've heard anything from Bonnie.

What Carolyn does is pack us a 'car picnic'. She makes sure I pack pyjamas and a toothbrush. She fusses about what revision materials I'm taking with me. She tells me how wonderful it is that I want to spend time with Valerie.

I try very, very hard not to feel guilty.

As promised, we don't hang around once the decision has been made about going, but I have a free half an hour while Valerie drives to the library to drop off some of the books she'd been using to revise with while she was here. I use the time to try and get a more exact location from Bonnie, but it's not really very successful.

Me

Where are you staying atm?

Ivy

This tiny house at the end of a terrace.
It's like a sub-sub-let, so totally secret ☺

AND CHEAP! Like, peanuts cheap. The living room window is all boarded up and it's a bit bare iykwim. I still love it, though!

Ivy

And omg, there's a cat cafe down the road and it's called the HOUSE of the CAT KINGS. CAT KINGS! How cute is that?

Me

Um, pretty cute?

Haven't gone in yet, just in case. But Jack says we can *just before we leave*. So we'll be leaving anyway if they recognize us and snitch.

Are you planning on leaving already???

Not right now. Probs in a few days. It's a good place to hide – no one pays any attention to us around here. We're going to lay low until it blows over.

Yeah, good idea. Stay for a few days, at least.

I'm nervous about pushing too hard for an address, so I decide to wait and speak to Connor before I try again. And anyway, Valerie is calling up the stairs that she's ready to go, so I sling my weekend bag over my shoulder and head downstairs.

'Drive safe and keep me updated,' Carolyn says to Valerie. They're standing in the open doorway, Valerie swinging her keys between her fingers. When I approach, Carolyn smiles, reaching to touch my face. 'Have a good trip, OK?'

It's just after three when we set off, which is good because we should get pretty far before rush hour hits. All in all, we should be in York by eight. It probably won't even be dark yet.

But still, I'm fidgety and nervous as we pull up outside Connor's house and watch him come jogging down the driveway with a holdall in one hand and a bottle of water in the other. So many things could still go wrong. It would be just my luck if there was a huge traffic jam on the A1 and we got stuck for hours or, worse, had to turn around and come home again.

'Hey, Valerie,' Connor says as he climbs into the back seat. 'Thanks for letting me tag along.'

'No worries,' Valerie says. 'The more the merrier, right?'

I look sharply at her. *Sarcasm?* Her smile is so innocent. No way. Valerie McKinley doesn't do sarcasm. Does she?

Connor leans forward to drop a kiss on my cheek as Valerie puts the car back into gear and eases off down the road. 'Hey,' he says. 'I checked the traffic reports for the whole journey. It's all clear to York.'

I turn my head so he can see my grin. Connor is the best. The actual perfect best. I don't say this out loud because Valerie is sitting right there, but I'm pretty sure he gets it anyway because he wiggles his nose at me as he sits back down and puts on his seatbelt. It's adorable.

My phone buzzes as we turn on to the main road out of Larking, and I open the message to see a ton of exclamation marks and a lot of sad-face emojis. Daisy.

'Daisy's upset we've gone without her,' I say to Valerie, unable to keep the affectionate smile off my face as I send back hugs and a promise that she can come next time.

'Aw,' Valerie says. 'Poor Daze. I guess she's not used to being left out of sister stuff.'

I glance at her, but she's smiling, so I decide that her words weren't the dig they sounded like. 'Daisy doesn't like to be left out of anything,' I say.

'Tell her we'll bring her back a York hoodie, or something,' Connor suggests from the back seat.

If everything goes to plan, the only thing I'll be bringing back from this trip is Bonnie, but I grin and nod anyway. Who knows, maybe we'll have time to actually visit Valerie's uni, and we really can buy a present for my little sister.

'This is pretty exciting,' Valerie says with a smile. 'It'll be so great to show you the university, Eden.' She pauses. 'And you, Connor.'

'Great!' Connor says cheerfully. 'And there's a castle too, right?'

I glance over my shoulder and give him a look, trying to remind him telepathically that we're not actually going to spend much time in York, but he just grins at me.

'Yeah,' Valerie says. 'There's a lot of that kind of thing in York, if that's what you're into. There are old city walls that we can walk along, if you like?'

'Great!' he says again. 'What made you choose York for uni?'

I stop listening, settling back against my seat to watch the road signs pass as we gradually leave Larking, and then Kent, behind.

We stop for petrol at an Esso garage not long after we leave, which turns out to be more about refuelling Valerie – with coffee – than the car. We hit some traffic when we first join the A1, but apart from that the first couple of hours are smooth sailing. Valerie and Connor chat about A levels and university and what kind of careers Connor can go into that involve birds. I don't contribute much, just watch the road and think about Bonnie. Specifically, her address. A random end-of-terrace in Glasgow doesn't seem like much to go on, even with a cat cafe nearby. But I can't exactly speak to her or ask Connor for help while we're sitting in the car next to Valerie, so I try to put it out of my mind for now. There'll be a way to get the address somehow.

The next time we stop to stretch our legs it's just after five and we're right on schedule. Valerie finds a space in the car park so we can get out of the car for a few minutes and remember what fresh air smells like. I hop a little on my feet outside of the car, winding my arms around my shoulders.

'Are you hungry?' Valerie asks, glancing up at me. She's sitting sideways in the driver's seat with the door open, feet on the concrete as she fiddles with the satnav, a little frown of concentration on her face.

'Not massively,' I say. 'Are you?'

'No, but I'm trying to figure out if it's better to eat now or wait until we get to York. We'll probably get there about eight. Is that too late? We could grab some pizza or something.'

'Sounds fine to me,' I say, shrugging. I'm finding it hard to care about food, partly because of Carolyn's car picnic, but mostly because my stomach has been keeping up its low-level churning of anxiety since we left Larking. 'Connor?'

'I can wait,' he says.

'Cool, we'll wait till we get there, then,' Valerie says. 'I'm just going to run in and grab a drink. Back in a sec.'

I watch her jog off towards the shop, then turn to Connor. 'Hey,' I say. 'How can I get Bonnie's address without outright asking her?'

He looks up from his own phone. 'You don't already have it?'

I shake my head, feeling heat rise in my cheeks. It's not that much of a problem, is it? There'll be a way to get it.

'How come you *can't* just ask her?'

'She'd get suspicious, wouldn't she? What if they leave Glasgow and don't tell me where they've gone?'

He looks at me for a long moment, and for a second I think he might actually be annoyed with me. 'Eeds, did you not think about this *before* we left on the cross-country trip?'

'There was a lot to think about!' I say, instantly defensive. 'You know, logistics and stuff.'

'The address *is* logistics,' Connor says. 'Do you know anything specific about where they are? Anything at all?'

'There's a cat cafe on the same road.'

Connor's eyebrows go up. 'She's a literal runaway, you're the only one who knows where she is, and she told you about a *cat cafe* and nothing else?'

'Yeah, she thought it was cute. It's called House of the Cat Kings.'

'Girls,' he mutters.

'What was that?'

'Valerie's coming,' he says. 'I'll look it up and see if it's easy to figure it out from there.'

I look up to see Valerie stepping out of the shop and heading towards us, a takeaway cup of coffee in her hand.

'You drink a lot of coffee,' I say when she reaches us.

'Is that a problem?' she asks, opening her door and sliding inside.

'Just an observation,' I say, getting into the car.

Valerie rolls her eyes a little. 'Right.' She fumbles with the gearstick and glances in the rear-view mirror as she pulls out of the parking space.

'What is this music?' I ask once we're back on the motorway.

'It's Christine and the Queens,' she says, smiling in that way people automatically do when they talk about music they like. 'Isn't it great?'

'Why is it in French?'

'Because . . . she's French?' She glances at my annoyed expression and laughs. 'I like to listen to French music because it helps me keep up with the language now I'm not learning it in school any more. Besides, this is a mix of English and French lyrics. Just listen to it, it's good. Promise.'

See, this is why Valerie and me aren't close. This exact thing. I can barely count to ten in French, and she chooses to listen to French music. 'Whatever,' I say.

And then she starts singing along. In French.

'Oh, my God,' I say. 'Can you just not?'

From the back seat, I can hear Connor laughing, as if Valerie is doing this to be funny instead of trying to wind me up.

'*Détendez-vous, mon petit choufleur*,' she says.

'Show-off,' I mutter.

'Cheer up, grumpy,' she says. 'We're away from Kent, just like you wanted. Can't you be a bit happier?'

I shrug and look out of the window, the countryside zipping by. Nearly three more hours of this to go.

'Look, we don't have to listen to music,' Valerie says. 'We can just talk instead, can't we?' There's a pause, which I know I'm meant to fill, but I just carry on looking out of the window. Finally, she says, 'Hey, Connor, how did you find your exams this week?'

I try not to sigh too loudly as he begins to answer. The last thing I want to talk about is exams and Kett Academy. The whole 'I need a break from Kent' thing might have been a ruse to get Valerie to agree to drive us, but that doesn't mean it's not a bit true as well. I run my fingers along the sides of my phone, wondering whether I should message Bonnie, or whether that would be a terrible idea. I don't even know if she'll be happy to see me. What if she thinks I'm just there to spoil the party? I mean, I kind of am trying to spoil the party. But in a good way, in the long run.

'What are you thinking about?' Valerie asks.

'Bonnie,' I say, then regret it.

'That makes sense,' she says, with a kind of sympathetic tone that annoys me. 'Maybe she was on this exact road. Did they ever figure out how they've been getting around since they left their car at Portsmouth?'

'They probably just paid cash for a cheap one,' I say, then regret it, worrying I've given too much away, but Valerie is nodding.

'Yeah, they must've,' she says. She lets out a disbelieving kind of laugh. 'God, it's so crazy. Your little friend Bonnie, you know? Doing something so . . . wild.'

'It's not that crazy,' I say, which is stupid, because it *is* that crazy. But the last conversation I want to have right now is the same old 'But Bonnie's so good!' one I've been hearing all week.

'Sure it is,' she says easily. 'One of my friends at uni was actually talking to me about it on Sunday, not knowing that I know Bonnie, and she was saying how she had a thing with one of her teachers, but after she'd left school. She says she's glad he never tried it on when she was younger, because she'd probably have thought it was a great idea, and that would have been a disaster.'

'Why? If she ended up getting with him anyway?'

'Because there's a huge difference between getting with your actual teacher and getting with an adult who used to be your teacher when you, yourself, are also an adult.'

'Why? How much difference does a year or two really make?'

'Depends. Are you talking morally, ethically or legally?' The voice she uses to say this is like a cheese grater to my nerves. And then she glances at me and says, 'You don't actually think what Bonnie's doing is a good thing, do you?'

Of course I don't, but I don't want to agree with her more. 'We can't all be perfect,' I mutter.

I practically feel her bristle at the words. 'What's that supposed to mean?' she asks.

'Just that you don't have to rub it in,' I say. From behind me, I hear Connor give a nervous little rustle in his seat.

'How am I rubbing anything in? I'm talking about Bonnie, not you. Why do you have to take everything so personally?'

'Bonnie's like a part of me,' I say, which doesn't really make much sense when I hear it out loud, but whatever. 'So you are kind of saying it about me.'

'What are you even talking about?' And then she lets out a small laugh, like I'm just oh-so-hilarious, and it pushes me over the edge.

'Oh, just stop it, OK?' I snap. 'Just stop. You just don't *get* it, and you never will, so just *stop*.'

'Get what? What don't I get?'

'Screwing up!'

'You think I don't get . . . screwing up?'

'Everything's always gone right for you.'

Valerie lets out the short, sharp bark of an *as-if* laugh. 'What the fuck does that mean?'

'That your life is all clean and neat,' I say, the words spilling out like they've been just waiting there all this time. 'You don't know what it's like for things to be messy and fucked-up and hard.'

'You think my life has just been plain sailing?' There's disbelief in her voice. 'Is that seriously what you're saying to me?'

'You've never done anything *wrong*!' I burst out. 'God, did you ever even get a detention in school? Did you ever get caught bunking off? Did you ever even get a *C*?'

I glance at Valerie to see that her jaw is tense, her eyes fixed on the road. She shakes her head slightly, like she can't believe what she's hearing.

'Even your first *break-up* was like some kind of feminist powerhouse move,' I say. 'Deciding you were better on your own, breaking up with your boyfriend, and then travelling by yourself. *God*. Has anything *ever* even gone wrong for you?'

'Oh, come on, Eden,' she snaps. 'Don't be so naïve.'

'What?' I demand. I'm so ready for a fight.

'That boyfriend you're talking about? He cheated on me.'

'He what?'

'He cheated on me. In Thailand. I went back to the hotel with a headache, and he ended up getting off with some American tourist in a bar. And then on the beach.' She looks at me as if she thinks I might not get what she means, and then adds, entirely unnecessarily, 'I don't mean just kissing "getting off". I mean they had sex.'

I open my mouth, but nothing comes out.

'Her name was *Lou-Ann*,' she adds, wrinkling her nose. I've never seen such an ugly look on her face before.

'But you *said* . . .' I try. 'You said you realized you were better on your own.'

'I said that to save face. I didn't want my little sister knowing I was so undesirable my boyfriend cheated at the first opportunity. Of course I didn't tell you – why *would* I? You want to know how awful it was, having to decide about travelling on my own? Telling Mum and Dad? You want to know how completely heartbroken I was?'

I try to picture this, but I can't. Valerie, broken-hearted and helpless, alone in a hotel room in Thailand. Yelling at her cheating boyfriend, throwing his clothes across the room in a rage. She's *Valerie*. She has a cool head at all times. A solution for everything.

'You already think I'm the most boring person alive,' she adds, smacking her hand against the indicator far harder than necessary and then changing lanes. 'I didn't want you thinking I was pathetic as well.'

'I don't think you're the most boring person alive,' I protest, but a little meekly, because even though it's not true, I know why she thinks it is. And that's pretty horrible, isn't it?

'And actually, you know what?' she continues, talking right over me. 'You want some more proof that I'm not as weirdly perfect as you seem to think I am? OK, fine. I actually find plants really boring. I always have, and I give away the orchid Dad gets me for my birthday every year to my housemates so I don't have to take care of it. I walk past homeless people and try to pretend I don't see them, even though that's a shitty thing to do, and I know it is. I never stick to my skincare regime, even though I spent loads of money on the stupid expensive night moisturizer. Sometimes I just can't be bothered to recycle, so I chuck everything in the bin. Last year I slept with my housemate's boyfriend.'

'Valerie!' I gasp, unable to stop myself.

'I tell myself that I was really drunk, but I actually wasn't that drunk and they're still together and I never told a single person it happened.'

From the back seat, Connor lets out a loud, unsubtle cough, like he's hoping Valerie will remember he's there and stop all this over-sharing.

'There,' Valerie says. She's breathing hard, her hands tight to the wheel, eyes fixed on the road. 'Has that done it? Do you still think I'm perfect, Eden?'

I don't know what to think, let alone say. I just sit there in silence, twisting my hands together, staring at my fingernails.

'No?' she prompts. 'Nothing to say? No comeback?'

Again, she waits for me to reply, but I don't know how. I hear Connor shift again in his seat. The car trundles on.

'Look,' Valerie says, her voice softer. 'What I'm trying to say is, you can't be so distant from me, and act like you don't have any interest in who I am or what my life is, and instead judge me on whatever it is you're making up in your own head.'

I open my mouth, lick my lips, swallow and say nothing.

'Maybe you don't see people as well as you think you do,' she says. 'Maybe you should stop thinking your impression is the right one, just because it's yours. People won't always tell you everything.'

I hadn't realized I thought they did.

'And that goes for Bonnie, too,' she adds. 'In case that comparison wasn't obvious.'

'This isn't anything to do with Bonnie,' I say, finding my voice again.

'Of course it is. She pulls this shock move on everyone, and you're still talking like you know her so well, when clearly you don't. I know that must be hard to take, but it's true. She obviously had her reasons for doing what she did, and because you don't understand what those reasons are, you're pretending they don't exist.'

'That's not what I'm doing.'

'No?' Her voice is a drawl. '*Really?*'

'*Stop talking to me like that!*' I almost shout the words, the fire that had eased off inside me flaring right back up again. Her patronizing disbelief is fanning my rage like fireplace bellows. 'You don't get to call *me* judgemental and then talk to me like you know me so well and I'm just so *stupid*.'

From behind me, I hear a muffled, slightly panicked, 'Oh *God*.' Poor Connor.

'I'm just saying—' Valerie begins.

'Well, *stop* saying. You don't know Bonnie, and you don't know me.'

'*You* stop saying *that*,' she throws back. 'I'm your *sister*. Stop acting like that doesn't matter to you; it's fucking *devastating*, don't you get that? It *hurts*.'

I falter. 'Of course that matters to me.'

'Like fuck it does.' Her breathing is a little ragged, her fingers drumming in agitated patterns against the steering wheel.

There's a long, horribly awkward silence.

OK, it's not like I didn't know that Valerie and I had a fair amount of emotional baggage to unpack between us, but did we have to start digging into it *now*? In the middle of the motorway? But now we've started, I don't know how to stop, how to push everything back into its case and lock it up for a more appropriate time.

'I always wanted a sister, did you know that?' Her voice is thick and tight, like she might start crying, and I hope she doesn't because I don't know what I'd do. 'I was so, so happy when you and Daisy came to live with us. But that's the thing – it was already and always you and Daisy. You were the sisters. I wanted to be a big sister to you, but it felt like you didn't want me to be. You never let me try.'

I shake my head. 'Me and Daisy are different. It's just different. You can't understand.'

'I can try, though. Why won't you let me? Daisy does.'

Until she was five, Daisy slept in my bed every night of her life. There are sisters, and then there's Daisy and me. 'Daisy's young. She doesn't remember stuff like I do.'

'*I* remember,' she says. 'I remember the day you arrived. I got home from school and Mum said, "We'll be having two guests joining us this evening. They might be staying with us for a while." That's what she always called the kids we fostered. Guests. And when you came through the door you were wearing this raggedy blue dress with a button missing and your hair was all tangled and I told you my name was Valerie and you scowled at me and said, "That's an old woman's name," and Dad *laughed* and said, "Yes, yes it is. Valerie's an old soul."'

I don't even remember that. Which is weird, because I thought every detail of that time was lasered into my brain. I never thought about Valerie then, not really. It was all about making sure Daisy was OK, and learning what Carolyn and Bob expected in their home, and a new school and new friends and my social worker, Marisa. Valerie was always just . . . there.

'We don't have to be like you and Daisy to have a relationship,' Valerie says. 'The only thing stopping that happening is you and your bullheadedness.'

'Can I say something?' Connor's voice comes from the back

seat, and both Valerie and I jerk in surprise, like we'd forgotten he was there.

'Go ahead,' Valerie says.

He's going to say something monumental, isn't he? Connor's an observer, and he's touched on something profound that Valerie and I just can't see because we're too—

'I need to pee,' he says.

19

We stop at the first motorway service station we find, having driven in total silence for the ten minutes it took us to get there. Connor disappears into the toilets while Valerie and I go to the coffee shop and find a table.

It's Valerie who breaks the silence. 'Sorry,' she says. 'About all that in the car.'

'That's OK,' I say. What I mean is that the person who should apologize is me, because as usual I was the one lighting all the fires and then acting surprised when they blew up in my face.

'I don't want to fight with you,' she says. She sounds tired.

'I don't want that either,' I mutter, keeping my gaze on the table so I don't have to look at her.

'Eden . . .' She hesitates. 'Should I just stop trying? Tell me.'

Just this morning, I think I would have said yes to this. I probably wouldn't even have given it much thought. But now . . . 'yes' doesn't feel right.

I tip some sugar on to the table and swirl my finger in it, stalling. 'I don't know why you do,' I say eventually.

'Try?'

'Yeah.'

'I told you,' she says. 'I always wanted a sister.'

For some reason, my throat kind of closes up at these words. I press my fingertip against the sugar crystals and feel them dent my skin.

'Shall I get the coffees in?' Connor's voice sounds from beside me, and I look up in surprise. He smiles at me. 'Or hot chocolate, or whatever.'

'A coffee would be great,' Valerie says. 'Thanks, Connor.' He walks off in the direction of the counter, hands in his back pockets, and she turns back to me, a cautious smile on her face. 'Connor's such a sweetheart.'

I smile back, because this is easy. 'Yeah, he is.'

'I've never really got the chance to even speak to him much before. He's not like most sixteen-year-old boys.'

'Nope,' I say, proud. 'He's special.'

'How long have you guys been together now?'

'Over a year.'

She smiles again. 'Are you guys in it for the long haul?'

'Oh yeah,' I say, nodding. 'We've got it all planned.'

'Yeah?'

I can tell that she's sceptical but trying not to show it, her mouth twitching with the I'm-so-much-older-and-you're-just-a-teenager smirk that is so endlessly annoying. But I mean it about Connor and me. We have everything going for us to be together forever, and who really cares if that's unrealistic or idealistic or whatever '-istic' word it is adults use when what they mean is 'cute but wrong'. I said once that Bonnie's like the light in my life, and that's true, but Connor is like the earth. Constant. Permanent. Safe. And we're going to have the perfect life. I'm going to be a landscape designer, maybe even taking on Carolyn and Bob's business one day. Connor is going to be an ornithologist, probably working for the RSPB. We'll live somewhere near the Downs – either the ones in Kent or in Sussex, we're not fussy – or near the woods, anywhere there's nature on our doorstep. We'll take holidays to faraway places with the coolest native birds and flowers. South America, for the quetzal bird. Japan, for the gardens and the cherry blossom.

'It's just right with him and me,' I say.

'That's so nice,' she says, and I can tell she means that bit, even if she doesn't believe we'll actually be together forever. 'Especially as the two of you are so different.'

'We're not,' I say. 'Not really. It just looks like we are, from the outside. But we both want the same things, and that's what's most important.'

'Like what?'

I paraphrase the chunk of my thoughts. 'An outdoorsy life. As little drama as possible.'

Valerie laughs. 'How's that working out for you right now?'

A reluctant smile twitches on my face. 'Yeah, yeah. Who'd have thought Bonnie'd be the one who'd bring the drama?'

'You never had any idea she was secretly like this?'

'Not a runaway-in-waiting, no.' I hesitate, then offer a little more. 'That's part of why we were friends, I thought. The no-drama bit. That's why I love her so much. She's steady.'

'That works both ways, though, doesn't it?' As she speaks, Connor slides on to the seat beside me, pushing a tray of takeaway cups across the table. 'That was quick. Thanks, Connor.'

'No queue.' He takes one of the cups and puts it in front of me. 'What works both ways?'

'Eden was just saying that she loves how steady Bonnie is. And I was thinking, well . . .' She turns back to me. 'If you chose her because she's steady, it stands to reason that she chose you because you're . . .' She makes a face. 'Er . . .'

'Not steady?' I suggest.

She looks relieved. 'Yeah. Exactly. She's not friends with you by accident. She obviously likes a bit of edge, you know?'

'Do I have edge?

'Eden, you're all edges.'

Connor chokes on whatever it is he's drinking, and then laughs, shaking his head and nodding at the same time.

'Right?' Valerie says to him, encouraged.

'Is that a good thing?' I ask, unsure whether I'm offended or not.

'Yes,' Connor says, at the same time Valerie says, 'Sometimes.'

'Well, anyway,' I say, hoping to steer the conversation safely away from me again. 'Bonnie's obviously not as steady as I thought.'

'Even steady people have rocky moments,' Valerie says. 'Life's hard for everyone.' She takes a sip from her cup and taps her phone. 'Do you guys mind if we head off again soon? I really want to get to York before it gets dark.'

I'm very aware that we never finished our original conversation, and I never told her that I don't want her to stop trying, but I don't know how to bring it up again, or even whether I should. But she and Connor are standing up, she's gathering her bag and pulling it over her shoulder; the moment is long gone.

We head back out into the car park together, Connor twining his fingers through mine, and Valerie looking at her phone. The silence stretches heavy and awkward. We're halfway to the car when Connor stops suddenly. 'Oh no,' he says, a little too loudly. 'I forgot a toothbrush. Is it OK if I just run back in and get one?'

Valerie shrugs. 'Sure.'

He runs off back towards the main building, leaving Valerie and me alone, and it occurs to me that he's done that three times since we got out of the car, and that he's probably doing it on purpose.

When we reach the car Valerie leans back against the bonnet, sipping from her cup. It's sunny and warm, so I sit down on the concrete, closing my eyes and allowing myself a deep breath in and out.

After a few minutes, Valerie speaks into the quiet. 'Eeds, how come Connor's here?'

'Because I wanted him to come,' I say, opening my eyes. What other answer is there? 'Why?'

'I was just telling my friend that I'm heading back up to York,' she says, waving her phone as evidence. 'And she was like, "Vee, they've obviously suckered you into being their chauffeur on some teenage shag weekend."'

I should probably find this offensive, but something about the way Valerie relays this message, plus the idea of Connor and me having any kind of a 'shag weekend', makes me crack up. 'No,' I manage, trying to gather myself. 'That's not why he's here.'

Valerie throws me a sideways grin. 'No? You sure?'

'Totally sure.' I shake my head, picking up a stray pebble and bouncing it against the ground.

'I mean, I'd understand,' she says. 'There aren't that many opportunities for . . . *alone time* when you're sixteen.'

As she talks, I register that the friend called her *Vee*. I'd thought she was Valerie to everyone. Vee sounds so much friendlier, so much more fun. I look at her, leaning against her car bonnet, clasping her cup of coffee between her hands.

'We haven't,' I say.

She looks at me. 'Haven't?'

'Had sex,' I say. This is the kind of thing sisters tell each other, isn't it? This is how I should talk to my big sister.

'Oh,' she says.

I smile. 'You're surprised?'

'No!' she says, too quickly, then reconsiders. 'Well, yeah.' She smiles hopefully at me, an *Is this OK?* kind of smile, and I smile back. 'I just thought, you know, you've been together for a long time.'

'We sort-of-almost did,' I say. 'Right at the beginning. But it was because we thought we should, you know? And it . . . wasn't great. So we agreed to wait until we were ready, and that just hasn't happened yet.' This is, by far, the most personal information I've ever given Valerie.

'That's so mature,' she says.

'You're surprised?' I ask again.

'A little,' she admits. 'Sorry.'

I shrug. 'That's OK.'

'Not because of you,' she adds. 'Because you're sixteen. I wouldn't have been that mature when I was sixteen.'

I want to ask her about this – the Valerie at sixteen that I remember was the essence of 'mature' – but Connor is walking across the car park towards us, and so the conversation has to end.

'Thanks,' Valerie says as she slides off the bonnet and takes a final gulp from her coffee cup.

I don't need to ask for what. In fact, I don't actually need to say anything. I just nod, pull myself up off the concrete and get back into the car.

We arrive in York not long after eight. Valerie is quiet as she drives us slowly through the evening traffic to the student house she lives in, her elbow resting on the window frame, chin in her hand. Even after our mini Connor-related heart-to-heart, she's probably thinking that this whole thing is a mistake, that she's got three more days of this, that I'm the worst sister ever. And I haven't even told her about Glasgow yet.

I feel like I should say something to warm everything up a bit, but I don't know what. Connor is silent too, apart from the occasional self-conscious clearing of his throat. Basically, it's all very awkward.

'Here we are,' Valerie says finally. We've pulled up outside an unremarkable terraced house on an unremarkable street. There's a gnome smoking a pipe outside the door, a campaign poster for the Green Party in the front window.

'It's nice,' I say, and she looks at me like she thinks I'm being sarcastic. 'Um. Are your housemates in?'

'No, not right now. Emma's pulling an all-nighter at the library. Chlo's at home this week. She says it's easier to revise there and she only lives in Hull. Neesh is at work, but she might be back later, unless she goes to her boyfriend's house. Come on.' She unbuckles her seatbelt and opens her door without looking at me, as if she's sensed that I'm wondering if Neesh's boyfriend is the one she slept with and wants to avoid that conversation.

I glance back at Connor, who smiles at me. 'All good?' he asks. Thank God he's here.

'Ish,' I say.

We get out of the car and follow Valerie to the front door, which she's lifting her key to open. 'I'll show you the—' she begins, but she's interrupted by the door swinging open and a tall, beaming figure who comes bounding over the threshold.

'Hi!' the figure says, stopping in front of me. She radiates cheerfulness, which after the stifling quiet of the car feels like actual sunshine. 'Vee! Is this Eden?!'

Vee. 'Yeah,' Valerie says. 'What are you—'

'It's so great to meet you!' the figure interrupts, sticking out her hand for me to shake. I do, a bit dazedly. 'I'm Emma. And you're Connor, right? Hi!'

'What happened to the library?' Valerie asks, sweeping her hair back from her face.

'I took a break,' Emma says. 'I wanted to meet the famous Eden.' She grins at me. 'I couldn't believe it when Vee said you were visiting! After three years! And with all that shit happening with your friend!'

'Um,' I say.

'Did Vee tell you I shagged my teacher once?'

We're all still standing outside the front door. At these words, Connor coughs.

'Uh . . .'

'I was nineteen. Home for Christmas. Saw him in a club on New Year's. I'd always fancied him, so I was like, go for it, Emma!'

'Emma—' Valerie says.

'And let me tell you, it's one of those things where you don't realize what a shit idea it is until you do it. The guy was in his thirties! And he had such a tiny knob.' She cackles, eyes dancing, and I can't help it – I laugh right along with her. I look over at Connor, whose face is bright red. 'Anyway, you live, you learn, right? Do you have any bags? I'll help you bring them in. Vee! We had a party while you were gone. You missed Badger falling down the stairs! He's fine, though. Just a couple of stitches and he says the scar will make him cooler.'

'Stitches?' Valerie repeats, looking alarmed.

'Just a couple, don't worry,' Emma says, throwing back a smile, and I realize two things. One, that even when she's Vee, Valerie is the responsible one who worries, but that Emma genuinely likes this about her. Two, that 'Badger' is Emma's boyfriend, and that he's the one Valerie slept with. There's just something in both their voices that gives it away to me, and then Valerie glances involuntarily at me, and I know for sure. 'Where are you all sleeping?' Emma asks, leading the way into the house. 'I'm doing an all-nighter and then going straight to Badger's, so one of you can have my bed, if you want?'

'Would you mind?' Valerie asks. 'I can take it, then Eden can have my bed, and Connor can sleep on the sofa.'

She can't seriously think Connor will actually be sleeping on the sofa if I'm in an empty bed just down the hall. Does she think that just because I told her we haven't had sex yet that we wouldn't want to share a bed?

Emma snorts, clearly thinking the same thing. 'Sleep on the sofa. Sure.'

Valerie rolls her eyes at her, but it's affectionate. 'I was going for plausible deniability. Don't you have somewhere to be?'

Emma sighs. 'Yes. Woe.' She picks up her bag from where it's been resting by the door. 'Hey, Vee?' Valerie turns and Emma grins. 'I missed you. Glad you're back.' She opens her arms and Valerie steps immediately into them, the two of them sharing a quick, tight girl-hug. I think of hugging Bonnie, the quick hugs and the silly hugs and the crying hugs. So many hugs. I miss her so goddamn much.

'Right!' Emma says, swinging her bag up over her shoulder. 'I better go. But I'm going to take a break tomorrow night so I can hang out with you guys. We can go to The Bell! They won't try and ID you or anything.' This girl is a *talker*. 'You can tell me all about your runaway friend and the dodgy teacher. And what you think of York. And what it's like being Vee's little sister. I mean real little sister. We all feel like her little sisters, even though we're all the same age here.' She laughs, light and happy, tucking her hair behind her ears as she speaks. 'OK, I really have to go. Have fun! See you later!' And she finally leaves.

There's a long pause. 'Well,' Connor says. 'She's chatty.'

'Yeah,' Valerie says. She doesn't elaborate. 'Let me show you the rest of the house, and then I'll go and get us a pizza.'

It doesn't take long, because the house is pretty small. The living room and kitchen are all on the ground floor along with Valerie's bedroom, and the three other bedrooms and bathroom are all on the first. When we're done, Connor disappears off into the bathroom, leaving Valerie and me standing in the living room, our eyes almost meeting but not quite, awkward in the silence.

'Look,' Valerie says eventually. 'There's a lot going on here, obviously. And I'm just too bloody tired to try and deal with it all now. So can we just . . . not?'

I look at her. 'Not?'

'Just for now.' She gives a drained little smile. 'Let me go out and get us some food. I'll bring it back, we'll stay up and chat about bullshit, nothing heavy. We'll put all this –' she gestures vaguely around us – 'on pause. OK?'

'OK,' I say.

Valerie dips her head a little, forcing me to meet her gaze. 'Happy?'

I nod. 'Happy.'

Valerie is gone for almost an hour. Connor falls asleep on the sofa in front of old episodes of *The Big Bang Theory*, and I try out the shower. When I come back into the living room, wearing the clothes I'd brought to sleep in and with a towel wrapped around my head, Connor is sitting up, looking on his phone.

'Any news?' I ask.

He shakes his head. 'Not really. Mr Cohn's dad has done a press conference, asking him to send Bonnie home. Poor guy. He looks wrecked.'

The front door opens and we both turn to see Valerie holding a pizza box and a plastic bag. 'God,' she says, coming into the living room and sinking straight down on to the floor. 'I'm exhausted.'

'You were gone for ages,' I say.

'I went to the supermarket for some wine –' she holds up the bag and I hear the distinctive clinking sound coming from within – 'and then the first pizza place I went to was closed.' She rolls her eyes at me. 'Sorry to keep you waiting.'

'Thanks, Valerie,' Connor says.

'Well, thank you, Connor,' Valerie says, raising her eyebrows significantly at me.

'Thank you,' I say, a little meekly. 'And thanks for driving us, too.'

She shrugs. 'Help yourself to the pizza. I just got plain cheese, so that better be OK. Can you grab some wine glasses? There should be some in the cupboard.'

Connor is already standing and moving over to the kitchen. 'Um, do you mean the wine glasses that are in the sink?'

Valerie makes a face. 'Are they clean?' she asks hopefully.

'Uh . . . no.'

'Great,' she mutters. 'Fine, whatever. Any drinking receptacle will do.'

Connor comes back holding what looks like plastic children's cups. 'Er . . . even these?'

Valerie rolls her eyes. 'Oh my God, is that really all that's left? You wouldn't think it would be so hard for a bunch of actual adults to do some washing-up, would you?' She lets out a loud sigh and reaches out a hand to take the cups from him. 'They'll have to do.' She opens the bottle and pours out three cups of wine. 'I'm capping you both at two cups each,' she says, giving me a mock-stern look.

'But these cups are tiny,' I protest. 'It's basically a shot!'

'Fine. Three cups each.' Valerie lifts her cup to her lips, takes a swig and then looks back at it, frowning. 'Four,' she amends.

I end up drinking six; Connor – not much of a drinker – has three. I have no idea how many Valerie gets through, but by midnight both bottles are empty and she's dancing around the room, singing something from *Cabaret*. She is loose-limbed and relaxed in a way I've never seen before. After what she'd said in the car about me not knowing her like I thought I did, I'm noticing things about her I never have before. Like how thin she actually is. Who is this person, my sister, really?

As agreed, we've talked about nothing heavy all night. This is good because there haven't been any more tears or minor breakdowns, no shouting or swearing, but it's also bad because I haven't been able to bring up the tiny matter of us needing to go to Scotland tomorrow. And I have no idea how to do that. Like, literally no clue. To be honest, the thought of having to tell Valerie the truth is giving me heart palpitations, so I just . . . haven't.

She's going to say no, isn't she? She's just going to see right through me and shoot me down. Send me straight home and tell everyone what a deceitful, ungrateful liar I am.

Maybe I should tell her *now*, while she's drunk. Yeah, that's what I should do. What could go wrong?

'Valerie?'

Valerie spins around to face me from where she's standing by the window, stumbling a little on her foot. '*Oui?*' she says.

'We should probably go to bed,' Connor says loudly. I glare at him and he gives me a look that says, *I know what you're going to do, and no.*

'Yes. Right. Yeah. Bed.' Valerie nods a little, swaying to whatever music is playing in her head. '*Oui. Je vais aller au lit.*' She gathers her loose hair into a ponytail, then drops it again, stretching out her arms and then dancing across the room towards the bathroom. 'I'm going to wash my f-a-a-a-ace.' She sings this last word, loud and elongated, before disappearing through the bathroom door.

Connor looks at me. 'Wow.'

'Yeah,' I say, shrugging helplessly. 'I guess this is Valerie on wine?'

'Valerie on wine after a long day of driving and arguing,' Connor replies. He scoots across the carpet so he's next to me.

'Oh God, don't bring that up,' I say, shaking my head. 'Sorry you had to . . . you know. Be there.'

'It was quite intense.' He makes a wincing face, then adds, 'And she doesn't even know about—'

I put my hand out to shush him just as Valerie comes parading out of the bathroom, barefoot and with moisturizer blobs on her face, holding a toothbrush. 'You guys heard me earlier about the bed situation, right? I'll be in Emma's bed, but you guys . . .' She wiggles her finger at us. 'Bed and sofa. Separately.' Out of the corner of my eye, I see Connor's whole face go bright red. And then Valerie adds, grandly, 'No hanky-panky on my watch.'

I wait until she's gone back into the bathroom before I risk speaking. 'I was going to tell her about Scotland about two minutes ago, but you ruined it.'

'You can't tell her now!' Connor retorts, his voice hushed like mine, cheeks still flaming. 'Not when she's drunk. You don't know how she'll react.'

'She's not *drunk*,' I say. 'She's just a bit . . . merry.'

'She just used the word "hanky-panky". She's definitely drunk. My gran wouldn't even say "hanky-panky".'

Valerie comes out of the bathroom again, her face scrubbed clean. 'Bedtime, children,' she says, dancing over to the stairs and then gliding – and I mean gliding – up them.

Connor looks at me.

'OK, fine, she's a bit drunk,' I say.

'It must be you,' he says. 'You pushed her over the edge. You broke Valerie.'

'Oh God,' I say, looking at the empty stairs. 'I did, didn't I? I'm . . .' I turn to him mid-sentence and then his mouth is on mine, his lips soft and familiar. I loosen against him, my tongue touching his as his hand moves up my body and cups the side of my face.

We lose ourselves to each other for a while, and at some point I realize we're both lying on the floor, tangled together, and that our kissing has reached the point of escalation where it's not enough, suddenly and all at once, to just be kissing. It's like we both realize it at the same moment because we break apart, breathing hard, and look at each other. His hand touches mine. I can feel his heart beating in the space between us. And I can feel . . . well, something else.

'Should we . . . um . . .' Connor's face is red, his voice breathy. He swallows. 'Do you want to go and lie down for a bit?'

I nod. 'Let me just . . .' My voice is crackly and I clear my throat, trying to steady it. I point at the stairs Valerie walked up who-knows-how-long ago. 'Um. Check.'

We both stand up and I creep up the stairs as silently as I can, leaving Connor staring after me. I push open the door that has *EMMA* written on it in pink chalk and poke my head around it. I can see Valerie lying on her side on the bed, clearly fast asleep. I close the door and pad back down the stairs, feeling a smile spread over my face as I look at Connor and nod the all-clear.

He takes my hand, his face a shiny, happy pink, and we walk across the living room together and into Valerie's bedroom. The wine has made me feel buzzy and warm, somehow more alive than usual. And there's electricity, too, in this room, between Connor and me, in his eyes and in his smile.

We lie down on the bed, curling together, his fingers sliding over my cheek and down to my chin as he leans in to kiss me.

Certain things happen when you're sixteen and you're lying on a bed with your boyfriend and you've had some wine and your sister is asleep in another room. I know it and Connor knows it, and the knowing it is all part of it.

The first and only time Connor and I sort-of-almost had sex was rushed and a bit frantic. We had about a half-hour window while his mother and gran were downstairs watching *Poldark*, for one thing. And the thing about first-time sex, at least if you believe in the whole virginity-loss as a thing and not just some stupid concept, is that it all becomes about it being over and done with; the thing being *lost*. There's no savouring or, God forbid, enjoying it.

But this time, everything is different. In the time since that sloppy anticlimax we've learned how to kiss and touch each other, and so we do, slowly, properly. When it comes to the moment, when our clothes are all off and the condom is on, I can tell that Connor is still a bit nervous, but for some reason I'm not. This is all right in every sense.

I take the lead and he lets me, the two of us together in the dark. I am simultaneously thinking *Why haven't we been doing this the whole time?* and *I'm so glad we waited until right this moment.* That is, until I stop thinking, and it's just him and me and heat and love for this absolute perfect moment that I can't quite believe is real, even when it's happening.

After, we lie on our backs, staring at the ceiling, quiet. I can hear him trying to slow his breathing to a normal speed. I'm thinking *hanky-panky*, and smiling in the dark. Finally he says, 'That was . . .' and I say, 'Yeah.'

Sometime later – I don't know how long because time seems looser somehow, less relevant – Connor has fallen asleep. I ease myself out from under the covers, dress and creep across the floor towards the door. The living room is still and quiet in the dark, the pizza box and empty cups on the floor where we'd left them. I tidy up on a kind of autopilot, savouring the silence and the being alone for the first time in twelve hours.

It occurs to me as I slosh water into the cups that I'm the closest I've been to Bonnie since she left. It's a weird thought. I could message her now, tell her about me and Connor. But how can I say just that bit and miss out all the rest, like the not-so-small fact that we're in York right now, on a mission to collect her? Maybe I *should* tell her exactly what I'm doing, let her know I'm on my way. I think about finding my phone and sending her a message: *Guess where I am!*

No. That's a bad idea. What if she tells Mr Cohn, and he gets spooked and they leave before I get there? What if she tells me not to come? Because that's what will happen, isn't it? She won't want me to come, no way. Turning up unannounced is really my only option.

And what about Valerie? How *am* I going to get her to drive us to Glasgow, of all places? Should I just tell her the truth? But the truth doesn't seem like any kind of an option, either. She'll just get right on the phone to the police, won't she? I'll be bundled into the car and driven back to Kent, and there'll be nothing I can do about it.

By the time I sneak back into the bedroom, I haven't come up with any answers. Connor is still fast asleep in bed, and I hesitate, looking at him. I'd intended to wake him up and remind him to sleep on the sofa, but that seems a bit mean. Maybe *I* should sleep on the sofa? I'll just lie down for a minute first.

I slide under the covers and curl up close to Connor, listening to the sound of his breathing in the silence of the room. He stirs a little and puts an arm around me, nuzzling his head against mine, and I smile. The moment is so nice – just plain *nice* – that I sink into it, warm and soft, and close my eyes. I can't help thinking, lying here next to Connor, about how I got here. This time last week, I was in my own bed in Larking, and everything was ordinary. Now, I'm in my adoptive sister's house in York, a place I never thought I'd see. I'm on a covert mission to try and bring my runaway friend back to England. I just had sex with my boyfriend. And it all comes back to Bonnie, the person who was my constant, the most reliable, my best friend.

Tomorrow, I will see her again. This whole strange, unlikely week will end with us in the back seat of Valerie's car, all of us on our way back to Larking. I can see it so clearly. Connor in the front seat, Valerie smiling and shaking her head in the driver seat, still not quite believing that her dipshit younger sister managed to pull it all off. And Bonnie beside me, shell-shocked perhaps, but there, squeezing my hand and saying, 'You were right. Thank God you came.'

This is the image in my mind as I fall asleep. Bonnie's earnest, familiar face and the words, comforting validation, echoing into my dreams.

Conversations That Took on a New Meaning after Bonnie Disappeared

The Last Edition: one day before

'Do you want to come back to mine?' I asked, pulling my bag over my shoulder and following Bonnie out of the classroom and into the hall. It was our last revision session before the weekend, and I felt instantly lighter.

'I've got a flute lesson,' Bonnie said. 'Sorry.' She paused outside the door, leaning against the wall, trying to stuff her papers into her notepad. 'Shit.' Her pencil case slipped from her grasp and hit the floor. 'Can you pick that up for me?'

'What's up with you?' I asked, obeying. 'You've been stressy all day.'

Bonnie lifted her free hand to her face, sweeping her side fringe out of her eyes. 'Just . . .'

'Exams?' I supplied.

For a second, an expression passed over her face that I couldn't read. 'I can care about other stuff, you know.'

'OK, sure,' I said, shrugging. 'Like what?'

For a moment she just looked at me, and I had no idea what it was she wanted. 'Forget it. You're right. I only care about revision and exams.'

'Why've you got a flute lesson this late on a Friday?' I asked. 'I thought you'd done the assessment already?'

She shook her head, her face pink and flustered. 'This is an extra thing. For the written exam.'

'But—'

'I have to go; I'm late.'

'OK, fine, go,' I said. 'See you tomorrow, then.'

Bonnie, who'd already started to turn to walk in the

opposite direction, paused. 'Tomorrow?'

'Yeah. Canterbury, right?'

'Oh. Oh, yeah.'

'You didn't forget, did you?'

'Of course not. I'll text you later.'

'See you tomorrow,' I said again, watching her departing back.

She glanced behind her and smiled. 'See you.'

Friday

20

I wake up groggy. I'd thought I hadn't had much wine, but what I did have seems to have floated up into my head and settled there in a heavy, uncomfortable weight.

'Eden?'

Someone is saying my name. Who is it? Valerie?

'Eden!' No, not Valerie. Connor. He's standing – I realize when I lift my head – in the doorway, not quite in the room.

'What?' I demand, not particularly nicely. I am not a morning person.

'Where's Valerie?'

I half sit up. 'I don't know. Isn't she just upstairs?'

Connor shakes his head. 'I went to ask if she wanted tea when I got up. The door's open and the room's empty.' He ducks out of the room and I hear his voice drift from the living room. 'Her shoes are gone. She must have gone for coffee or something.'

I throw on some clothes and join him, the thin carpet more scratchy than soft against my bare feet. 'I hope she brings some back for—'

That's the moment the front door opens and Valerie appears, holding a carrier of four cups in one hand and a paper bag, sunglasses and keys in the other. She smiles in surprise when she sees us. 'Hey, guys,' she says, swinging the door closed with her hip and coming into the house. 'I didn't think you'd be up yet.'

'Connor got me up,' I say. 'He was wondering where you were.'

Valerie holds up the paper bag. 'Sustenance! Breakfast sustenance, which is the best kind.'

She looks way too fresh for someone who had about a bottle and a half of wine the night before. 'Aren't you hungover?' I ask.

Valerie smirks a very un-Valerie smirk at me. 'It's not my first time.' She sets the cups on the kitchen counter. 'I always wake up early when I've been drinking. I've been up since six. OK, who wants what? I have two croissants, two chocolate twists and an apricot Danish.'

We divide up the pastries between us, leaving the entire Danish for Valerie because she looks heartbroken when Connor attempts to cut it in half. I try to eat some of the croissant, but the nervous churn in my stomach is making everything taste like dust.

'So, what's the plan?' Valerie asks me, smiling. 'Do you want to just head out into York and explore? There's loads to see in the city, or we could go to the uni and I could show you around.'

I try and swallow a chunk of buttery pastry. I have absolutely no clue what to say.

'And if we do that stuff today, tomorrow we could go for a drive and go to Whitby, or something. I *love* Whitby. We could have a day by the sea.'

Honestly, a part of me is tempted to just forget about Glasgow and Bonnie and the whole stupid idea and just hang out in York for the next two days. That wouldn't be so bad, would it?

'Or did you have something else in mind?' Valerie prompts. Both she and Connor are staring at me from the other side of the breakfast bar, waiting.

I cannot bail out on this now. I'm not a wuss.

'I did have an idea,' I say eventually. Or try to say. It comes out as more of a squeaky, questioning choke. I cough. 'But it's a bit . . . um.' I swallow. Come on, words. 'Not Yorky.' Oh, great. Well done, Eden.

'Not . . . Yorky,' Valerie repeats slowly. She glances at Connor, who immediately goes bright red. She looks back at me, eyebrows lifting. 'Oh . . . kay. What is it?'

'Could we go to Scotland?'

Valerie lets out a surprised, breathy half-laugh. 'Scotland?!'

'Yeah.' There's no other way to play this than just to go all-in.

'You mean, like, Edinburgh?'

'No, I've been there, done that. Climbed the hill, saw the castle, Royal Mile.' I'm blabbing. Shit. Get a hold of yourself, Eden. 'I was thinking Glasgow.'

Valerie's eyes go even wider. '*Glasgow?!*' She sputters a laugh. 'Why?'

'Because I've never been, and we're way closer than I usually am. I know it's a bit random, but I really want to see it.'

'You really want to see it,' Valerie repeats, deadpan. 'You just thought this morning, *Oh hey, why not go and see Glasgow?* That city you've always dreamed of seeing.'

The weird thing is that she doesn't even seem that surprised. Bemused, maybe. But not surprised.

'I like big cities,' I say. This is a complete lie, but I'm counting on the fact that Valerie doesn't know me well enough to know that.

'Do you?' she asks, forehead crinkling. 'How about you, Connor? You like big cities?'

Connor coughs.

'They have botanic gardens,' I say, which I know is true because I saw it on the Glasgow Wikipedia page yesterday in the car.

'So does York,' she says. Shit. This really isn't going well. 'Eeds. Let me just get a hold on this. Are you telling me you came to York because you want to see a city in Scotland?'

I scan my possible answers to this for anything that might give me away. 'Yes.'

'And this has nothing to do with Bonnie.'

'No.'

Valerie looks at me. 'Eden.'

'It doesn't.'

'*Eden.*' When I don't say anything, she lets out a groan of frustration. 'Stop treating me like I'm stupid, Eden. I know this is about Bonnie. Can't you just drop this ridiculous charade and be honest?'

My hands are starting to feel clammy. What is the right answer to this? Is she talking like she *would* take me to Glasgow if it was to do with Bonnie, or that she wouldn't?

'Do you know where she is?' Valerie asks. Her voice is hard, her eyes fixed on me.

'No,' I say, automatically. Connor is making eyes at me, like, *Try a new line, Eden*. 'Well, I . . .'

There's a long silence. Valerie is nodding a little at me, coaxing out the truth. No. I can't tell her that I know exactly where Bonnie is; she'll just send the police to Glasgow and me home. And I have to get to Glasgow. It has to be me.

'I don't *know*,' I say finally. 'But I *think* they could be there.'

'You think,' Valerie repeats.

I nod.

'They *could* be there.'

Another nod.

'And why do you think that?'

'Because Bonnie used to talk about Glasgow. I just have this . . . feeling.'

'Why didn't you share this "feeling" with the police?' She makes air quotes and everything.

'It would sound stupid. It's not much to go on.'

'But it's enough to try and trick me into driving you there?' she asks flatly.

A guilty flush rises in my cheeks. God, when she puts it like that, I sound horrible as well as stupid. 'I just . . .' I don't know how to finish.

'You just what, Eden?'

'I'm sorry,' I say.

This surprises her, I can tell. She lifts a hand and tugs her fingers through her hair, frowning.

'I just need to do this,' I say. 'For Bonnie.'

'Eden . . .' she says softly, then shakes her head. 'Glasgow is a long way to go for a hunch.'

'I know, but . . .'

But what?

'If it's more than a hunch, you should just tell me,' she says. 'Right now. Just tell me.'

I try very hard not to look at Connor.

'I won't be mad,' she says. 'I promise. But I know there's more going on here. Just tell me.'

'There isn't.' Lying to Valerie's face like this doesn't make me feel good. It makes me feel small, and cold, and rotten. 'I just thought . . . as we're here . . . and it's not that far away . . . The police aren't finding her. And this is my chance to have a go.'

Valerie lets out a long sigh, bites her lip, then rolls her eyes to the ceiling. I glance at Connor and he makes a clueless face at me.

'OK,' she says.

I blink. Connor's mouth drops open. 'OK?' I echo uncertainly.

'OK,' Valerie says again. 'Fine. If that's what you want, that's what we'll do. But just today. We're coming back tonight. I don't want you thinking we can get there and then you can be, like, "Oh! Let's go to Loch Ness, it's only another three hours away!" or something. OK?'

'OK!' I say, disbelievingly thrilled. 'Oh my God, Valerie. Are you sure?'

'Yes. Go get your stuff. If we're going to go, we should go now.'

She takes a big bite of Danish just as I lunge around the breakfast bar to hug her. '*Oof.*'

'Valerie, you're the *best*,' I blurt, actually meaning it. I feel dizzy with excited relief. 'The actual, actual best.'

Connor is just standing there, his forehead crinkled slightly, his expression unreadable. His eyes flit from Valerie to me like he's trying to understand something, and I widen my eyes to say, *Don't say anything. Don't risk this.*

Valerie pats my shoulder, then disentangles herself. 'I'm going to run out and get some more coffee,' she says. 'When I get back, be ready to go, OK?'

Connor waits until she leaves before he says it. 'Well, this is weird.'

'Just go with it,' I say, shoving the remains of my croissant into my mouth. It suddenly tastes amazing. 'I'm just glad she said yes.'

'Don't you think that was a bit too easy, though?'

'Better too easy than a no,' I point out. I think this is a pretty clever response, but he still looks troubled.

He leans over and picks up the coffee cup she'd brought in with her. 'There's still coffee in this,' he says.

'That'll be cold by the time we leave,' I say. 'She's getting some for the journey, which is why we need to be ready when she gets back. Quick, go and get your stuff together.'

He doesn't move. 'Do you think she's calling Carolyn?'

I almost pause. 'No, she'd just tell me, wouldn't she? Stop being so paranoid.'

Connor glances down at the cup again and then back at me. 'You're going to have to tell her the truth at some point. You know that, right?'

I'm already halfway across the living room, gathering up my things. 'It'll be fine,' I say, even though I know it won't be. 'I just have to wait for the right moment.'

*

The thing is, I don't really know what the right moment is going to look like. At first it seems a good idea to wait until we're out of York, and then until we're out of England altogether. But when we cross the border into Scotland, it still doesn't feel right. And then I realize, it doesn't make much sense to confess until we're actually in Glasgow. And anyway, there are so many other things for us to talk about. Why spoil it with an inevitable fight?

When we first drove out of York, Valerie overruled Connor and me, and put on one of her playlists, and that turned into the soundtrack for the four-hour trip, underpinning our conversations as we zipped from one to another. Everything felt as free as the countryside surrounding us: unfamiliar but open; new but somehow ours.

The Song: David Bowie, 'Starman'

The Conversation: GCSEs (Part 1 of 6)

Valerie: When's your next exam?
Me: Oh my God, can we not?
Connor: Tuesday. Maths.
Valerie: Yikes.
Me: Who says 'yikes'?
Valerie: I do. How are you feeling about it?
Me: [*Mimes choking to death.*]
Connor: How does anyone feel about a Maths exam?
Valerie: I quite liked Maths exams.
Me: Oh my God.
Valerie: I mean, relatively speaking. I liked that there were actual answers. It's not like an English exam, where it's all subjective. There's a right and a wrong.
Connor: That's true.

Me: It's not so great if you only have the wrong answers.
Valerie: You're so defeatist.
Me: I prefer 'realist'.
Connor: I like this song.

The Song: George Michael, 'Faith'

The Conversation: Daisy
Valerie: Do you ever worry about Daisy?
Me: All the time.
Valerie: I mean at school, specifically.
Me: So do I! She's a menace.
Valerie: Mum said she's been in and out of detention all year.
Me: Pretty much.
Valerie: That's not great, is it? She's only in Year Seven.
Me: No, but the other side of it is she finds schoolwork really hard and they don't deal with that well enough.
Valerie: Really?
Me: Yeah. She acts up to save face.
Valerie: Is that what you did?
Me: Sure. Who wants to look stupid in front of everyone? At least when you're acting up you've got some kind of control.
Connor: Daisy's got more of a mouth on her than you ever did.
Me: Hey, watch it.
Valerie: Only McKinleys are allowed to say anything bad about Daisy.
Me: Yeah!
Connor: Did you two just . . . *fist-bump*?
Valerie: I bloody love this song. Turn it up.

The Song: Viola Beach, 'Boys That Sing'

The Conversation: The ABC Game

Valerie: Let's play the ABC game.

Connor: What's that?

Valerie: You have to name something in a certain category beginning with A, then B, then C, etc. It's a McKinley staple for car journeys. What topic shall we go with? TV shows?

Me: Flowers!

Valerie: Eeh. OK. But only if we can do trees too. I'll start. Ash.

Me: Begonia.

Connor: Uh . . . chrysanthemumums?

Me: That's not how you say it.

Valerie: It still counts. Daffodils.

Me: Eremurus.

Connor: Show-off.

Me: That doesn't begin with F.

Connor: I know a phrase that does.

Valerie: Children, children.

Me: You have ten seconds.

Connor: Fruit.

Me: Fail.

Connor: Whatever. I don't like this game. Turn the music up.

The Song: Leonard Cohen, 'Everybody Knows'

The Conversation: Badger

Me: So. Badger.

Valerie: Oh God.

Connor: Huh?

Me: *Badger?*
Valerie: His real name is David.
Connor: Who?
Me: I can't believe you . . . with someone called . . .
Valerie: It wasn't planned.
Me: And you never talked about it?
Valerie: Never.
Me: Wow.
Valerie: I definitely shouldn't have told you.
Me: I'm glad you did, though.
Valerie: Yeah?
Me: Yeah.

The Song: Prince, 'Kiss'

The Conversation: GCSEs (Part 4 of 6)
Valerie: God, we should all be revising right now.
Me: Should we, though?
Valerie: Yes! Especially you! I'm so irresponsible.
Me: Bad Valerie.
Valerie: It's very rude to mock your chauffeur. Shall we turn around and go back to York?
Me: No! Why don't you quiz me on something? Quiz me on French. Your favourite thing.
Valerie: Still with the mocking. But OK. Translate this: 'I am in a car with my sister and my boyfriend.'
Me: Uh. *Je suis . . .*
Valerie: Good start.
Me: *Une voiture . . .*
Valerie: You are a car?
Me: *Avec . . . ma soeur . . . et mon petit ami.*
Valerie: Close enough.

The Song: David Bowie, 'Heroes'

The Conversation: Fostering

Me: How old were you when Carolyn and Bob started fostering?

Valerie: Six.

Me: Wow. That's young.

Valerie: It's older than you were when you were *being* fostered.

Me: True. Was it weird? Having random kids in your house all the time?

Valerie: No. And they never felt like 'random kids'. Remember how I said that Mum used to call them our guests? It was more like that. How was it for you? Going into random houses all the time?

Me: Shitty.

Valerie: Oh. [*Long pause.*] You didn't . . . feel like a guest?

Me: I didn't mean shitty in your house—

Valerie: *Our* house.

Me: You know what I mean. [*Pause.*] But thanks. I just mean it could only ever hit a certain level of good, you know? However nice the foster carers were, it was still a shitty situation.

Valerie: Is it different when you're adopted?

Me: Yeah. Just having things be permanent instead of temporary all the time, you know?

Valerie: Yeah.

Me: Wasn't it weird for you having two new family members without having any say at all? Like a family invasion?

Valerie: I did have a say.

Me: You did?

Valerie:	Yeah, of course. Mum and Dad sat me down and said, 'We're thinking of adopting Eden and Daisy. How would you feel about that?'
Me:	What did you say?
Valerie:	I said I thought it would be the best thing they'd ever done.
Me:	Did you actually, though?
Valerie:	Yes! Why is that so hard to believe?
Me:	Because I'm a brat.
Valerie:	You're not a brat. You're just a bit difficult sometimes.
Me:	Uh, same thing?
Valerie:	I like difficult.
Me:	Do you?
Valerie:	Yeah. You know I'm a massive nerd. You don't get that way from liking things to be easy all the time.
Me:	That's true. You are a massive nerd.
Valerie:	Well, all the best ones are.

21

The journey up to Glasgow is so different from the one we took yesterday that I almost forget why we're there and what we're doing. I just want to stay sitting in the front seat of Valerie's car, snacking on a bag of sugared almonds I found in the glove compartment, laughing and talking about things that matter and things that don't. I've never had fun like this with Valerie. I didn't know I *could* have fun like this with Valerie.

But then we stop for petrol, and Valerie gets out of the car, leaving Connor and me alone. He leans over my seat, his hands on either side of the headrest, to hiss in my ear. 'We're nearly there, you know.'

I shove my fingers into the bag of almonds, but they scrabble around the corners, the bag empty. 'How far?'

'About half an hour. But that's just getting to Glasgow. It's a city. It's big. Did you get anything more specific about the address?'

I watch as Valerie finishes filling the car and heads towards the shop to pay. I can see a queue leading up to the till, so I calculate we have at least five minutes before she comes back. 'Uh, no.'

Connor makes a noise like he's unimpressed but also not surprised. 'OK, well, I found the cat cafe.'

'Yeah?!'

'Well, it wasn't hard. It's near-ish the centre of the city and when I Street-View it, I can see a few terraces nearby. I guess we could just knock on every end-of-terrace within a few minutes' walk?'

'I guess . . .'

'That's the only option, unless you can narrow it down somehow.' He waits for me to say something, then sighs, and adds, 'Did she not mention anything at all about the house?'

I try to think, watching Valerie near the front of the queue inside the shop. 'She said the living-room window was boarded up.'

Connor doesn't say anything, so I twist in my seat to see his face, which is scrunched. 'Boarded up?'

'Yeah, I didn't ask why.'

'Sounds romantic,' Connor says, rolling his eyes. It's not like him to be so snide, and I raise my eyebrow at him.

'If we ever run away, we'll stay in five-star hotels,' I say.

'With a swimming pool.'

'And a concierge.' I'm not even sure what a concierge is. 'And room service.'

He smiles. 'A boarded-up window should be pretty obvious, so long as it's as close to the cat cafe as Bonnie said. We should be able to just see it.'

'OK, well, that's something.'

'Yeah . . .' he says slowly. 'You know what you need to do first, though, right?'

I watch Valerie walking across the concourse, purse in hand. The last hurdle. 'Yeah,' I say.

Ten minutes later, I still haven't figured out how to even bring up the subject. My whole body is tense with anxiety and my mouth is dry. There's not going to be any way around it this time. I have to tell Valerie the truth. And all of the light-heartedness between us, all of the tentative, teasing progress, is going to collapse. I'm no longer sure why I'm doing this, if any of it is going to be worth it, or even what 'worth it' means any more.

But . . . Bonnie.

Connor keeps giving me a look in the rear-view mirror. An increasingly stressed look. But it's all right for him, sitting in the back seat, far away from the danger zone. I'm going to be the one who gets bludgeoned.

'Hey, Valerie?' I say, aiming for casual, and missing.

Connor's eyes go wide. Valerie glances at me. 'Yeah?'

'Can we stop and get lunch?' I ask.

'Now?'

'Yeah, I'm pretty hungry, and it's almost one. Can we stop at a cafe or something?'

'Don't you want to just wait until we get into the centre?' Valerie says. 'We're not that far now.'

'It'll be really busy in the centre,' I hear myself say. 'And . . . um . . . more expensive.'

There's a pause. 'OK,' Valerie says finally. For a second, I think I see her roll her eyes. 'If that's what you want.'

'Can we get McDonald's?' Connor asks.

'No!' Valerie says, and this time she definitely rolls her eyes. 'I draw the line at McDonald's.'

'Valerie can choose the place,' I say to Connor. 'That's fair.'

'Well, thank you, Eden,' Valerie says. 'That's so generous of you.'

'Scotland really brings out the sarcasm in you,' I say.

'Sure, that's what it is,' she says. 'Scotland.'

We end up in a cafe on the way into the city. She orders stovies for all three of us, which turns out to be a kind of meat and potato stew, and then tells us a story I don't really listen to about her first week at university, when her flat had a party and she walked into her room to find a couple of strangers having sex on her bed. Usually this kind of story would hold my interest, but my stomach is so tight it's distracting. There's no more time for excuses. I have to do this now.

'So,' she says after two more stories I also don't listen to, 'what shall we do when we get into the centre? Is there somewhere we could start looking for Bonnie and Mr Cohn?'

And here we go.

'Um,' I say.

There's a long silence. Connor coughs. Valerie digs her straw into the ice in her glass of Diet Coke.

'I have to tell you something,' I blurt.

Valerie lifts her eyes to mine. 'Go on.'

My heart is hammering. 'I actually know where they are.'

Valerie's expression doesn't even change. 'Right. I have something to tell you, too.' She waits for barely a beat before saying, 'I know you do. And so does everyone else.'

All the air leaves my body in one big gasp of shock. 'What?'

'The police have been tracking us since we left Kent,' she says. Her face is still set, her eyes never leaving mine. 'There's an unmarked police car that's been following us the whole time.'

'What?' I say again. 'How . . . What?'

'There's a tracking device on my car.'

'Valerie.'

'They're trailing us about ten miles behind.'

'I don't understand.'

But I do.

'They're letting you lead them right to Bonnie and Jack Cohn,' she says, spelling it out.

There are so many questions to ask at this point, but what comes out is, 'When did anyone put a tracking device on your car?'

'Before we left home. Remember I told you I was going to the library?'

I don't know what to say. I don't even know what to think.

'So this was all you selling me out.' My voice, when it comes, is flat. 'You betrayed me.'

'No, Eeds. I'm protecting you. You and Bonnie. The police wanted to force it out of you, you know. They've suspected that you've known where she is ever since she first left. And when you suddenly wanted to go off to York – somewhere you'd never shown any interest in; you thought we didn't notice? – they wanted to bring you to the station, try and scare you until you told them the truth. I was the one who said I'd take you to York and go wherever else you wanted to go, and they could keep tabs on us from a distance, *instead* of them pulling any of that shit on you.'

'But you lied to me.'

'And you lied to me,' Valerie replies, her voice firm. 'And you did it because you felt like you had to, just like me. Eden, it was either this or nothing. You'd still be at home in Larking, except with added police pressure, and no one would be any closer to getting Bonnie home safe.'

'Why didn't you tell me from the start?'

She half laughs, but it's humourless. 'Really? Why didn't *you* tell *me* from the start?'

I don't have an answer to this.

'You know, this is so stupid, but there was a part of me that was really hoping you actually didn't know. That you weren't lying to me.' She lets out a sigh, running her fingers through her hair. 'God, but of course you were. You're not even good at it.'

I'm still too shocked to be offended. (Besides, it's true.) I look at Connor, who is slumped in his seat, shredding a napkin into tiny pieces, not looking at either of us. I think about the last twenty-four hours all three of us have spent together, running it through this new filter of truth.

'Was that why you got the wine?' I ask, my voice coming out a little shrill. 'Were you trying to get me drunk so I'd spill?'

For a moment Valerie just looks at me, bewildered. And then she laughs. 'No, Eden. The wine was for me.'

Well, I guess that's something. Not a lot of something, but something. She's been lying to me, but she hasn't actually tricked me, not like I tried to do to her. Who is in the right here? Or are we both wrong? And what does it actually matter now we're here?

'So what happens now?' I ask.

There's a silence. Valerie picks up her fork and twirls it between her fingers. 'I don't know,' she says.

'I think we should go and see Bonnie,' Connor says. It's the first time he's spoken since we sat down, and both Valerie and I turn in surprise at the sound of his voice. 'That's why we're here, isn't it? Whether the police are following or not.'

'But they *are* following us,' I say. 'As soon as they see the house, they'll just come in and arrest Mr Cohn. I won't get a chance to talk to Bonnie.' I sit back, my throat suddenly tight, shaking my head. It's over. I failed.

'Do you really think you could convince her?' Valerie asks.

'I just want a *chance*,' I say. I want to explain to her, face to face, the mess she's caused. To show her I've come all this way, that this is how much I care. I don't just want her to come home. I want her to *want* to come home.

'Well,' Valerie says slowly. 'They're following the *car*. They're not following *us*.'

I look across the table at her, and her eyes meet mine.

'How specific is your information?' she asks. 'Do you have an address?'

I nod, cautious, not quite letting myself hope. 'Connor found it,' I say.

She turns to him. 'How far away is it?'

Connor fumbles with his phone and I wait, holding my breath tight inside. 'Google Maps says a half-hour walk,' he says. 'From here, I mean.'

'If we leave the car here,' Valerie says, 'they wouldn't know where we'd gone. We could go and see Bonnie, just us. No police.'

'No police,' I repeat. My voice is a little shaky. 'But . . . what about after?'

'Well, we'd have to talk to the police after,' she allows. 'But if you talk to Bonnie first . . . if you get through to her, it won't matter.'

'What if I can't?'

'If you can't, you might realize you *want* the police to catch up with them.'

That doesn't sound likely, but I nod anyway, because there's no way I'm risking this fragile understanding. The answer seems to be that failing to convince Bonnie is not an option, and didn't I know that already?

'Are you going to get in trouble for this?' I ask.

One side of Valerie's mouth lifts into a smile. 'Nah,' she says. 'Everyone has to choose a side eventually.'

I'm not sure exactly what she means, but I don't ask.

'So . . .' Connor says. 'We could leave the car here and walk there?'

Valerie looks at me. 'If that's what you want,' she says, 'that's what we'll do. It's up to you.'

There's only one possible answer to this. 'Let's go,' I say.

22

We don't talk much for the next half an hour. Connor walks slightly ahead, his eyes on his phone, leading the way. Valerie and I walk side by side without speaking, not because there's nothing to say, but because there's too much. She walks with her hands in her pockets, shoulders back, just like she always has, but she somehow looks so different to me. I should feel like I know her better now, but I don't, not really. I look past her to Connor, so focused, an unlikely leader. In all of this confusion and change, he is just the same. Thank God.

And in the midst of thoughts like these, I get sharp shocks of *Why the hell are you thinking about this when you're about to see Bonnie?* that jolt and confuse me so much I almost trip. Everything feels upside down. My priorities have warped.

'Does she know you're coming?' Valerie asks.

I shake my head. 'I thought it was better not to give them a chance to leave.'

She nods. 'Smart.'

And then we're silent for another ten minutes.

'Is Carolyn angry with me?' I ask.

'No,' Valerie says without even hesitating. 'She's just worried about you. That's all.'

And silence falls again.

I'm letting Connor lead us without paying much attention to our route or how long everything is taking, so it's a surprise when we reach the cat cafe. The House of the Cat Kings. The logo features a black-and-white cat wearing a crown, a sceptre tucked between its paws.

'Cute,' Valerie says.

It's open; I can see people milling inside, surrounded by cats. Maybe when we're done, and Bonnie's with us, we can go in for a bit, I think. I have a sudden, vivid image of the four of us sitting on the sofa I can see through the window, laughing, taking a selfie or five with the cat that looks like a tiger.

'This means we're near where they're staying,' I say. 'It's an end-of-terrace. Look for a boarded-up window.'

Connor is already a few metres ahead of us, jogging from one end of each terrace to the other. I watch him, rather than join in the search, my hands suddenly clammy.

'Do you have an address?' Valerie asks, but before I can reply, Connor puts his hand up and waves, pointing at a house.

My heart gives a sudden, painful clench. Oh God. I'm not ready for this.

Valerie and I walk across the street to join him, and I know immediately that he's right. The boarded-up window is unmistakable, even if nothing else about the house is. There are steps leading to the front door and a small, dirty-looking wind chime hanging beside it.

'So, is this it?' Valerie prompts.

'Uh-huh,' I say.

'Go on then,' she says. 'Knock.'

'I need a sec,' I say.

'You don't have a sec,' Valerie says bluntly. 'The sooner we get in there, the less likely it is anyone in uniform is going to catch up with us.'

When I still don't move, she puts her hand between my shoulder blades and physically pushes me towards the doorsteps so hard, it's either go up them or fall on my face. I stumble, right myself, and then hammer on the door before I can second-guess myself.

My head is going *Oh God. Oh God oh God oh God.*

No answer.

I knock again.

Silence.

I glance back at Connor and Valerie, who both shrug at me. Now my head is screaming *Oh God oh God oh God* because – *OH GOD* – what if they're not here? What if they've left? Why didn't that possibility even cross my mind? All the way across the length of the goddamn country, and not once did I think, *Hey, Bonnie might move on without even mentioning it.*

My hands are cold. I feel a movement beside me, and it's Connor, bounding up the steps and pressing his face up to the window by the door.

'Seems kind of . . . quiet,' he says.

This can't happen. I can't have dragged Connor – let alone Valerie – over hundreds of miles for an empty house. Bonnie can't have left without telling me. She wouldn't do that.

Would she?

'When did you last talk to her?' Connor asks me.

I barely hear him. Maybe she knows. Maybe she guessed, somehow, that I was on my way. Maybe the fact that I didn't message her for so long made her suspicious. Maybe she told Mr Cohn that I knew where she was, and he made her cut off all contact with me and leave. Maybe this was all for nothing.

'Eden?'

We're going to have to turn around and go back home, Bonnie-less. And this time there'll be no hiding what I know, or knew. I'll have to face everyone's disappointment and judgement, and I won't even have Bonnie to show for it.

'Eden?' This time it's Valerie, cautious but gentle.

The house is empty. I know it is. I feel a hand on my arm, someone guiding me away from the door and easing me down into a sitting position on the top step.

'It's OK.' Valerie's soft voice. 'Take a second. It's OK.'

'Maybe they're just out,' Connor says. He sounds worried. 'They might just be out, right?'

Tears are streaming down my face. My nose feels all bunged up. I am clutching my knees with my fingertips, trying not to actually sob or wail or do anything even more embarrassing than what I'm doing right now. This is all very un-Eden-like behaviour. I'm not meant to be a crier. But I'm crying now.

'They're not here,' I manage. I wipe my nose with my sleeve, which makes precisely zero difference.

'It doesn't look like it, no,' Valerie says.

'I thought they'd be here.'

'I know you did.'

But how can they not be here?

We stay there together on the top step for a while, Valerie occasionally rubbing my arm, and Connor kind of hovering above us both, making a concerned face.

'What happens now?' I ask.

'I don't know,' Valerie says.

'Maybe you should call her,' Connor says. This is actually the third time he's said this, but it's the first time it really registers for me. He's right, of course. I should call her.

I unlock my phone and open my contacts, looking at the mostly blank 'Ivy' entry. Is this person really anything more than a stranger to me? Why am I putting myself through all of this, really?

'Eden—' Valerie starts.

'I know; I'm going to call her,' I say impatiently. 'Just give me a—'

'No, *Eden*,' she says, insistent. 'Look.'

I glance up to see that she's facing away from me, looking down the road. I follow her gaze and spot two figures walking close together, one tall, one short, both holding carrier bags. The short figure has red hair. The tall one is wearing a baseball cap.

I walk back down the steps, my breath loud in my ears. It's Bonnie. It's Bonnie, it's Bonnie, it's Bonnie. I want to call out to her, but I can't form words. I just stand, waiting for one of them to look up and see me.

Thirteen seconds later, Bonnie does. She's close enough for me to see her whole face jerk with shock. '*Eden*? Oh my God, Eden!' She drops the bags she's holding and runs the last few metres towards me, throwing her arms around me for a hug. She steps back to look at me, hands still on my shoulders, a huge grin on her face. She is uncomplicatedly, genuinely happy to see me, I can tell. That is, at least, until she registers the tears and expression on my face. 'What's wrong?!'

What's wrong? *What's wrong?!*

'You!' I say. I don't even know what I mean. Without even thinking about it, I reach out my arms and hug her again, feeling her arms curl around my back. Bonnie. Hugging her feels just the same.

When we break apart again, I look behind her at Mr Cohn, who has gathered up the bags Bonnie had dropped and is approaching us. His expression, from this distance, is hard to read.

'Eden Rose McKinley,' he says. 'Now this is a surprise.'

'Hi, sir,' I say. I don't even do it on purpose – it just comes out. 'I mean . . . uh . . . Mr . . . um . . .'

'Why don't you call me Jack?' Mr Cohn says, looking like he's trying not to laugh. There's no way I will ever call him Jack. 'And Connor! Well. You've made quite the journey.'

Connor gives him a kind of uncomfortable half-smile, and I'm relieved that it's not just me who's feeling how completely weird this whole scenario is. Bonnie's just standing there beaming.

'Let's go inside, shall we?' Mr Cohn adds. He tries to hide it, but I see him look up and down the street, searching, no doubt, for police. And once I've seen that, I also notice that his jaw is pretty tight considering he's smiling, like underneath it he's clenching his teeth.

'This is my sister, Valerie,' I say, gesturing, partly because it seems polite to introduce them, and also because I'm belligerent, and stalling someone who's obviously in a hurry is in my nature.

'Shall we make the introductions inside the house?' Mr Cohn says. 'Lead the way, Bonnie.'

Bonnie obeys immediately, looping her arm through mine and ushering me towards the front door. 'I can't believe you're here!' she whispers, squeezing my elbow. 'Why didn't you tell me?'

What's the right answer to this? 'Surprise!' I say.

She laughs, pushing a key into the lock and opening the door with a *clunk*. 'Well, I'm definitely surprised!'

We go into the kitchen, which is small and cramped, and cluster around the table. There aren't enough chairs for all of us, so Valerie and Mr Cohn stand on either side of the room, him unpacking the bags, her leaning against the sink, frowning.

'Shall I make us all some tea?' Mr Cohn suggests.

No one says anything, but he starts filling the kettle anyway.

'So what brings you to Glasgow?' Bonnie asks and, though she laughs, it sounds more awkward than anything else.

'We came to see you,' I say. 'Well, *I* did.' I glance at Connor and smile. 'Plus guests.'

'How did you find us?' Mr Cohn asks, all casual, like he's just curious.

I glance at Bonnie, but she's looking at him instead of me. I open my mouth, but before I can speak Valerie answers. 'Does it matter? We're here now.'

'I'd like to know whether to expect any other visitors,' Mr

Cohn says mildly. 'If this particular location is . . . common knowledge.'

'You mean like the police?'

He coughs. 'Well . . .'

'No need to be vague, *Jack*,' she says. 'Aren't we a little bit past euphemisms at this point? Let's call this what it is, shall we? A crime?'

'Valerie,' I hiss.

'What?' she demands. 'Did you expect me to come here and act like this is all OK? Let these idiots play happy families right in front of me?'

'Now, wait a—' Mr Cohn starts.

'No. No waiting,' she interrupts, actually pointing an angry finger at him. 'Abducting a minor, that's a prison sentence right there, for a start. How many cups of tea in a little Scottish kitchen does it take to make you forget that? This isn't a love story; it's just a stupid mistake. One that's going to ruin both your lives.'

The silence in the kitchen that follows these words feels almost alive. It crackles with electricity. By now, Bonnie is half standing, her expression as she stares at my sister a mix of anguish and horror. *Reality, thy name is Valerie.*

'I love Bonnie,' Mr Cohn says, and I think he means to say this with gravitas, like the way it would sound in a Richard Curtis film, but he gets the delivery wrong and it comes out all thin and weedy.

'So?' Valerie says, actually shrugging.

'So we wanted to be together,' Bonnie says.

Valerie closes her eyes and lets out a groan. 'Oh my God,' she says. 'Is that as far as the reasoning went for you two? I'm in love, therefore this bullshit is OK?'

'The "reasoning" is not your concern,' Mr Cohn says, suddenly sounding more like the teacher I remember. 'And neither is it welcome, quite frankly.'

'Quite frankly,' Valerie replies without hesitation, 'as the only other adult here, I don't care how welcome you think my concern is. You're operating on *levels* of wrong. *Multiple levels.*'

'Age gaps—' Bonnie begins.

'This isn't about age gaps!' Valerie interrupts, appalled. 'Is that the bit he's made you focus on? Has he done the whole "age gaps are taboo" crap? This is about things like power imbalances and taking advantage of authority and – oh, hey – *boundaries*?!'

'Stop it,' Bonnie begs, her voice shaky. I see her hands have clenched into fists. 'Valerie. Stop.'

For a moment I think Valerie is going to carry on, but instead she actually does stop. 'You're right,' she says, and Bonnie's face pops in surprise. 'There's no point in me going on like this. Eden's come all this way to see you. It's her who should be talking to you.' She looks expectantly at me. 'Right?'

Everyone looks at me and I feel my face flush a slow, deep red in response. I hadn't expected that I'd have to give a speech to an audience of anyone but Bonnie. 'I . . .' I falter, then look helplessly at Valerie.

'Bon, why don't you give Eden a tour of the house?' Mr Cohn suggests. 'I'll make some tea for Valerie and Connor while you both . . . chat.'

I'm not sure exactly why he suggests this – whether he means it out of kindness to me (unlikely), if he wants to have it out with Valerie while Bonnie isn't in earshot (possible), or if he thinks I'm just not a threat to his and Bonnie's relationship because I'm such a nonentity (most likely) – but I decide it doesn't matter. When Bonnie nods and smiles at me, I smile back. And when she reaches out a hand to me, like she did when we first met, when we were two little eight-year-olds from different worlds, I take it.

23

'There's not much to see,' Bonnie says, pulling me down the hall, not letting go of my hand. 'It's really just the kitchen, the living room and the bedroom. And the bathroom, of course. It's small. Cosy, I mean. We don't need much, the two of us.'

'How are you paying for all this?' I ask, ducking my head obligingly into the bathroom as we pass, and then following her up a small flight of rickety, winding steps.

'Jack got cash before we left,' she says. 'The bedroom is the only room up here, so this is it. Watch your head! The door frame is pretty low. On our first night here Jack hit his head on his way in. It bled and everything!'

'How much cash?' I ask. The bedroom is small, basically just a bed and a single wardrobe. The sheets are messy and rumpled – ew, ew, ew – and there are two suitcases on either side of the room, but not much else. It's kind of bare, actually.

'Enough for a while,' she says.

'Did you guys plan this?' I ask, wondering what 'a while' means.

She shrugs. 'Not really. I mean, we talked about it, yeah. And Jack got the money out in cash all ready for us to go a bit before. But we didn't know for sure we were going to do it until we did.' She smiles at me, spreading out her arms like she's gesturing to the whole room all at once. 'Pretty good, right? For a couple of fugitives?'

I try to smile back, but it doesn't quite land on my face.

'It's not forever, anyway,' she adds. 'We'll be moving on soon, probably.'

My stomach tightens. Not likely. 'Were all the places you've stayed like this?'

'No, the place in Tenby was so cute. Like a proper holiday cottage. I could've stayed there forever. But then we got busted.' She sighs and sits down on the bed, pulling her legs underneath her.

'What about Yorkshire?' I ask, hovering awkwardly, not really wanting to sit on the crumpled sheets.

'Oh, we didn't actually stay anywhere there.'

I feel my face scrunch. 'You were there for a couple of days, weren't you?'

'Yeah, we slept in the car.'

I pause. 'What?'

'We slept in the car,' she repeats. 'We couldn't find somewhere that was safe that took cash, so we just slept in the car. That's basically why we left and came up here.' Seeing my face, she shrugs. 'It's not that weird. It was good, actually. Proper cosy.'

I stare at her, searching for traces of the friend I knew who would be able to hear how ridiculous she sounds, and laugh. Connor was completely right about her being in denial. It's like she's putting everything that's happening through an 'adventure' filter in her head before she lets herself think about it too hard.

'Sit down,' Bonnie says, nodding at the space beside her, and I do, because refusing would be weird. It's strange how awkward I feel around her, even though Bonnie is meant to be one of the people I'm most comfortable around in the world, and I'm not even a shy person. But I thought I'd know what to say, and I just . . . don't.

'This is so bizarre,' I say finally, and I laugh out some of my nerves. 'You feel like a stranger.'

Bonnie grins. 'It's the hair, right?' She puts two hands under her new red bob and then laughs. 'I'm still me, though.' She reaches over with open arms to hug me, her head settling on my shoulder. 'See?'

I lean my head against hers, like I have a thousand times. 'It feels like you've been gone for so long.'

'It feels like that for me, too.'

We lift our heads at the same moment so we can face each other again. 'Do you miss it?' I ask. 'Home?'

At this, Bonnie looks away, shrugging. 'What's to miss?'

'Um, your family? Me? Not having to hide all the time?'

'Firstly, we don't actually have to hide all that much,' she replies, her chin jutting slightly. 'It's not like it looks in films and stuff. Secondly, you're right here, aren't you? And honestly? No, I don't really miss my family. Home wasn't exactly a fun place to be.' She must read the sceptical surprise on my face, because she lets out a bitter laugh. 'Oh, I know they've been pulling the perfect family bit for the press. I've seen the press conferences. Mum crying and Dad looking all stoic, or whatever. Please. They just don't like the embarrassment. Being shown up in front of their friends at church. A daughter with a mind of her own? The horror!' She shakes her head. 'This is the best thing for everyone.'

'I didn't know you felt that way about your family.'

'It's not a "thing". I'm not trying to say I've got some secret childhood trauma. I obviously don't. It just wasn't a very happy place, that's all.'

'Why didn't you tell me?'

'After everything you've been through in your life? It'd be like complaining about a headache to someone with a brain tumour.'

I frown. 'Um, what?'

'You know what I mean.'

'No, I don't. You're saying that because I was adopted, you didn't want to talk to me about not being happy at home?'

'Well, yeah. It would just have been a bit insensitive, you know?'

'Bonnie. That's so stupid.' The more I think about it, the stupider it sounds. 'And who cares if it was insensitive, anyway? You got to the point where you actually ran away. *How* could you not tell me that?'

She's calm even as I'm starting to get worked up. 'Because the running-away bit – and I hate that phrase, by the way – was all to do with Jack, and I couldn't tell you about him.'

'*Why not?*' The big question. 'Didn't you want to tell me? Didn't you trust me?'

'It had to be a secret,' she says. 'It's nothing to do with trusting you – it just had to be a secret. I know that must sound crazy to you from the outside, but that was the only way it could go. It was always about just the two of us. The only ones who get it. And that's OK. That's part of us being together. The two of us against the world.'

I resist the urge to tell her that she sounds completely delusional, because even I can see that that won't help me to convince her to come back home with me. She needs a dose of reality, but not too much, or I'll lose her completely. 'Do you think that's why you did this? Like . . . it's a big adventure you're both having?'

'Sure!' Her face lights up, like she's excited that I understand.

'But what about when the adventure . . . ends?'

'Who says it has to end?'

'Don't all adventures end?'

'Not this one. Not with Jack and me.'

'You want to be running away forever?'

'Sure,' she says again. 'Why not?' Her eyes are bright; too bright. There's a touch too much energy in her voice. 'We're like outlaws.'

'And that's a good thing?' Frustration is thickening in my

throat, and it's getting harder to hide. This isn't going how I expected, and this Bonnie is not a girl I recognize. I don't know how to navigate this conversation; there are none of the usual signposts in her voice or her expression to guide me.

'If I can be with Jack, yes.'

'But, Bon . . . you slept in a *car*.'

'So?'

Great. This isn't going well. 'Are you even a little bit sorry?' I ask, changing tack.

'Sorry about what?'

That's a no, then. About the mess you caused, I could say. Or, about starting a national manhunt. I say, 'For lying to me.'

'I didn't lie. You didn't ask.'

'You mean, I didn't ask if your secret boyfriend was actually Mr Cohn?' I try to swallow down my sudden anger, but I can feel it rising in my throat. She wants to put this on *me*? 'That's bullshit, and you know it. The biggest thing that had ever happened to you was happening, and you didn't tell me. And then you buggered off and left me – and everyone else – to deal with the fallout. You know everyone thought I knew all along? And why wouldn't they? I *should've* done.'

'I just explained,' she says. 'I couldn't tell you. It had to be a secret.'

'From everyone else, sure. But me? I thought we trusted each other.'

'What would you've said if I actually told you?' she challenges. '*Great, go for it*? No. You would've freaked out, just like you did when you found out. Remember what you texted me? *Holy fucking shitballs*?'

'That reaction is totally valid,' I say. 'Yeah, I would have freaked out. It's a freak-out-able thing. But I would still have kept it a secret, if that's what you wanted. Just like I have all this week – by the way, you're *welcome*.'

'Exactly,' she says. 'You kept it a secret. So you obviously don't think it's that bad, do you?'

'I *do* think it's that bad,' I say, trying to keep up with the twists in the conversation. 'It's *completely* wrong. Can't you see it?'

Bonnie raises one eyebrow. 'Is that what you came all the way here to say? That you think I'm wrong?'

I hesitate. 'Well, yeah.'

To my surprise, she smiles. 'Do you know, that's why you're so great, Eden. That's why I told you about leaving, and where I was, even after we nearly got caught in Tenby. Because even though you think this is wrong, you still kept the secret. You didn't tell anyone. You trusted me to know what I'm doing.'

I know I'm meant to feel pleased about this. What she's saying is everything I've thought over the last week, the way I reasoned with myself every time I hesitated over keeping her secrets safe within me. But instead, Connor's face pops into my mind. That point he'd made yesterday (*that was only yesterday?!*) about Bonnie acting selfishly.

Everything she's said is great, I guess, but isn't it all a bit . . . one-sided? She's listed everything I'm doing for her, but what exactly is she doing for me in return? Forcing me to collude with her in this trainwreck of mistakes? I've lied to my family, been shouted at by journalists, dragged my sister more than halfway across the country. And for what? This dewy-eyed schoolgirl, infatuated by some false idea of love.

I feel, suddenly, really, really stupid. What am I doing here? What the actual fuck am I *doing* here?

'I love that you did this,' Bonnie continues, oblivious. 'And I forgive you for just dropping in on me without a warning first.'

I blink. 'You *forgive* me?'

'Jack won't be happy about that. But this was the only way to do it, right? If you'd told me you were coming, I would've had to have told Jack, and he'd probably have said we should leave before you got here. Especially if we'd known about Connor coming too. And *Valerie*?! Did you have to bring her, Eeds?'

'She's the driver,' I say, which is minimalist, but accurate.

'Since when do you even talk to Valerie?' she asks, and something about her tone makes my hackles, already prickling, rise.

'She has a car,' I say. 'And she's been pretty great, actually.'

'Really? All that stuff down there about boundaries and abducting a minor? It's so cold, you know? Doesn't she have feelings?'

I frown. 'She's right, though.'

Bonnie shakes her head. 'Only from one point of view, which is if you completely disregard the emotional level. I love Jack, and she's saying that doesn't matter? How does that make any sense?'

'I'm not sure that's what she—'

'It's all technicalities, Eden. How old I am *right now*, what his job is *right now*, that stuff. It's so arbitrary. Did you know the legal age of consent in Denmark is fifteen? Doesn't that just say everything?'

I wait for her to elaborate on what this 'everything' is, but she doesn't, so I say, 'But we're not in Denmark.'

She rolls her eyes. 'Yeah, I know that, Eeds. What I mean is that there are all these, like, caveats to us being in a relationship, but none of them factor in the most important thing, which is that we love each other.'

This doesn't sound right to me, but I don't know how to say so. I feel hot and fizzing with confusion and frustration, and it's making my brain, which doesn't work fast enough to keep up with her at the best of times, panic and freeze. And anyway, isn't Bonnie the smart one? She's the one in the top sets, the one with all the As. Why am I questioning her? Of course she'd know better than me.

'You understand, don't you?' she prompts. 'You get it.'

I could agree. It's what she wants. I could tell her that she's right, that all of this is worth it in the name of love. I could leave with all her secrets intact, give them a head start on the police. I could save our friendship in letting her go.

'Not really,' I say.

Bonnie frowns. 'You agree with all of them? You think that because some random guy fifty years ago decided that the age of consent should be sixteen, I shouldn't be allowed to choose to be with the man I love?'

I swallow past the tightness in my throat. 'But it's not just about that, is it?' What was it Bob said a few days ago? Something about power? What was it? Come on, Eden. 'I think it's more of a thing that Mr Cohn is your teacher, and so he's, like . . .' Her darkening expression is twisting my insides into knots, but I steel myself. 'I read this thing about grooming—'

'Oh my *God*,' she bursts out. 'No way. Not you, too.'

'OK, but listen—'

'I don't have to listen to another person talking like they know my own relationship better than I do. Grooming! For God's sake! You only say that because you don't know him.'

'Well, of course I don't know him,' I say. 'He's my teacher. I'm not supposed to know him.'

This silences her. She stares at me for a moment, and I'm proud of myself for getting in such a killer, inarguable point before she starts shaking her head, all slow and disappointed.

'You don't understand,' she says. 'And you're not even trying to.'

'I've been trying to understand all week,' I say, stung. 'I basically haven't done anything else *but* try and understand.'

Her eyebrows lift, like, *Yeah, right*, and it's so unfair, after everything I've done for her, that for a second I want to stand up and leave. I don't, though. I try again. 'But Mr Cohn is your teacher, Bon. He's in, like . . . a position of authority, so he has a kind of power over you. It's not equal, and *that's* the problem.'

'His name is Jack,' she says coldly. 'And our relationship is totally equal. He loves me. He respects me. He'd never, ever hurt me. He's given up everything to be with me. And just because you don't get that, it means it's not real?'

'It's not—'

'You don't understand that because you don't feel that way about anyone, and no one feels that way about you.'

Words like a sucker punch. They feel physical. But I don't crack. I take the hurt inside and hold it there, ready. Pain is fuel. 'I have Connor, actually.'

She rolls her eyes. 'Oh, please. *Connor*.'

OK, now I'm mad. 'What the hell is that supposed to mean?'

'Come on, Eden. You can't compare Connor to Jack. Jack's a man. Connor's a boy.'

'Yeah, that's just one of the great things about him,' I say.

'You're not passionate about Connor,' she accuses. 'You don't have sex. Do you even fancy him?'

My instinct is to tell her that, actually, Connor and I just had sex. Like, literally last night. But that would feel too much like point-scoring, like taking something perfect and special and turning it into a weapon. The whole thing is just so *wrong*. Bonnie's my best friend. She should have been the person I spoke to afterwards, to gasp and shriek and discuss every detail with. And I should have been that person for her. But look at where we are instead.

'I *love* him,' I hiss out through gritted teeth. 'And that's about more than how much sex we're having, for God's sake.'

'So no, then?'

'What is *wrong* with you?' I yell, surprising myself and, judging by the look on her face, Bonnie. 'Why are you being like this? This isn't you. You're not stupid and selfish and mean.'

There's a moment when I think she's going to yell back at me, but then her face crumples and she turns away from me. I hear the hitch of her breath before she says, quietly, 'I'm sorry. You're right. I'm sorry.'

I wait, my heart feeling strangely heavy in my chest, for what comes next. Is this the moment of revelation?

'I just . . . I love him so much.'

Nope.

'But it's still been so hard. And I just have to keep telling myself – *reminding* myself, I mean – that it's all worth it.'

I let this digest, then translate. 'So you're being mean because you feel guilty?'

'No. I don't feel guilty.' She says this with far too much conviction for it to be completely true. 'It's just not easy. And knowing everyone is against me and I have to try so hard to explain everything.'

'Bon,' I start, then hesitate. 'Bon, are you sure you're not just in denial?'

There's a silence. 'Denial?' she repeats, but quietly, like she's saying it to herself and not me.

'About whether this is really the right decision,' I say. I try hard to keep my voice soft and gentle. 'And the effect it's having on you.'

'What difference does it make anyway?' she asks, finally raising her gaze to meet mine again. 'It's done now.'

'It makes a big difference,' I say. 'You can change your mind, you know. You can come home.'

She half laughs. 'No, I can't.'

'Of course you can. You can just leave with me. We'll drive home together.'

A pause. The wheels turning in her brain almost visible on her face. Oh my God. Oh my God. This might happen. I might actually turn this around.

'I can't leave Jack,' she says.

'You can,' I say. 'And this isn't even about him. It's about what's best for you. Isn't that what he wants, too? The best for you?'

Bonnie's whole face is a crease of confusion now. 'But I love him.'

'Bon, you can love him in Kent.'

'They're going to arrest him if we go back.'

'Then he can get a good lawyer,' I say. 'And you can—'

'Girls.' And there he is. Mr Cohn, standing in the doorway. How the fuck long has he been there? 'All OK in here?'

'Everything's fine,' I blurt, but Bonnie is already untangling her legs and easing herself off the bed, an instinctive smile on her face at the sight of him. And more than anything else, it's that smile that does it. I know I'm not going to convince her, and what's more, it was never a possibility, not really. I lost her to Jack Cohn a long time ago. I was the one in denial.

'I heard some shouting,' he says, smiling back at Bonnie and reaching out a hand.

'Sir?' I say, and he frowns.

'Jack,' he corrects.

'Can you get my sister for me?'

Mr Cohn glances at Bonnie, who nods like she's vouching for me or something. He hesitates a little – what does he think I'm going to *do*? – then turns to leave.

I wait until he's gone before I reach for Bonnie's hand and pull her back down beside me. 'Bon, I love you, but I'm going to go.'

Her smile disappears. 'Already?'

'I can't stay here. Unless you want the police looking for me, Valerie and Connor as well.'

'You'd be good company,' she says.

'I thought you had all the company you needed?' I can hear the sound of footsteps coming back up the wooden stairs.

'I miss my best friend,' she replies.

'Hey,' Valerie says, sticking her head around the door. 'You requested my presence?'

'To let you know that I'm ready to go,' I say.

Valerie hesitates, her eyes flitting from me to Bonnie. 'Just you?' she asks.

I nod. 'Just me.' I take a deep breath and turn back to Bonnie. 'Listen. I'm not going to cover for you any more. When I get home I'm going to tell them what I know, OK? So wherever you go next, you'll be on your own.'

Bonnie closes her eyes, then slowly opens them again. 'Eden,' she begins.

'No, seriously,' I say. 'I've said everything I can say. If I can't convince you to come back, that means I can't be part of this any more, either. You can understand that, can't you?' When she doesn't say anything, I add, 'If you want to be running forever, this is what that means.'

As I say this, Valerie comes into the room to stand beside me. I feel her hand, steady and reassuring, touch my shoulder. 'Eden's right, Bonnie,' she says. 'This can't last, what you have here. It's going to fall apart.' As she speaks, Mr Cohn appears in the doorway and, beside him, Connor, eyes full of questions. I watch Valerie look directly at Mr Cohn. 'There's no happy ending here.'

'Bonnie,' Mr Cohn says. 'We have to go.'

A helpless kind of confusion takes over Bonnie's face. She looks, suddenly, like the schoolgirl she is. 'What? Why?'

Valerie's hand clenches over my shoulder. 'Let's go,' she says to me.

Bonnie and I look at each other.

'Bonnie,' Mr Cohn says again, his voice tight and tense.

'We have to go. Now.'

What the hell. If this is over, I might as well say it. 'Are you really going to choose him over me? Me and your whole family?'

Bonnie's mouth opens, then closes again. Mr Cohn makes a motion to come further into the room, but Connor – sweet Connor – puts out his hand and stops him.

'Come with us,' I say.

There's a moment of total silence, all of us suspended in it. Enough time for minds to change and the rose-tinted glasses to fall off and Bonnie to come back to me.

But they don't, and she doesn't.

'No,' she says, softly.

Everything inside me deflates, slowly, like air from a balloon. Disappointment and failure and sadness and heartbreak and that dull, heavy ache of something lost forever. 'OK,' I say. I stand up and walk straight towards the door, grabbing Connor's hand and squeezing it so tight it must hurt him, but he just squeezes back. I can feel Valerie following me without a word, and we all walk down the stairs together, leaving the fugitives alone together in the bedroom, like they wanted. My heart is pounding into pieces.

'What now?' Connor asks, but quietly.

'We have to leave,' Valerie says, grabbing her shoes. 'Whatever we do, we have to do it before they do.'

I don't know what she means by this, but in this mess she is the only one whose judgement I trust, so I just nod.

Valerie pauses for just a second to tilt her head and meet my gaze. She touches her hand to my face, gentle like Carolyn would. 'You're OK,' she says. A statement, not a question.

'Let's go,' I say.

So we do. All three of us together, walking out of the house and out on to the porch, ready to face whatever it is that comes next.

Except we're not. Because what comes next is the police.

24

Dozens of police, all waiting in front of us, on the driveway, on the lawn, on the street.

Connor, Valerie and I all freeze, right there on the top step. She looks as shocked as I feel, but still I hear myself say, 'You called them already?'

There's a clatter behind me and Bonnie's voice, 'Wait, just—', which is all she manages before the tableau in front of her registers and she makes this tiny whimper that sounds a lot like 'Eden?' that pierces my heart, and there's just one more second of frozen agony before life bursts back into full action and *all hell breaks loose*.

Split second one: A police officer holding a taser – a *taser* – shouts something that my head can't translate because . . . *taser*.

Split second two: Both Connor and Valerie jump in front of me, crashing into each other so hard that Valerie falls down the steps.

Split second three: Three police officers run forward.

Split second four: There's a crash behind the house – a door slamming against its frame – and the sound of someone running.

Split second five: Everyone starts shouting.

Split second six: Five police officers take off in that direction.

Split second seven: Bonnie lunges after them.

Split second eight: A police officer catches her before she's made it two metres down the drive.

Split second nine: Bonnie lets out a noise I've never heard before, a wail of pure, defeated pain that cuts across the mayhem and stops it dead. Everyone freezes, turning to look at her, bent double, caught in the police officer's arms.

Somehow I'm still standing on the top step. Connor has both his hands on my upper arm. Valerie is grimacing in pain on the concrete below. I hear a crackle of static from a radio, and then a voice saying, 'Suspect secured.'

And just like that, it's over.

Except it's not, of course, because the end of something is always just the beginning of something else. This is the end of Bonnie being missing, the end of her 'adventure', but I know there are countless questions to come, not just from the police all around us, but from our parents, journalists and basically everyone back home. There'll be a court case. Lawyers and statements and a judge. Recriminations and blame. Tears. Heartbreak. Acts of destruction are usually pretty brief, in the long run, but it's the fallout that lasts. Not just months, but years.

Right now, though, there's Scottish soil beneath my feet and a frenzy of confusion all around me. The police swarm, and I lose track of Bonnie, and strangers come out of their houses to gawp at the circus, and Valerie tries to walk on her foot, and it's so painful that she cries, and my music teacher is being pulled into a police car in handcuffs, and my phone is vibrating with a call from HOME, over and over and over, and Connor is taking my hand and squeezing, and someone is taking pictures, and we're being guided into a police car, and no one will tell me what's going on.

We get driven to a police station, where Connor and I sit in timid silence while Valerie argues with a liaison officer about whether she should go to the hospital for her foot or not. It's through this conversation that I learn that we're going to be put on a plane home, along with Bonnie, who is being looked after somewhere else in the station, as soon as physically possible.

Valerie wants to come with us and deal with her foot back home, but she's worried about her car, and the liaison officer – whose name is Lorraine – is worried that a potentially broken foot should be dealt with straight away.

'I don't want to get stuck here with a car I can't drive if my foot really is broken,' Valerie says. 'But I also don't want to leave my car behind.'

'We'll get your car driven back to you,' Lorraine says. 'That can be done.'

I'm surprised and impressed by this level of service for about ten seconds, until I remember that Valerie was basically working for them for the last couple of days, and delivering her car back is really the least they can do. Especially as it now seems clear that the police never actually trusted her. At least, not as much as she thought they did. They weren't just tracking her car; they were tracking her phone, too. There was never a moment when they didn't know exactly where we were. It seems like everyone involved in this whole mission was double-crossing someone. Except Connor, of course.

Lorraine leaves us alone for a few minutes to get an ice pack and painkillers, and Valerie turns to me. 'Are you OK?' she asks, which is sweet, considering she's the one in actual pain.

'I don't understand what's happening,' I say. 'Where's Bonnie?'

'Getting checked over and debriefed, most likely,' she says. 'But they'll be getting her on a plane back home as soon as they can.'

'Why?' I ask. I'd assumed they'd want to do loads of questioning before bothering about planes.

'It's faster. It'll be best for everyone if they can get her back home before the press finds out where she is.'

'Why can't we go back to York?' I ask, which is stupid, because I don't even want to go back to York. What I want is some kind of sense of control back.

Valerie just grimaces and points at her swollen foot. 'Look, don't worry,' she says. 'Everything's being taken care of. We'll be home tonight. All of us.'

'And Bonnie?' I say. I can't quite believe it.

She nods. 'And Bonnie.'

The first time I ever travelled on a plane, I was nine years old. Mine and Daisy's adoption was almost official, and we all went on a 'We're a family!' holiday to Portugal. Bob spent ages before we went explaining to me how flight worked, and why I shouldn't be scared because flying is the safest form of travel. The thing was, I wasn't scared. I was excited. I didn't even care about the rest of the holiday – I just wanted to fly.

I got to have the window seat, and Bob sat between Daisy and me. (I thought that was just because he wanted to carry on explaining lift and drag, but I learned years later that Carolyn is afraid of flying and she was worried we'd pick it up from her.) When we were airborne, and England began to shrink at an alarming rate below us, Bob pointed out of the window. 'See how small it is, Eden?' he said. 'You remember that, if life ever feels too much. It's all so very small.'

This is what I'm thinking of as our plane takes off. Connor, Valerie and I are all on one row, with me by the window and Connor in the middle. Valerie's foot is swathed and tightly packed with ice; at each small jolt of take-off turbulence, her eyes squeeze shut and her forehead crinkles slightly. Connor's head is leaning around mine, watching Glasgow disappear beneath the clouds. All three of us are silent.

On the other side of the plane, Bonnie is sitting between Lorraine and another police officer. Even though we waited for and boarded the same plane at the same time, she hasn't even looked at me; not once. Her face is set and blank, eyes on the back of the seat in front of her. She looks like someone who has lost everything. Someone I don't know at all. All I can think of is Bob's voice, warm and calm, saying, 'See how small, Eden? It's all so very small.' Which is funny, because I hadn't thought of those words and that moment since I was in it.

I imagine unbuckling my seatbelt and going over to speak to her. All the things I want to say. That I'm sorry, that I didn't mean it to work out like this. But that I'm also not sorry, because it was always going to work out like this, and how could she not know that? I'd tell her that I did it all for her, because that's what best friends do. I'd say, hey, did you notice that when you got wild, I got steady? Look at us, bucking the stereotypes everyone had of girls like us. I'd say, God, I missed you. I'd say, don't worry. I'd say, your parents will forgive you. I'd say, *I* forgive you.

But I don't move. I know there's no point. The Bonnie from before, the Bonnie I thought I knew, would have listened, but that Bonnie is gone. If she ever existed at all. In her place is this angry stranger who probably hates me, the girl who ruined the party, the one who broke her promise.

I don't know what's going to happen when we land. I can't imagine what the new normal is going to look like, just that there's no way to go back to how we were. But here's the thing I realize: I know what it means to lose someone you thought was forever. I've done this before. The people that you let into your life are a choice, and sometimes that choice changes. I look across the aisle at Bonnie, still staring fixedly in front of her. I think about how I never told her I liked her red hair, that it suits her, in a weird, unexpected kind of way. I think, if she looks at me, just once, I'll tell her.

She doesn't.

Later, when the plane starts its descent, Valerie takes another round of painkillers and cranes her neck to try to look out of the window. 'I am so ready to be back at home,' she says.

'Me too,' Connor says, with feeling. 'I'm going to drink the fuck out of a cup of tea.'

Valerie and I both crack up at the same moment, both of us no doubt slightly giddy on hysteria (me) and codeine (her). Connor's ears go pink, but he's grinning, slouched down into his seat. I lean over so I can rest my head briefly against his shoulder as the loud *clunk* of the landing gear extending sounds below us.

'You ready for this?' Valerie asks me. Out of the window, England looms large, the buildings suddenly life-size.

'Do I have a choice?' I ask.

'Nope.' She flinches as we hit the tarmac with a bump, then visibly relaxes. 'Home!' she says, a smile blooming on her face.

We're all escorted off the plane in a group, flanked by the police who'd flown with us and a new set who meet us on the tarmac. There's a wheelchair waiting for Valerie and she lets out an audible whimper of relief when she slides into it. I let the group guide me through the terminal, my eyes on the back of Bonnie's downcast head. I'm half expecting her to make a break for it, or at least do something suitably dramatic, but she just walks, hands at her sides, silent. The only word for her is 'defeated'.

'Where are we going?' I ask one of the policewomen who is flanking us, realizing as I turn to look at her that it's DC Doyle, who'd sat at my kitchen table and taken notes instead of talking. The one who'd winked like she'd seen right through me way back at the beginning of all of this.

'To a safe meeting place,' she says, which sounds ominous until she adds, 'To see both your parents.'

These words seem to do something to Bonnie, because she stops dead in her tracks. Lorraine, walking beside her, puts a gentle arm around her and guides her on. 'It'll be just fine,' she says, gratingly soothing.

'I don't want to.' I hear Bonnie's voice, raspy and quiet, tinged with panic.

I have a sudden flash of Bonnie's mother in her hallway, blazing with anger, snapping at me about priorities. I wouldn't want to be facing her in Bonnie's shoes right now, either. In fact, I'm not really sure *I* want to be in the same room when the explosion happens.

Somehow, with Bonnie's dragging feet and most everyone else stepping back, the two of us end up entering the room side by side. We're so close that I feel Bonnie's whole body convulse when she sees her parents, who are already up and moving towards her before we can even walk properly into the room.

'Bonnie,' her mother says, her voice all cracks. She reaches forward, cupping both her hands around her daughter's face. 'My Bonnie.'

There's no explosion here. I glance up at Bonnie's dad to see that there are tears on his cheeks. He's reached past his wife and has one hand on Bonnie's shoulder, squeezing down. As I try not to watch, I see Bonnie crumple into them both, a heaving sob muffled against her mother's arms. I hear, 'I'm sorry, I'm so sorry,' and her mother saying, 'It's OK, it's OK,' and her father saying, 'We love you.'

My vision is all blurry, but I see Carolyn making her way towards me, a smile on her face. She reaches for me and I let myself be gathered into a hug, closer than she'd usually attempt, closer than I'd usually allow. She whispers into my ear, 'Well done,' before she pulls back, her eyes scanning behind me for Valerie. I can tell by the way her face lifts again that she's spotted her. She turns back to me and gives my hand a tight, Carolyn squeeze, her eyes on mine.

'You're home,' she says.

August

THURSDAY

The school is bustling. Busy in a way that feels completely wrong for a Thursday morning in August; a time when school isn't meant to exist.

Connor and I walk through the main reception doors together and head into Room 14A, which is where we used to take Science, but is now the official Results Room. I head towards the third row, where the 'M' box is, and Connor steps up to the first, for the 'E' box. It's Mr Hale who's manning the 'M' box, and he smiles at me as I approach.

'Ah, Eden,' he says, friendlier and warmer than he ever has been before. Affection, apparently, is earned with hindsight. He rifles through the box and pulls out an envelope that he hands to me with a flourish. 'All the best to you, Ms McKinley.'

I know it's the last time I'll ever see Mr Hale. It feels weird and kind of sad and right all at once. I make sure to smile back before I walk away to open my envelope. It's not possible to find a quiet spot, and I want to see my results before I find out Connor's, so I turn my back on the room and create a quiet corner of my own.

It's as I expected. My results are mostly Ds, with a handful of Es and a couple of Cs. I stare down at the letters, waiting for some kind of feeling to hit me. Relief? Joy? Sadness? But to be honest, I just feel the same as I did before. Nothing's changed.

I fold up my results sheet and slide it back into the envelope, turning to look for Connor in the crowd. He's making his way through the throng to reach me, a smile on his face.

'All good?' he asks me. He's holding his own results in his hand, but still he thinks of me first, because he's Connor.

I shrug and smile. 'All fine. No surprises. You?'

'Eight Bs,' he says. 'Two Cs. Not bad, hey?'

'That's great,' I say, leaning up to kiss his cheek.

'Connor,' someone calls, and we both turn to see Connor's Art teacher waving at him to come over.

Connor glances at me and I nod my permission, leaning against the wall to watch the room buzz, running my fingers absently over the fold of my envelope. I'm just wondering if I should call Carolyn now rather than wait until I get home, when my eyes fall on a figure on the other side of the room, standing quiet and somehow unnoticed, beside her mother.

Bonnie.

As I watch, she unfolds her own sheet, glances at it, and then hands it straight to her mother, her expression unchanged. She looks small. Shoulders hunched, eyes downcast under her glasses. But her hair is still, impossibly, red. Bobbed, as it was the last time I saw her.

In the end, Bonnie only missed the two exams that took place in what the rest of us all call 'That Week'. The remaining exams she took on schedule and without fuss, though she had to take them in a room on her own with private supervision, instead of in the hall with the rest of us. Even after everything, she's probably still ended up with far better grades than me.

Not that I'll know. We haven't spoken a word to each other since that Friday afternoon in a Scottish city in May. She's gone from Facebook, gone from my phone contacts, disappeared all over again, but permanently this time. I don't know anything about her life. And I mean her real life, not just the stuff that gets leaked to the press even now, three months after she was headline news. I don't know what she thinks or feels. Whether she blames me for them getting caught and, if so, if there's a chance she'll forgive me one day. The Bonnie I once knew would have understood that I did it all for her. Part of me thinks that version of Bonnie is gone forever, but there's another small part that still believes in her, that is still waiting.

Rumour has it that she's going back to Kett in September to take her A levels, alongside the retakes she'll need for her GCSEs. It sounds about right to me. Anywhere she goes she'll be gossip fodder, so she may as well be it somewhere that's familiar. She won't be Head Girl, of course. I wonder if she minds.

Everything between her and Mr Cohn ended when we first got back home, obviously. But I don't know how much of a say in it she had, if she realizes now what a mistake it all was, or if in her head she still thinks it was worth it, because she hasn't said a word publicly about him since. His trial is due to start next week, and Bob says he'll probably get a few years in prison. Sometimes I wonder if Bonnie is just being quiet in public. Maybe in private, or even just in her head, they're still together. Maybe they send each other secret letters while Mr Cohn is in prison – who knows?

This is what's left of Bonnie being missing, and of me missing her. Rumours. Questions. That feeling of something half forgotten, half finished, that comes with loss.

I watch as Mrs Wiston-Stanley says something to Bonnie, who nods. The two of them start to make their way towards the door, and that's when Bonnie turns her head and looks straight at me, like she'd known I was there all along. Her face doesn't burst into any kind of an expression at the sight of me. She doesn't even smile. Her head tilts ever so slightly, and then her hand lifts into a brief, silent wave. Before I can even react she's turned away, following her mother out the door, disappeared into the crowd. It was nothing more than an acknowledgement, really. But it was there.

'Ready to go?' Connor asks, reappearing at my side.

'Definitely,' I say.

There was an independent investigation into the school to try and find out how it happened, and why, and it found 'serious failings' at a 'senior level', which basically means that no one was checking up on Mr Cohn and his possibly-too-friendly relationship with his students, even when people like Rebekka Bridges raised the alarm. She wasn't even the only one who'd done it, it turns out. Schools are meant to have all these procedures in place, and Kett messed them all up. That's not supposed to happen, and they promise it won't, not ever again.

Still, I've made Daisy promise that she'll tell me if any one of her teachers ever tries to give her their mobile number or email address or anything even slightly personal. She rolled her eyes and called me an old nag, but then she sat on my lap to hug me like she was still six years old, and whispered that she'd never run away from me or our family.

It's a beautiful day, bright and warm, and it makes me smile as Connor and I walk out of the main door into the sunshine. I glance back at the building as we walk down the steps, passing a group of the clever bunch posing for a picture with the local paper, their results in their hands and grins on their faces. Bonnie would have been part of that group, no doubt. She'd have been front and centre. I wonder if that knowledge hurts her, if it makes her regret everything that happened. Livia Vasin catches my eye and smiles, automatic but genuine, and I smile back before I feel Connor's hand squeeze around mine and we head out together into the car park.

Just like that, Kett is a part of my past.

'Off to work then?' he asks me, his eyes scanning for his gran's car.

'Not until after lunch,' I say. 'Are you free tonight?'

He nods, smiling, and leans down to kiss me goodbye. I watch him jog over to the car, open the door and slide inside. Connor will be coming back to Kett in September to join the sixth form, which is weird to think about, but then again a lot of the future is weird to think about. Me, I'll be going to college to study horticulture; something I'm actually interested in, something I'm actually good at, for the first time ever. The course is approved by the Royal Horticultural Society, and everything. And one of the best things is that I had a place there, regardless of today's grades. It just makes it even sweeter.

Last month, I started working part time at the local garden centre. Carolyn got me the job, and I thought I'd hate it, but it's actually pretty brilliant. I mostly work in the cafe bit, making tea and spooning out soup portions, but it's still great to be officially part of the gardening world. I'm usually on-shift with Layla, who's my age and likes to jive across the tiny kitchen area singing made-up songs about soup ('Oh potato and leek, you make my week, so green and sleek, la-dee-da-deek'). This Saturday, we're going into town together after work so I can get my nose pierced like hers.

I head across the car park, my results envelope light between my fingers, the sun on my back. Valerie smiles as I approach, pushing herself up from where she'd been leaning against the bonnet of her car.

'Hey,' she says, sliding her sunglasses up on to her head. I can tell she's excited, because results days are exciting for her, though she's trying not to show it. 'How was it in there?'

I hand over my envelope and she beams, pulling out my results. 'Busy,' I say. 'Bit weird.'

'You passed Maths!' she bursts out, and she's thrilled, I can tell. Sweetly, genuinely thrilled. 'Eden! That's amazing!'

I can't help grinning back at her. 'Yeah?'

'Yeah!' She leans over and nudges my shoulder with her fist. 'Congrats.'

I take the paper back and fold it away. 'Thanks.'

'Ready to go for lunch?' she asks me, reaching up to slide her sunglasses back down over her eyes.

I glance back one last time at my old school, my old life, and then turn back to my sister.

I smile. I say, 'Ready.'

ACKNOWLEDGEMENTS

First and foremost thanks, as ever, to Claire Wilson, without whom I wouldn't have one book to my name, let alone three. (People ask, what does an agent *do*? And the answer is *everything*.)

Thank you to Rachel Petty, for your unflappable brilliance, and the team at Macmillan Children's Books, for once again going above and beyond for me and my books. Particular thanks have to go to Rachel Vale, who creates the kind of covers I once only dreamed of. Thank you, Kat McKenna, George Lester and Jess Rigby, for every seamlessly organized event, each appropriately giffed email, and especially your unfailing support. And thank you, Bea Cross, for just about everything. It just doesn't feel like work, guys.

Thank you to the UK YA community for being a constant source of joy, camaraderie and friendship. There are just too many of you to name, so I won't try! I hope you all know how valued you are.

My dear friends Mel Salisbury, Holly Bourne and Katie Webber, who were all tapping away at their laptops beside me at one time or another – you're brilliant, and I adore you. And to all my writer friends, always just a DM away – Harriet, Holly, Jess, Ellie, Non, Cat, Lexie, Christi, Lauren and Anna – thank you.

Thank you, Tracy King, for once again being both my unwitting life coach and my friend. And thank you to the good ship DT, and all who sail in her. Weathering the storms with you is a privilege.

Thank you to my family, especially my parents, who never made me feel like 'perfect' was desirable, let alone essential.

And thank you to Anna, Lora and Tom, my three favourite people. You make me, my life and my books better, and I love you very much.

ABOUT THE AUTHOR

Sara Barnard lives in Brighton and does all her best writing on trains. She loves books, book people and book things. She has been writing ever since she was too small to reach the 'on' switch on the family's Amstrad computer. She gets her love of words from her dad, who made sure she always had books to read and introduced her to the wonders of second-hand bookshops at a young age.

Sara is trying to visit every country in Europe, and has managed to reach thirteen with her best friend. She has also lived in Canada and worked in India.

BEAUTIFUL BROKEN THINGS

Sara Barnard

CADDY AND ROSIE HAVE ALWAYS BEEN INSEPARABLE. BUT THAT WAS BEFORE SUZANNE.

Now Caddy wants to be more than just the quiet one.
She wants something to *happen*.

I WAS BRAVE . . .

Suzanne is trying to escape her past and be someone different. Someone free.

SHE WAS RECKLESS . . .

But sometimes downward spirals have a momentum of their own.

WE WERE TROUBLE . . .

And no one can break your heart like a best friend.

A Quiet Kind of Thunder

Sara Barnard

Steffi doesn't talk.
Rhys can't hear.
They understand
each other perfectly.

Love isn't always a
lightning strike.
Sometimes it's the
rumbling roll of
thunder . . .